beyond the horizon

beyond the
horizon
EOIN LANE

**BLACK
STONE**
PUBLISHING

Copyright © 2020 by Eoin Dolan Lane
Published in 2020 by Blackstone Publishing
Cover and book design by Sean M. Thomas
Original artwork by Eoin Lane

"The Lost Heifer" by Austin Clark used with permission from
Carcanet Press Limited. "Dirty Old Town" by Ewan MacColl
used with permission from Sony and EMI Music Publishing Ltd.
Various quotes from Paul Henry used with permission
from Yale Representation Limited.

Printed in the United States of America

First edition: 2020
ISBN 978-1-982641-54-2
Fiction / General

1 3 5 7 9 10 8 6 4 2

CIP data for this book is available
from the Library of Congress

Blackstone Publishing
31 Mistletoe Rd.
Ashland, OR 97520

www.BlackstonePublishing.com

For Cormac, Maggie, and Pepe

In 1946 the painter Paul Henry fell ill, and as a result his eyesight was severely damaged.

He never painted again.

His timeless landscapes have provided inspiration for artists ever since.

But every artist fears their blind spot …

"I was alone in the world with the mute fish."

—Paul Henry
"The Basking Shark"

contents

I

fresco

The man is not elderly, but his gait is stooped. She does not think the little dog is elderly, but he seems to be lame. He lifts up his left back leg and hops. Then he puts it down for a while and trots beside the man. The man has a muffler, and his head is shrunk in the folds like an egg in a cup. He walks with his hands in his pockets against the wind. There is no one on the sands. There hardly ever is at this time of the year. The beach is for visitors and most of those have gone. The waiter comes with her breakfast. Scrambled eggs and toasted soda bread. She watches the man and his dog. They are like a stick and a twig in the wind. It is the third morning she has seen them. Today she was waiting. The Lobster Pot looks out on the beach and the sea. She cradles her cup and watches. They move closer to the waves spilling on the sand. The same spot again. The same as yesterday. The man lifts his head and stands looking out to sea to some invisible point. Some golden eye of his own. The dog mooches about. Then they turn and head back across the sands and the stones. The window is fogging up. There is drizzle on the wind. A gust catches the dog on his three legs and blows him over. He cannot stand up. The man bends down slowly as if in a mime and picks up the dog. He holds him in his arms and carries him back to the verge and the road. They head away, the man stooped, the dog lame. Their shadows blur as they fade into the rain. She sits back and passes her fingers through her hair. The beach is empty. The sea is drenched with grey. She stares at nothing in particular.

seagull

"There is over and above [the] remoteness and beauty of the place ... an air of romance impossible to describe or to resist, intangible, alluring and tender."

—Paul Henry

1

They say a watched pot never boils, but that was a thought that came much later. The day was fine with no rain, clouds jostling overhead in a sky of pale blue and sun catching the sand through a filter of gauze. A wild chorus of seagulls and water was casting an Elysian spell and a strange, mercurial feeling was hovering in the air. The boy's hair was shining like white silk in the sun. He had skinny freckled arms that whirled like an octopus, and mischievous, fairy-tale eyes.

"My name's not Colin, and you don't know who I am."

"Well, who are you then?"

"Shush," he whispered, bursting into giggles. "My name is Lal."

"Is that right?" said his father, tousling his hair.

"And I live on a moonbeam way up there." Then he jiggled around like a plane coming in to land. He was four foot two. He was six.

"Whoa," laughed Jim. "I think that's what they call a crash landing." His father was six foot three.

They say the power of waves comes from the wind rolling over the sea.

Eileen Larkin already knew the tide was coming in.

"Don't be long, Jim," she said. "Don't stay in too long."

She smiled at Colin. "And don't you get cold, or you'll be shivering when you come out."

"I'm a plane, I'm a plane, I'm a plane," he sang, and his words danced back on the air.

They say the force of a wave comes from the strength of the wind.

She watched them leave. The man and the boy across the shells and the pebbles, then across the hard sand. They stood for a moment as the foam licked their feet, then raced in.

They say the crash of a wave comes from how far it has traveled.

She could hear them laughing, Jim hollering, Colin squealing. Her husband and child. Like father like son.

Some waves travel thousands of miles.

But it only takes three minutes to boil an egg.

Jim struck out, his arms scissoring the surface. She watched him for a while until he was a wriggling tadpole. *He always goes too far*, she thought and unpacked the picnic things. She glanced up. Colin was floating like a water lily, the water jigsawing around him. *He'll be cold*, she thought. She took out the colored plates and plastic spoons. A shadow curtained the sand and then it was gone. The sun returned. She poured a tumbler of tea and hugged her knees, her eyes closed. She held her face up to the sun. "Hold your face up to the sun," her mother had always said. "Get the benefit while you can. We don't get much of it." The water was changing, but she wasn't looking. There was sun on her eyelids and the tang of seaweed in a freshening breeze. She moved her hand slightly, spilling the tea, and opened her eyes and watched the colored tumblers rolling like tulips on the sand. The wave began to rise.

She closed her eyes again. She scooped up a handful of sand and let it fall through her fingers like an old-fashioned egg timer. When she opened her eyes, a phosphorescent light had enveloped the beach in blue. She inhaled the freshness of the moment. The waves were rolling in now and she watched them surge and break and foam.

It took her a minute. The clouds shivered.

"Colin?" She stood up. "Jim?" A stone stabbed her foot as she started to run. She ran crooked in the wind down to the water's edge. The beach was slanted. She hadn't noticed that before. She shouted their names. The waves slapped her ankles as she waded in. A surge of water hit her. She was wet through before she saw him. He was upside down and bobbing like a duck in the bath. She pulled and dragged him, stumbled and fell. The water was in her mouth, her nose, her hair. They made it to the shore. She shook and slapped him, but his eyes were shut. She got him on his side and rocked him gently. Her eyes strayed out to sea. Kneeling on the ground she was at eye level with the waves. But there was nothing to see except the undulating walls of waves advancing. Colin was coming back to her now. His limbs were twitching. She held his shoulders. He began to cough. A mix of sea and bubbles and sick. She ran to get towels.

They say the energy of the wind moves the waves.

The wind was stirring. The colors were changing. There was no sign of Jim. She would need help. She grabbed towels, clothes, and ran back to Colin. There was no one around.

"You will need to stay here. I have to get help. Do you understand? Colin?"

But he didn't reply. He was just staring at her.

Poor child, she thought. But inside her a voice was beginning to scream.

"Wrap these around you," she said, tugging the towels around him. "Don't move," she warned him. "Stay here. Do you hear me? You must stay here."

She ran back into the water. She couldn't see anything. She couldn't swim. She was wasting her time. She shouted his name. "Jim!" Over and over. "Jim!" It only came back to her on the wind. She would need to run to the village.

She left Colin sitting on the beach, the towels wrapped around him like the wings of a sleeping bat. Eileen couldn't look at him. She couldn't think. She could only run. She had grabbed her shoes and when she got to the path to the car park, she balanced on one leg then the other like a heron and squeezed them on. A collie spied her from the grassy bank and ran with her as if it were a game or a race. She reached the paper shop first. Annie McGovern was behind the counter, sorting jellies and bull's-eyes into glass jars. Eileen stood in the doorway, trying desperately to catch her breath in fast raw gasps. Annie McGovern looked up and saw that something was not quite right. Eileen's shoulders were heaving, and her hair hung limp and wet like strands of seaweed around her cheeks. Annie called for her brother out the back, then she put the jars on the shelves and took hold of the situation.

*****

JP McGovern had gathered some men. Annie had offered tea, which Eileen declined. The other children, Peadar and Mick and Aine, had gone into the hills looking for the wild donkeys. They would have to be found and told later. She had to get back to the beach.

A crowd had gathered out of a queer mix of curiosity, sympathy, and foreboding. A couple of rowing boats had ventured out. People murmured bits of prayers and words of consolation, most of it lost to her on the wind. She had stopped calling his name. But every now and then she shouted it out as if from some delayed and desperate sense of duty or even a kind of guilt that she had stopped calling it out in the first place. Colin held her hand, his head tucked under her arm, like a bird in a nest.

The waves seemed slower now.

She watched the curves of water flow and suck back, the sea growing heavy and dark and green. The waves were making her head sag and her eyes ache. The waves slipped from green to gunmetal grey.

The light had changed. The sky was disappearing.

Soon there would be a sea mist.

The crowd began to pull apart and drift away. She could feel the cool sea air settling on her arms and she hugged Colin to her side. The boats had returned, and the fishermen were hauling them over the stones. The priest came and spoke a few words. She didn't really take anything in that he said. But she had the feeling he wanted her to leave.

Someone had gathered her things.

Father Sheehan put his hand around her shoulder and led her gently away.

*****

The first night, they stayed late with the priest and his housekeeper. Eileen hadn't wanted to stay for dinner, but she hadn't wanted to go back to the cottage either. Sylvia Gallagher was a woman of few words, but she was generous and kind, and Eileen was grateful for the meal but glad of the lack of conversation. The children were naturally subdued and there were tears at night. Colin hadn't spoken a word and clung to her whenever anyone appeared. She hadn't pressed him. Time enough for that, but she kept him close. It was as if she believed he might hold the key to where his father was. But she knew that to be nothing less than a desperate hope to unscramble the irreversible truth. His sister, Aine, normally a chatterbox, was unusually quiet and seemed to have acquired new manners of politeness and reserve. Colin's two older brothers, Peadar and Mick, kicked a ball around in the field and kept out of the way, apart from meals.

They returned earlier to their cottage on the second night.

Sylvia had given them a beef stew to heat up and after they had eaten what they could, everyone drifted off to bed. There seemed to be nowhere else to go. Nowhere that was safe. At least when they closed their eyes, it was with the vain belief that their father was still around and might reappear at any moment.

Eileen lay in bed, conscious and half conscious. Not asleep. Not awake. The doctor had given her an injection, so that she lay quite still like an injured bird, her arms splayed out like broken wings. Her mind was draped in darkness, her thoughts fumbling in and out of focus like a camera lens not quite working. So, she lay.

Numb.

Dull.

Blunt.

Breathing faintly. But feeling as if she too were dead. Drowned. She turned her head on the pillow. Drowned in deep, dark fathoms of dense, black water.

And then he was there. But wasn't.

But she could see his face.

He was in his suit and they were standing at the altar. She could see the carnation in his buttonhole, his shaved face splashed with cologne, his hooked nose and slicked hair and dancing eyes. He was lifting her veil. Her bouquet dropped to one side as he kissed her on the lips with the priest and the guests looking on.

She opened her eyes, but the wedding was gone. It had vanished as quickly as it had appeared. Jim's presence had dissolved. And now her eyes found nothing except the dull fuzz of dawn that was filtering through the dust in the air.

She stirred herself to rise and wash and dress.

Automatically and slowly like a patient in hospital. When she pulled the curtains back, she could see the cows in the field and she stood watching them, feeling the sun warm the panes and brighten the sill. The cows ambled slowly around. It was going to be a nice day. She could tell from the sky. It was time to get breakfast, but she stayed at the window reluctant to leave, just watching the cows mooching on the hill. Then she heard him.

Laughing.

Telling one of his jokes. One of his silly, incorrigible jokes.

She could hear him working his way to the punch line. Doing the different voices.

Telling the milkman, the butcher, the postman, anyone who would listen, and she laughed for a moment and the sound of her laugh was strange, disturbing the silence here in what was meant to have been their room for the week. *Must have been the cows*, she thought. *Must have been the cows on the hill*. Every day now, she walked the beach very early at dawn. But there was no trace and no sign.

*****

The rains came and the clouds settled low on the horizon. A week passed.

And then on a clear and bright morning a body was found.

A woman walking her dogs had come across what she first mistook for a half-submerged rock in the sunshine. But the dogs had known better and she had to pull them away. The beach was five miles farther down the coast.

When the two Gardai in their crisp blue uniforms came to Rose Cottage, Eileen was clearing up after breakfast. The boys were in the field. Colin had gone with them for a change. Aine had walked to the shops to get milk. She was on her own and she was thankful for that. Father Sheehan had come with the two young men and they held her when she began to sway. But after a cup of tea laced with sugar, she felt a little stronger and less sick. She would have to rally.

The guards had gone to collect the boys from the field, and they arrived now sullen and morose, with their hands in their pockets and their eyes cast down. Aine came back and found them all in the hall.

Eileen opened her arms and they all pulled together. The guards stepped back and Father Sheehan watched them quietly.

They were a new unit now, Mother and boys and girl.

They were folded together like the bud of a flower and in the center was Colin, almost lost in the weave of arms. Someone was sobbing and then Father Sheehan realized they were all crying now. And he knew it was their time to break. This was their moment together alone.

He turned to head to the garden to wait when he spotted little Colin looking at him. The boy's eyes were dry and he was staring at the priest. Staring at him with wide open eyes, like a puppy that has strayed out of bounds and can't find his way home.

Father Sheehan walked out to the garden and stood looking over the wall. The sky was billowing with clouds and the summer was alive in the ditches and fields all around.

A death in summer, he said slowly out loud and thought of Colin and sighed. The boy still hadn't uttered a word. Father Sheehan shifted from one foot to the other, and all he could see were those vacant, frightened, staring eyes.

*****

They left the next day to go home.

Eileen's brother, Thomas, came for them. "I don't know what to do," was all she said. He held her in his arms and pulled her close. The children were packing. She gripped his arms and sank her head on his chest, as if for a moment, he was Jim.

The car was nearly packed.

Aine and the boys were sitting together on the wall, their legs dangling in the sunshine. "Have any of you seen Colin?" she asked them.

They shook their heads and she sighed and went back into the house to look for him. He was curled up on the window seat, his fingers tracing the glass. She watched him from the doorway, the sun kissing his curls. It was as if he hadn't heard her calling. Perhaps he hadn't, and she wondered what if anything he chose to hear these days and what on earth was passing through his mind. She stood still. He was intent on what he was doing.

His fingers were moving delicately over the glass. He was making patterns and curves and circles using his fingers like a brush on the page. He blew on the glass and let it fog, then smeared a finger through the mist and began to draw slowly and then with added vigor, stabbing at the heart of the glass.

She drew her hand to her mouth.

He was drawing a wave.

*****

Sylvia Gallagher called to see them off.

Eileen felt an odd ache about leaving, as if she were somehow abandoning Jim. His body was returning home, but she felt in a way that they were leaving him here.

Forever running down the sand, holding Colin's hand.

"Father will be saying Mass for you all in the morning," Sylvia said, touching her arm, and Eileen could feel herself becoming upset again. She nodded briefly and smiled.

As the car pulled away, the last impression Eileen had was of Sylvia shaded by the trees, her face like a fresco under stained glass leaves. It was an image that was to stay with her for years, reconnecting her with Jim's final days. But for now, she turned and fixed her eyes on the road. Everyone seemed conscious of the significance of leaving as the car turned up the sea road, the beach slanting away to one side, the water this morning a gently waltzing blue.

*****

Back in Dublin, their house in Ranelagh felt strange, as if they had been away for a year. The front lawn needed cutting. The dog daisies by the gate had blackened in their absence and emitted an odd, unsettling odor. The cats were disgruntled and demanded food.

Neighbors called.

The house became full, at one point bursting at the seams. The children had their tea with the next-door neighbors, which took their mind off things. Colin followed the other three around, ate what he was given, but otherwise remained silent. But Eileen had enough on her mind.

"As long as he's eating," she said to her brother. "That's all that matters. If it continues much longer, I'll have to take him to the doctor."

"He'll come round," said Thomas. "I'm sure of it."

"I hope you're right," she said. "For his sake, I hope you're right."

The rooms had become quite crowded now.

People squeezed in wherever they could. Even the kitchen was packed. At one point, there was a crowd of people standing out on the road by the front gate, like cows gathered for a milking.

The Fitzpatricks from across the road had come to pay their respects and were talking to her now. Yvonne Brannigan handed her a sherry. For a while Eileen felt almost relaxed. It was like a suspension of grief. The sherry added a velvety warmth and had brought a flush like rouge to her cheeks. As she looked around, she found the whole affair quite surreal. The strange mix of people gathered under one roof.

*****

When the children were in bed and everyone had gone, she lingered in the drawing room. The room was perfectly still with the embers glowing faintly in the grate. The moon lit the garden and the window framed the scene. She opened the lid of the piano. Her fingers traced the keys and trickled out a tune. A few notes, then reduced to two.

She let her fingers dip the keys. One and two.

Cuckoo.

Again. Cuckoo.

Now deeper, slower, quieter still.

Cuckoo.

Cuckoo.

She sat motionless and still, her fingers playing out the mono rhythm.

One and two. One and two.

It numbed her mind. Cuckoo. In the moonlight. An echoing tribute to two.

Cuckoo. Cuckoo.

The minutes drifted.

Her hands began to falter.

Then she added a third note. Colin.

And it lingered in the air.

The sound grew fainter in the dark. She sat utterly still.

She had no real wish to go to bed. But she gathered herself.
It was time to go.

But the next morning, in the early hours before dawn, she saw them again.

Father and son.

The wave was rising in the bedroom and she could see them running down to the water's edge.

They say you should never revisit the past.

She could feel the tug of the wind once more on her cheeks.

They say it is difficult to harness the wildness of a wave.

They are running in the sun and she hears them laughing, Jim hollering, Colin squealing. Water is splashing around. Droplets of spray are sparkling, tossed up high in the air. The wave is advancing.

They say the lure of the sea comes from an ancient sense of fear.

Jim is away like a seal through the water, weaving his way far out.

But they say it's never too late to turn back.

Colin is basking in the water, ebbing in the sway with the heat of the sun on his white, wet skin.

And she is running now, unsteady and unsure and a panic rising fast inside like when a breeze becomes a wind.

And there is nothing to see. There is no one to see. The water is rising and falling and the wave has broken. She cannot see them now. The room is drenched in the wave and the backwash pulls across the carpet, sucking across the sand to the door, and she is left on her own.

Awake and alone. Standing at the water's edge, calling their names.

The water and sky begin to merge. Into a fog of blue and grey and green. The scene starts to fade. Her eyes begin to close, heavy and drugged with unnatural sleep, and she sinks like a stone through the blur of grey water. Where is Jim now? Now. Now. Sleep washes through her. Now. Now. Where is Jim now? And her mind through the blur turns to Colin. Colin. Colin. Her limbs twitch with worry. What can she do for him? What? What? What will happen to him now? Now. Now. Now ……

the folds of clouds within the sky
soften the horizon
where a wind blows fast upon the tide
as waves keep slipping in
two hands entwine and then unwind
a boy and man
beneath the darkening glass of waves
and all is fused, the light is mute
within Ultima Thule
where the light is weft and the wind is warp
far out beyond that distant point
where the sky meets the water

2

They were climbing up the steps of the tall house on Marlborough Road. There was a large black lion on either side of the door. A woman in tweed ushered them in. The waiting room had magazines on a low table, shelves of leather-bound books, and paintings in ornate, gilt frames. Colin held her hand but let it go when they sat down. The armchairs were padded with brocade cushions edged with satin.

One week. Two weeks. Three weeks had passed. Days had slipped away like snow melting from a roof. Slow, heavy days dulled with repetition.

The events of that day in August pulled alongside them every-where they went, while at the same time appearing more distant and unreal, as if dreamt or somehow imagined. Days of shock had turned to grieving followed by days when her legs felt so heavy, it was like dragging them through mud. Peadar, Mick, and Aine had returned to school where their status had unalterably changed and they were viewed not with hostility but with an unspoken curiosity. Something had happened to them in the holidays that marked them out as different.

Colin had refused to go. But she hadn't expected him to.

She watched the three of them closely as she waved them off

every morning and observed them on their return. They tried hard to be as they'd been in the middle of August but it was as if they themselves were acutely aware that those carefree days were gone. They all seemed to exude a weariness far beyond their ages. But all in all, she felt they were coping as best they could. They cleared their plates at meals, did their homework, and did not complain.

But Colin stayed at home.

With her. Where she could keep an eye on him.

And she had cause to be perturbed.

He had taken to spending long hours in his room and sometimes she found him under the bed, where she presumed he felt safe from the world. One morning, he had hidden away in the wardrobe and she could hear him sobbing inside. She called his name and the crying stopped but then the banging began.

He was kicking his heels against the door. But worse, when she pulled it open, he was banging his head in his hands against the wood. She had to reach in and drag him out screaming and kicking at her like a wild colt, untamed or simply afraid. She wrapped him in her arms, and he struggled and wriggled and fought back, something terrible and feral inside him.

She had the temptation to slap him to shock him. But something just made her hold him and hold him until at last the awful sobbing began to slow and subside. Until he just lay in her arms like a simple, silent child. And they stayed like that for some time while she waited for the suck of the phantom wave to recede and disappear.

*****

Their appointment was for twelve.

But they had arrived early. She was a great believer in such things. Colin fidgeted a little, then got bored and walked around.

"Colin, don't touch anything," she said, almost whispering. It was that sort of room. He was standing in front of the fireplace gazing at the painting overhead. A blue mountain with a sea of turquoise rippling in waves to the shore. Seagulls hovered above the green water, hanging in the air like white kites.

She watched him nervously. The scene made her want to place her hand over her heart. It was too close to the bone. To the day.

She watched him. Suddenly, he raised his arms out wide and began to turn, waving his body in circles of eight.

"I'm a plane," he said, the words escaping from his lips like a parachute inflating midair.

She edged forward on her chair. He was still twirling around. She was about to say something, but no words came.

"I'm a plane, I'm a plane," he said, slowing and coming to a halt in front of her.

The door opened. The woman in tweed beckoned to him.

*****

Colin was in the chair staring at Dr. Morton when Eileen entered. She glanced at him sitting there in the big armchair, lost in the cushions, his legs dangling like a puppet, not even reaching the floor.

He seemed calmer today.

Perhaps it was the occasion of coming to see the doctor in the big house with tall ceilings.

Just that. The novelty.

She thought of him as she had found him last week.

Lying at an angle on the floor, one foot dangling in the stirrup of the rocking horse. Toy soldiers spewed all around where he had knocked them. She had heard him rocking through the ceiling.

Back and forth. Back and forth. The creaking sound of the rocking horse.

Then faster and faster. At first, she had smiled and thought at least he was having some fun. Then she realized.

Dropped what she was doing. Then came the crash.

"Colin!" she called. "Colin!" as she ran up the stairs. Past the clock. Past the Sacred Heart. And then she stopped at his door. For a moment she wondered, then he moved and the comforting began all over again. And that was when she knew she must act.

The room was dark, the carpet a tapestry of burgundy and gold.

There was a snow globe on the desk and Dr. Morton leaned forward. He turned it upside down and snow shivered in the air, falling gently on the houses and trees in the globe. Colin stared at the snow. Dr. Morton was watching him intently. Eileen stayed quiet. Colin leaned forward, his eyes transfixed. Then he wriggled back in his chair and turned his head to one side, burying his cheek in the cold, dark leather.

Dr. Morton cleared his throat. He pressed his fingers together, resting his elbows on the desk. Then he rang a bell. The woman in tweed reappeared.

"I wonder, Miss Montgomery, whether you would be so kind as to take young Colin to see the butterflies."

"Yes, of course," she said, smiling at Colin. "We have a wonderful collection, young man. Would you like to come?"

"Go on, Colin," said Eileen. "I won't be long." He got up reluctantly but took Miss Montgomery's hand. He looked back at Eileen. She gave him a wave. Then the door closed.

Colin dragged his feet down the carpet as if he was wearing oversized slippers. The lady was chatting away. Her words popped around him like bubbles in the bath. "Butterflies," she said. Her skirt was like purple heather. He could feel it brush against his hand as they treaded their way down the hall. She was opening a door. Still talking. "Beautiful colors," she was saying. She seemed very different to his mother. There was an orbit of perfume around her. She had hair like a doll and a string of pearls dangling down her blouse which had a sheen like a rose. Colin was mesmerized and followed her in. Miss Montgomery was turning lamps on left and right. The walls were sky blue and there were cabinets with gleaming glass doors filled with hundreds of butterflies, large and small. "How old are you, Colin?" she was asking. But he was staring at the butterflies encased behind glass, circles and bands of color patterning their wings. "This one," said Miss Montgomery, bending down beside him, "is called the painted lady." Her face was very close to his. He liked the words. "Painted lady." Miss Montgomery was a painted lady. "And this one," she said, "is from America. Do you know where that is?" He shook his head, his eyes widening. "This one," she said softly, "is very old indeed ..." There was a large book on a table and she began to turn the pages, all interspersed with tissue paper. Colin looked at the pictures. Golden brown, red umber, and shades of petrol blue and emerald green, all the colors like jewels on a chalice. "What age did you say you were?" she asked again. "Six," he said suddenly and emphatically, breaking his silence without realizing. "That's very old for a butterfly," she said, smiling. "Why?" he asked. "Because they are so little," she said. "Oh," he said as if he was not quite sure of this explanation. But she didn't expound further. She could see his face puckering with concentration, pondering the life spans of butterflies. Miss Montgomery kept turning the pages. "Here," she said. "You have a go." And Colin stood turning the pages as the butterflies danced in front of him. She bent down again close to his ear. "I'll be back in a few minutes," she said softly. But he looked at her blankly as if he had forgotten she was there. "You stay here with the butterflies," she said, "and I'll be back in a few minutes." His eyes followed her out but he made no effort to follow. She paused in the hall until she heard him turning the pages, then she walked briskly back to the consulting room.

"Well, how did we get on?" asked Dr. Morton.

"Happily looking through the book," she said. "He was quiet at first, but he's speaking now. I think he's completely enchanted," she said, smiling at Eileen.

Dr. Morton thanked her. "You go on back to Colin and we'll finish up here."

Eileen had been listening intently but said nothing. She was intrigued.

"Your son," said Dr. Morton, "is physically fit. From what I've observed and from what you've told me, he's a sensitive little chap who's had a hard time. There's really nothing to be overly concerned about. Normally," he said, rising from his chair, "for someone of his age in this sort of situation, I would prescribe plenty of fresh air and exercise like hurling and football. But in Colin's case ..." He paused. "I would encourage you to get him making things, drawing, collecting stamps, painting—anything visual—that's what he needs. Stimulation. Keeps the mind absorbed," he said, tapping his temple. "It will stop him from fretting."

"And reading?" she asked.

"Well," he answered, "to an extent. Of course, he must read," he went on, "but in Colin's case, that might be just a little bit too solitary and passive. He mustn't be let to go in on himself. We must keep him busy and amused. He has an artistic nature, Mrs. Larkin. Encourage that. And get him back to school as quickly as you can."

"And the speaking?" she asked, standing up.

"Oh, he'll not be long talking now," Dr. Morton said as he walked her to the door.

"The butterflies have been a distraction." He held open the door. "A diversion, that's what he needs. That's what he will continue to need."

Eileen nodded and shook his hand. He smiled at her. "Mrs. Larkin," he said, holding her arm, "don't be worrying. Is it any wonder after what you've all been through?" She paused, then nodded. Dr. Morton bowed his head a little and stood back and let her go.

She stood in the alcove window, staring at the garden where the roses and dahlias were catching her eye like brightly colored sweet wrappers. She could hear a door opening down the hall and Miss Montgomery talking to Colin. Eileen turned, surprised at how much she had missed him. It was almost as if she needed to be near him too for her own peace of mind these days. Colin was coming toward her. He had a bounce in his step and his eyes were smiling. Miss Montgomery let go of his hand and he ran to her. She touched his shoulder and he looked up. "Butterflies," was all he said. He sank his head against her waist and she held him close. Miss Montgomery nodded encouragingly. Eileen smiled and patted his hair. The spell had been dispersed and she hoped it would last.

Miss Montgomery opened the big, heavy front door and they emerged tentatively into the sunlight. Eileen turned and spoke a few words with the woman. Then she thanked her and took Colin's hand and they navigated the steps, a swan with her gosling gliding out on the water. Miss Montgomery watched them until they had faded away behind the hedges and garden walls. They walked in silence, hand in hand, mother and son. Eileen could feel Colin's hand glued to her palm and she could feel the young trust in his tightly clenched fingers.

The sky was painted with cumulus clouds and a sudden, sharp shiver shot through her. Jim was swimming through the water again. Such moments came often and out of the blue but subsided just as quickly as they came. She found a tearoom, and they sat by a window and had tea and hot buns and milk. A new distraction and a treat.

That night Colin went to bed earlier than normal. He seemed exhausted from the day. Eileen watched him trudge up the stairs, his head barely visible over the bannisters.

Colin climbed into bed and lay awake for what seemed like ages. It was a big bed. Brass posts with knobs and woolen blankets with pale green hemmed edges. In the blue of night, the bed was a like a ship in a bottle sailing along on a starlit sea. His bed was a bolt-hole and he felt safe under the blankets. During the day, he liked being under the bed, in his cabin, shut away from the world. But it was hard to go to sleep. The waves lapped the ceiling and he would lie awake staring at them over him as if he were underwater. In the end, his eyes would falter and close with the hypnotizing rhythm until he would wake with a jerk in the small hours, his hands clammy and clutching the sheets like limpets attached to rocks.

But there were no waves tonight. He turned his head to one side, then the other. Checking his moorings. He looked up at the ceiling. Wings.

Brightly colored. Fluttering like bunting in the breeze at a fair or the flap of napkins in the wind on the washing line. The butterflies were swarming, dissolving, reappearing, enlarging. His eyes began to fade, the lashes on the lids gently quivering. He fell asleep. Into a long, deep sleep. A darkness filled with butterfly wings. Whirling wings of organza like in *Swan Lake*.

*****

One night at twilight, Eileen paused in the drawing room and opened a small suitcase she had brought down from her room. It was full of Jim's paintings. Watercolors and sketches and oils from before they were married. Photographs as well. One in particular she was looking for.

The watercolors were delicate and faint with pale, transparent colors, the brushstrokes rapid, adept. The oils were small, awkward in places, but richly textured like butter, the colors singing of sun in the mountains, the heather humming with bees.

She studied them now. She had seen them before, but Jim had moved on and hadn't spoken of them much except in passing. Looking at them again, she considered that a shame. And yet he had always kept them. Under the bed. Close to him, she supposed.

He was quiet about such things.

The door opened behind her and Colin came in shyly, as if he wasn't entirely sure who she was.

"Were you not able to sleep?" she asked him.

He shook his head and slid down beside her onto the floor. He had spotted the paintings and she showed them to him one by one. His face brightened and his eyes began to smile and she wondered to herself. She could see the depth of his absorption and she wondered.

"Shush!" she whispered suddenly, curling her arm around him. "The foxes have come!"

The light had dimmed to an ethereal blue. They sat still, watching through the French doors, at the garden masked with dusk. A fox's nose appeared under the apple tree. Then he stepped forward tentatively like a soldier from the trenches, and Eileen and Colin held their breath. The fox looked up at the house, checking for signs of life. Then he dipped his snout and carried off a fallen apple in his mouth. Colin gasped. Eileen held him tight. The fox reappeared, hesitated and stopped, and then was gone again into the night like a ghostly dog from heaven. Eileen closed the suitcase over. "Time for bed," she said. Colin murmured a little but then slipped away quietly.

Eileen lit the lamp. She had found the photograph she wanted but had kept it back from Colin. An image snapped with a timer delay. Jim in front of a mirror.

And out of frame, another mirror. Mirror in mirror in mirror.

A triptych of portraits …… diminishing reflections.

He looked younger and fresher, high cheekboned. Looking straight at himself. Hair creamed and combed back. Tweed jacket, neat shirt, slim tie. His own self-portrait.

Still waters run deep.

The other photographs she looked at and smiled. He had an eye. An array of things caught on camera. A wooden gate ajar in a garden wall. A fence post with sheep's wool caught on barbed wire. A chicken grubbing soil behind a highly polished car.

She thought of Colin and she wondered. She wondered and began to hope.

*****

Colin was standing in the hall. His bag was packed. He was wearing a tie and had new shoes on. He was going back to school. The glow from the fanlight dappled the floorboards with shapes of colored glass and he stood quietly, transfixed by the patterns.

His mother took his hand and they went out together. She was asking him if he was alright. He nodded. He hadn't wanted to go to school. Term had already started and he was joining late. But now he didn't mind. His mother kept looking at him. She was wearing a blue dress like the Virgin Mary at mass. She was talking quite a bit. But he wasn't really listening. He was thinking about how to catch butterflies, but it was the wrong time of year. The walk to school wasn't very long but he was taking every detail in. The green grass speckled with golden leaves. The dog across the road chasing a cat. A friend of his mother's in a red coat with a handbag, stopping for a chat. The flowers at the Harrigans' gate. "They always have a lovely garden," his mother said. They passed on.

He was in an office. There was a tall man in a cape called a headmaster looking at him. Colin didn't much care for him but he was curious to see the other boys again. The headmaster led him down the long corridor. Colin looked behind him. His mother waved in her blue dress and coat. The classroom was full of boys. A teacher called Miss Rogan was looking at him and saying welcome. She smelled of soap and had chocolate brown hair. Colin remembered her from the year before. His desk was beside a boy with black hair called David. Colin stared at him. David smiled back and said, "Hello." Colin shrugged and sat down. There was a game of football in the yard at lunchtime but Colin just ate his sandwich. Cheese and pickle. David sat beside him eating his. Neither of them wanted to join in. There was drawing in the afternoon with crayons and pencils. Colin drew birds and butterflies and colored in the wings. Miss Rogan stood beside him admiring them and hung them up at the end of the day. David lived a few roads away and they walked home together, the sun dappling low through the trees on the road. They walked heads bent, like two little old men who had known each other a lifetime.

*****

The bus was sitting in traffic, the streets clogged with cars and bicycles and trams. Colin was staring out the window. It was a habit he had developed ever since he was small. He could see the two of them now walking home, kicking leaves along the path, scuffing their shoes. He remembered it all. The buns and the milk. The snow globe. The butterflies in cabinets and Miss Montgomery's pearls. The black lions at the top of the steps. The fox's snout twitching in the moonlight. His mother holding his hand.

He remembered the night the waves turned to wings. His first day back at school. The long corridor, classrooms on either side and the headmaster striding ahead. He smiled. He had liked Miss Rogan. She had eased him back in.

The bus was crawling through the streets like a caterpillar gnawing cabbage. He checked his watch. He wondered should he get off and walk. But he thought he might just about make it. His appointment was for eleven. He had a large folder in his arms which he was clutching tightly, as if someone might steal it. The bus was turning down Dame Street now, toward the mouth of Trinity College. The streets were crowded and he watched the people marching along like toy soldiers on the carpet when he was six. Eleven years ago.

Eleven years since the waves. Eleven years of feeling alone inside. But all the time, his mother looking out for him and he was deeply proud of her. And fiercely protective. He straightened his tie. It was important that he made an impression when his time came. He should be there soon. He began to get nervous and his foot began to shake. He held his knee to stop the shaking.

His father sat beside him on the bus and tousled his hair. "I'm proud of you, son." Colin bit his lip. He was once again Lal on the beach and he could hear the seagulls crying above the slap of the water. He was racing around and waving his arms and jigging about like a paper plane. His father was laughing in the sunshine. He had to rouse himself now. The bus was inching past Dublin Castle. Not that day. Not that day now. Not that moment all over again. He sat up in his seat.

His mother had found him a craft class on Saturday mornings. Colin had looked forward to it all week. He would wake early, at the crack of dawn, and be out of bed like a shot. His mother caught him once trying to leave the house at seven o'clock and he sulked while she made him wait. Stubborn as a donkey. Even then. He grinned. Their teacher was a nun in a grey habit. Small wizened face like a monkey nut under her wimple but with a big, bright, cheerful smile. He loved her very much and saw her as a kind of grandmother in a habit. The gateway to a dream with those early swirly pictures and the papier-mâché models of animals and felt glove puppets. Sister Aloysius on Saturday mornings had pointed the way like a signpost on a country road. When he was ten, his mother gave him a framed print of a Paul Henry painting. He had hung it over his bed. The blue, magic mountain, sacrosanct behind glass on the wall. He loved watching the mountain change color in the morning and darken with dusk in the evening. He was fascinated by the changes of tone as the light spilled in through the window. At night, the mountain seemed to take on a sacred mantle, as if it was watching over him. His Paul Henry mountain began to shape all his days. It became an intrinsic part of him. When he was twelve, Sister Aloysius found him a place in the adult group. Saturday mornings became afternoons with Wednesday evenings thrown in. About ten to fifteen of them, all different ages, but he was the only child in their midst.

They had eyed him curiously at first as if he were an orphan or a refugee. But soon they became accustomed to the quiet boy with white-yellow hair who painted with a vibrancy that made them stand around and stare. His favorite lady was Sally. She had grey hair in a ponytail and smoked a pipe. She painted mountains and bogs with the pipe wedged in the corner of her mouth and every so often the sweet smell of tobacco would waft through the room like smoke drifting from an open turf fire. He loved the silence in the room, the only sound the brush of bristle on canvas and the scrape of knife on board overlaid with the odd grump and harrumph at misplaced strokes, the clearing of throats caught on the fumes of turpentine and all the while the smell of that countryside pipe. Sally, Sally, Sally. He would miss all of them in that room. And he knew they would miss him. Last Wednesday they had given him a card wishing him good luck. Sally had slipped a pound in his hand. She had winked at him through the peat of the pipe.

The bus was rattling to a stop. People were jumping on and off.

A fat woman's shopping basket knocked against his folder and he frowned as if he was holding something breakable like glass. The engine coughed into action. He gave up his seat to an old man with a walking stick. The bus swayed along for a bit belching smoke out the back and then turned into Nassau Street.

It was time to get off now.

There was a wind whipping litter and leaves down the street. He walked along by Trinity College, the railings piercing the sky like bayonets stabbing clouds. He turned into Leinster Lane, a small street tucked in behind the National Gallery. There was a neatly lettered sign on a redbrick wall. He stood reading the words formally, his lips moving slowly as if in prayer. So, it was real then after all. The National College of Art. He took a long, slow, deep breath, then pulled open the heavy door and stepped inside. Into a tiled, shady corridor. A completely different world. A place where he would have to make his own way.

3

Dusk was dropping outside the tent, stars prickling the sky like May blossoms. Michael Murtagh was peeling off his shirt in the cool sea breeze. Colin could see his limbs twisting in the moonlight like a figure on an ancient cave wall. He folded up his clothes and crouched inside the tent.

"That's me," he said. "Are you asleep?"

Colin shook his head. "Not yet," he replied. "Just drifting." He could smell Michael's hair and skin close up. A warm amber aura about him. Michael collapsed on his sleeping bag, legs in the air. "Night then," he said, his breath crawling across Colin's neck.

"Night," said Colin, staring out at the sky. It was black as a coal pit and studded with diamonds. The Milky Way over the sea. Michael was breathing heavily, and Colin listened to the sound like a breeze across the pillows. And they stayed like that for some time, half asleep, half awake, limb against limb, like two calves looking for milk. Later in the darkness, their bodies closed together and their breathing turned fast and shallow. Then they slept.

When they woke in the morning, the sun was breaking through and the sea was embroidered with silver, like filigree lace. They lay without words, watching the sun on the water until it was time to make breakfast and pack up their things.

On their way down the hill, Michael strode on ahead whistling and carrying the tent. Colin dawdled behind with the paintings and easels. Everything seemed intensely serene as if plugged into a socket. The sea was viridian and rippling to shore, and it was like walking through a Nathaniel Hone painting of the sea and the sands at Malahide. Colin ambled along in the sunlight, lost in thought.

"What do you think about when you're painting?" the man at the interview had asked.

"This," he wanted to say now. "Days like this. Here, now on the hillside. This."

Instead he had stumbled, searching for words, unsure about the question. The man had stared at him, his head cocked to one side like Mr. Micawber. Colin could still see his face, the craggy, veined cheeks with the tufts of hair growing from his nostrils like rushes in a field.

"Birds," he had said. What made him say that? "Seagulls," he added. "Seagulls," he said again hesitantly, unsure of himself. His neck above the line of his shirt had flared red and the color crept up his cheeks.

The man closed Colin's folder and held out his hand. Colin took it. Stanley Fitzgerald had small stumpy hands. Colin remembered the feel of the fat fingers. His inability to speak for himself overshadowed as always by his eye for detail. He had left the interview room feeling downcast and useless. Outside, the next boy was being called. Michael stood up. Colin had seen him earlier. Tall, with grey eyes and hair slicked back like a wet paintbrush. He smiled at Colin who watched him head confidently into the room. The door closed. His walk back to the bus had been flat and unsteady, like a wobbly tyre.

"Well?" his mother had asked when he arrived home.

Aine had stuck her head out the sitting room door, and Peadar and Mick had gathered on the stairs. They all thought he was brilliant and were waiting for the news. He had just shrugged his shoulders and set the folder down. "I couldn't tell you," he said. "I have no idea."

"But didn't they like your paintings?" asked Aine. Eileen frowned at her and Aine disappeared. Peadar and Mick went back upstairs. "I'm sure it will be fine," his mother had said.

Colin sighed now at the thought of it. Everything had led to that day. Everything. The day had woken full of promise, the early spring air infused with lightness like a Turner watercolor and he had hopped on the bus, his face set and determined. But the day had dripped away to nothing like turpentine and he had gone to bed tense and afraid. Afraid of the curtains of failure.

"Are you coming or what?" Michael shouted now up the hill.

"Hold your horses," Colin shouted back. "I'm struggling here with two easels, you know."

"There's a pub in the next village. If you get a move on, we can make it for lunch."

"You're always dying to spend money," Colin called.

"Fine, you can fish for your lunch from the sea then."

Colin laughed and quickened up. Lunch beckoned, the day stretching ahead like a dog on a rug. A day without having to clean his brushes and palette.

"It's about a mile and a half," said Michael. "Do you want me to take an easel?"

"Here you go," said Colin. "I'm like a scarecrow with all this stuff."

They walked on then, along the winding road, the sun searing down and sealing the shirts to their skin.

"You're quiet," said Michael. "Planning a painting?"

"No, I'm thinking of lunch." Colin said, laughing.

"And a pint," said Michael. "I could murder a Guinness."

They trailed on in the heat like two pack mules in the desert.

*****

The weeks after the interview had passed slowly. Colin fidgeted at school. He had tried to keep sketching in his room, but his mind was overcast and elsewhere. His mother was aware. He was aware of her glances. No one spoke of it at dinner. The interview skulked in the shadows like an uninvited guest. One who had nothing to say. Their neighbor Mrs. Harrigan asked Eileen if Colin would do a painting for her and he brightened for a bit. She would pay him for it, his mother said. He completed the picture over Easter, which had come early. The weather was showery with dark clouds threatening the light but he painted with abandon, as if his life depended on it. His mother was delighted with the result. "Oh, lovely, lovely, lovely," said Mrs. Harrigan when he brought it to her framed. She paid him handsomely, but his room felt empty and strange that night. He realized he had sold his first painting, but it was an odd thought, like giving up a child for adoption.

When the letter came, Colin was at school. His mother propped it up on the hall table. But the envelope stared at her, so she moved it to the sideboard in the dining room and spent the morning dusting in silence.

Colin walked home late after sports with David, who had his own concerns now with the exams coming up. He wanted to be a solicitor and had ink-stained fingers and a bag heavy with books, but they were still best of friends. They had been since Miss Rogan's class in primary school.

"You'll get in," said David, when they reached the garden gate. "I know you will."

"Oh, I don't know," said Colin as he turned down the drive. He looked back. David waved and disappeared behind trees. The light in the hallway was speckled blue and green like a mosaic in the glow of the afternoon sun.

The front door kept opening and closing. First Peadar. Then Aine. A few minutes later, Mick came crashing in.

"Shush," whispered Eileen. "He's had a letter."

"Where is he?" said Aine.

"The garden," said Eileen. "Dinner's nearly ready."

They crowded around the window like they were in the dress

circle. Colin was standing under the pear tree fiddling with the envelope.

"What painters do you like?" Stanley Fitzgerald was asking him again.

"Constable, Turner," he had blurted out, unsure of himself but confident with the names.

"Irish painters?" snapped Stanley.

Colin looked at him as if stung by a wasp. His mind drew a blank and his leg began to shake.

"Na ... Nathaniel Hone," he stuttered.

"Wa ... lter," he added, "Os ... borne."

He scrunched the envelope now in embarrassment. He'd completely forgotten Paul Henry. His tie had been too tight, his leg shaking, and all he could see was Stanley Fitzgerald's face like a windfall crab apple quizzing him. He had never felt so stupid.

"Will he ever open the blasted thing?" said Peadar.

"Will you be quiet?" said Eileen. She noticed the window needed cleaning.

Colin slid his finger through the seal without looking. He took the letter out and unfolded it, trying to focus on the words. There was a pause, then he hung his head.

"Oh, my God," said Eileen and Mick put his hand on her shoulder.

"Oh, Jesus," said Aine.

"Don't say Jesus," said her mother.

Peadar was about to swear but thought better of it. Just then, Colin threw the letter up and they watched it catch the light like a paper plane. He turned around pumping his fist and started running to the house.

"I got in, I got in," he shouted.

And they jumped up and down inside the window, laughing and cheering with Eileen wiping her tears in their midst.

*****

That weekend, she took them out for lunch. To the Elk Lodge Inn. A long low dining room murmuring with conversation. Fresh flowers on tables, crisp waiters, and cut-glass crystal. A three-course meal and coffee afterward in a drawing room of low green sofas. The bill was more than a lot, but Eileen had been planning for the occasion. They drank a toast to Colin as the main course arrived and he reveled in the fuss for a change. Eileen watched him with pride. She looked at him laughing, his hair gleaming with oil. In a new shirt and tie, he resembled his father. *Oh, Jim,* she thought. *Oh, Colin.* He had come a long way. And she knew she would remember this meal. To see him happy and bright in himself for a change. She hoped it would last and turn out for the best.

*****

Michael and Colin had reached the pub, a stark white building baking in the sun with a dark inside and pelargoniums on the sills. They set down the easels and slumped in a corner and ordered stew and pints of Guinness. There were not many customers about, some men at the counter and a few tables of tourists in the courtyard. Flies buzzed intermittently through the front and back doors, but the lamb was delicious and they mopped up the gravy with homemade bread.

"*This* is it," said Colin to himself, pushing his plate away.

Michael sat back, wiping his lips. "What do you mean?"

"*This* is the life. I wish it could always be just like this. Sunny days by the sea, just painting away. The freedom of it all. That's why I wanted to be a painter. No hassle, no worries."

"You think?" said Michael.

"Mmmm," said Colin. "Days just like this."

But even as he said it, Michael thought his eyes seemed wandering and restless. "Ah, you'd need a bit of adventure," said Michael. "A few good old storms. You'd get bored with all this."

"Nah," said Colin. "I like it here by the sea. The peace and the quiet. You can keep all your storms and adventures."

Michael laughed and sipped his Guinness.

"I remember trying to explain it," said Colin, "to Stanley at my interview. Stanley asked me what I thought about when I was painting, and I didn't know what he meant. Afterward, I thought he must have been looking for a really clever answer, but when he asked me, I just said seagulls. I mean, can you believe it? He must have thought I was an eejit."

"Why seagulls?" said Michael, laughing.

"Because I was trying to say I felt free when I was painting … like a seagull way up in the sky. God, you probably think I'm a nutter as well."

Michael shook his head. "I reckon Stanley knew *exactly* what you meant. I mean, he didn't ask *me* any of that. And do you know why? Because your paintings stand out from everyone else's."

"Don't be daft," said Colin, cradling his glass.

"I'm being serious," said Michael. "That's why he asked you, because he saw something different in your work and he wanted to find out more … about where you were coming from. And I bet he could see you had no confidence in yourself."

"Well, maybe not so much then, but I do now."

"No, you don't. And you don't realize how good you are."

"Oh, come on, I'm not that good, for heaven's sake."

"Colin Larkin," said Michael, "listen to me, whether you like it or not you're a bloody good painter. Everyone in class has been talking about you. Your work is incredibly wild and different. No one else even comes close to it." He took a sip of his pint and looked at Colin. "I genuinely mean that," he said. "You're brilliant. Bloody brilliant."

Later that evening, they pitched their tent by a beach a few miles away.

"I think I'll go in for a swim," said Michael. "Want to come?"

Colin shook his head. "I don't swim," he said flatly.

Michael looked at him. "Why not?" he asked in disbelief.

"I'll tell you sometime."

"Are you sure?"

Colin nodded. "Yes," he said, "very sure."

"Alright," said Michael, "but I'm going in. The tide is just right."

Colin watched him cantering down the sands, then wading thigh high through the water. He watched him stretch then lunge and cut the surface like a knife. Colin drew a breath. But it was a clear, still night, the sea smooth as satin. There wasn't the hint of a wave. He hugged his knees. There was something about Michael that he couldn't put his finger on. From the day of the interview when he had first noticed those sea-grey eyes. He never seemed to worry or care. He just seemed to sail through.

They had met again in September in a class of new faces and found themselves drawn together from the start. The friendship had helped Colin settle. On Friday nights, they would drift around town with the others to favorite haunts like Grogan's and McDaid's. Colin had felt a bit nervous about taking up his place in the college. It was one thing being considered talented at school or encouraged by his family. It was another to find yourself surrounded entirely by artists, each one more skilled than the next. Michael's company had reassured him and given him a confidence he lacked. But Michael's words earlier had disturbed him a little and he didn't know whether to believe him or not.

*****

Michael came out and shook himself down like a dog out of water. He toweled himself quickly and jumped up and down to warm up. Colin had lit a small fire with driftwood and the flames crackled and spat around their shins. Michael lay down on his towel, lit a cigarette, and leant back on his elbows.

"What are you doing?" he said over his shoulder.

"Drawing a masterpiece," said Colin. "You look like something out of Caravaggio with the flames of the fire."

Michael exhaled. "*Chiaroscuro* ..." he said, coiling the syllables into smoke rings in the air. "That picture in the National."

"The Taking of Christ," said Colin as he sketched, the charcoal making short scratching sounds on the page.

"God, do you remember those first sessions?" said Michael. "I was terrified."

"Everyone was," said Colin, laughing, thinking of the first time they had to do life drawing sketches in ten, twenty, thirty seconds.

"We got quicker in the end though," said Michael.

"That was because we had to do them over and over," said Colin. "There you go," he said holding up the sketch.

"I'll frame it," said Michael, grinning. "Make sure you sign it."

"The angle of your left shoulder is a bit off," said Colin, "and your arm is too thin."

"I don't know how you can draw in the dark," said Michael.

"I know," said Colin, "it's like sitting in a Whistler."

"Nocturne, Blue and Silver—Chelsea," said Michael, remembering the title.

"Nocturne, Midnight Blue, the Burren," said Colin in return.

"Paint it," said Michael.

"I think I might," said Colin. "I love a good Whistler."

"Paul Henry studied with him, didn't he?" said Michael.

"Yes," said Colin. "That's why some of his work is so sparse."

Michael nodded. "Oh, right, I didn't realize that."

"That's because you're more into portraits."

"Well, you can knock them out quicker than anyone," said Michael.

"They're just doodles," said Colin.

"Nonsense," said Michael, throwing a stick at him, "you know they're good."

Colin ducked and laughed.

The fire churned orange and red. They sat chatting on in the dusk. Down on the shore, the waves rustled, breaking foam. It began to get late. Colin poked the last of the sticks in the flames. His mood seemed to have changed now. Michael looked at him and gave him a push. Colin shrugged him away. He was stirring the fire. Something was different. The lighter moment had gone. There were times like this when he seemed to just fold in on himself. Michael had seen it before. It was as if someone had quenched the light in his eyes.

"Come in for a swim," said Michael.

"No."

"C'mon, why not?"

Colin's face had tensed up, his eyebrows furrowing into his forehead. He hugged his knees up to his chest and sighed slowly.

"My father drowned," he said.

Michael stayed quiet. He knew he had died, but Colin hadn't talked about it before.

"I was six," said Colin. "It was a beach like this in Wexford. The first day of our holiday."

Michael listened.

"It was an Irish summer sort of day," said Colin. "Not hot like today. Warm. There was a bit of a wind." He paused. "We were fooling around on the beach. Mum was there. She had the rug and the picnic things. 'Don't be long, Jim,' she said." He bowed his head. He was beginning to mumble. His head was in his hands. Then he groaned.

"We went in for a swim. I can't remember. It was cold and blue and wet and we were mucking about in the water." He looked up at the sea, his eyes widening as if it were happening now in front of him.

Michael held his breath.

"Dad swam out and I ......   I was floating and ...... it all went black. There was a wave ...... I can't remember ...... I was underwater and there was a spinning sound in my head like angels singing. Then I came back up and the next thing my mum was dragging me out. She was calling for Dad and she was in the water and ...... and ......"

Michael stirred.

"He ...... he never came back. He never came back. One minute he was there and then he was gone. Mum ran to get help. I was on the beach in a towel and ...... and ...... it was raining by then."

Colin stood up. "He never came back," he said again.

"But didn't they find ..."

"They found his body washed up a week later." Colin's face was a mess and he rubbed his nose with the back of his hand. "Five miles down the coast."

Michael let out a deep breath and stood up. He put his hands on Colin's shoulders. They were standing close together in the warm night air. Neither spoke for a bit.

"Swim with me," Michael said out of the blue. He didn't know why he had said it.

Colin was staring out to sea and didn't reply. He could see his father running down the beach. Something in him stirred. He could feel Michael's breath on his neck.

He bent down and touched his toes, straightened up and stretched his arms. "I'm a plane, I'm a plane, I'm a plane." The words began to dance in his head.

"Alright, then." He pulled off his shirt and shorts and started running.

Michael stared, then raced after him.

Colin splashed through the water and fell awkwardly around, flailing his arms, sending up spray. Michael caught hold of him and folded him into the water. Colin gasped as the water washed over his face. He began to choke, the water spluttering through his nose, and came up coughing for air. Michael stood up in the water and pulled him close.

"We're not even out of our depth," he said.

"No," said Colin. "Not out of our depth," and he let himself fall back and felt the cold water slide on his skin like silk.

He could see the moon overhead, a naked bulb in the ceiling.

"My name's not Colin, and you don't know who I am," he said to the sky.

"What do you mean?"

"Shush," Colin whispered. "My name is Lal," and he closed his eyes and lay still. Michael floated beside him, the water bobbing and ebbing all around them, the ripples catching the moon like electric light. Michael stared at the sky and the fragments of a poem by Yeats came dancing back on the wind ......

O body swayed to music, O brightening glance,
How can we know the dancer from the dance?

4

The train had thundered through Wales and was clattering now to a halt in Chester station.

"And just remember," said Eileen, rising from her seat, "I know we haven't seen them in years, but Phillip and Edith have been very good to invite us. So, whatever you think, just go along with it."

Colin nodded and sighed. He had been reluctant to come but now he was here.

Phillip Larkin, like his brother Jim, was tall and instantly recognizable on the platform. He had a pipe dangling from his mouth but took it out to kiss Eileen, then put it back in and shook Colin's hand. They drove on pencil straight roads through flat open country, the light like a net curtain grimy with haze. By sunset they reached Frodsham, a market town nestled in hills.

Edith met them at the door. She had a pale, porcelain face and was wearing a broderie anglaise blouse. The Oaks was a rambling Victorian house with a garden of roses and flowers.

"It's like stepping back in time," Colin said as he looked around.

"Yes, we are rather old-fashioned here," said Edith, beaming.

They were shown to their rooms, Eileen's overlooking the garden and Colin's across rolling fields. There were seascapes either side of the bed and a round mirror like a porthole on the wall and the effect was like a ship's cabin. A painting of a lighthouse caught his eye, but he had no time to linger, just enough to freshen up. Edith had a supper laid out in the drawing room and he joined them again downstairs. All the way through the sandwiches, the lighthouse kept flashing through his mind. They were talking mostly about family and relations, and after he had finished his tea, he slipped away early to bed. The painting of the lighthouse intrigued him and he sat staring at it for a while. The room was peaceful and quiet like a boat on a calm, gentle sea and he lay back and dreamt of the summer.

*****

His days in the Burren with Michael at the end of June. They had parted at Limerick, Colin catching the train back to Dublin, Michael heading for Cork. They hadn't seen each other again all summer. Colin had found a job with a small gallery on Molesworth Street. On his days off he took himself down to Sandymount Strand, sketching studies of the sea and the changing expanses of light in the bay. He became a familiar figure to passersby who often stopped to watch him work. He worked through the drizzle and the rain with sheets of tarpaulin for cover, often coming home half drenched like a seal from the water.

One morning, a woman with six dogs had walked by.

She pulled up short and gave an ear-piercing whistle. The dogs froze. "Stay!" she bellowed, then took a step closer, looking down at Colin's work.

"Good Lord!" she exclaimed. The dogs stirred.

"Paul Henry is dead!" she roared in the wind.

Colin stared at her.

"Love your clouds!" she shouted. "Long live Paul Henry!"

The dogs began to pull.

"Got to go, got to go. Are you in the art college?" she fired back.

"Yes," Colin called, "the National."

"Then we'll meet again," she shouted, the dogs pulling her away, her striped coat flapping like a beach towel in the wind.

Colin watched her go, zigzagging across the sands. He paused for a while, startled by the circus intrusion. And by her strange words. Then he took up his brush and returned to his clouds, lost in thought.

He saw her on and off over the weeks. Crisscrossing the sands in the wind, with the dogs. She always brought a smile to his lips as she passed, clutching her hat in the breeze, and he wondered who she was.

*****

The next day Phillip drove them to a place called Port Sunlight.

Colin was skeptical at first but the visit became a revelation. Port Sunlight had been built at the end of the last century by a businessman called Lord Leverhulme as a model village for his soap factory workers. Wide boulevards of Tudor style houses stretched all around like a chocolate box picture.

"Over there," said Edith. "That's why we're here."

Colin and Eileen turned around and stood still.

The Lady Lever Art Gallery was an unexpected sight, like a lioness sitting on a village green. A large and impressive neoclassical temple.

"One of our finest," said Edith, smiling.

Inside, the rooms were packed floor to ceiling with sculptures and paintings. There were glass cabinets filled with ancient ceramics and vases and Wedgwood jasperware.

"He's in his element now," said Eileen with a smile as they watched him wandering about.

*****

Colin loved the silence which came with art galleries. The self-absorbed concentration that settled across people's brows as they drifted through. Reverently, as if they were in a church or at a holy shrine.

And it was the same sort of peace here. There were towering Pre-Raphaelite panels, large canvases by Constable and Turner, portraits by Gainsborough and Reynolds and horses by Stubbs. It was all a bit much to absorb at once and he tried to just stand back and let the pictures call him in. Turner's *The Falls of Clyde* could have held him all day with its spray-drenched atmosphere. There were many fine landscapes by British artists with whom he was entirely unfamiliar but the paintings soon spun a shimmering web of charm that he found hard to resist. The wetness of the waves in Henry Moore's *A Breezy Day* seemed to almost surge out of the frame. He could feel the wet cold of the deep in those waves as if he had fallen overboard. In *Two Boys in a Boat* by Jacomb-Hood, he stood transfixed by the calmness of light shot through with the shadows of the boys on the water. And there were others like Sir David Young Cameron's landscape of *Clunie*, with its searing cerulean-turquoise sky and richly painted bog pools of ultramarine.

Eileen and Phillip climbed the stairs to the balcony. The gallery was spread out below them like a marble hall. They could see Colin and Edith drifting around, oblivious to each other.

"I know Peadar and Mick are both working now," said Phillip, "but Edith and I would like to help with Colin's fees. He's going to be rather good, isn't he?"

Eileen nodded. She had suspected this was the reason for the invitation.

"We'll sort something out," he said. "If it helps with the fees, well and good, otherwise put some away for rainy days. Life," he said, looking down at Colin's head, "can be difficult for artists."

"Let's get him through the art school first," she said, patting his arm.

"He'll have rainy days ahead," he said. "You can be sure of that."

At the end of the afternoon, Eileen found Colin lost in thought, sitting by the Henry Moore. He didn't hear her when she called his name. And when he looked up, it was almost as if he didn't know her.

She was right; he wasn't there, he was busy absorbing every inch of the painting, sucking it into him in a form of osmosis that would help him remember when he returned to Dublin.

*****

And all the way home on the train and the boat, he was still in Port Sunlight.

Still in the gallery. Still in the paintings.

Standing on deck, watching Wicklow emerge from the drizzle, he listened to the sound of the engines, the slap of the water and shouts of the crew. The lights of Dun Laoghaire appeared like glow worms and every so often a ray from the lighthouse swept over the bay. He could still see the paintings and now he could feel the sea. The trip had given him wings and ideas.

*****

On the Saturday before classes resumed at the college, he called around to Michael's flat in Rathmines and they stayed up late going over the summer. Michael had worked in his uncle's pub in Kinsale using his spare time to fill notebooks with sketches of old men crouched over pints. Although neither of them mentioned their trip to the Burren it was still a shared memory between them, like a photograph tucked away in an album. Colin spent half the evening talking about Port Sunlight.

"Never heard of it," said Michael, lolling on the sofa, his long legs dangling across the armrest. " Sounds different though."

"I want to try and use some of it in the year ahead," said Colin.

"God, do you ever *stop* thinking about painting?" said Michael, refilling his glass. "I mean don't you ever switch off?"

"Switch off?" Colin looked startled. "What do you mean?"

"I just think if we're both going to do this for the rest of our lives, we should learn to switch off," said Michael, finishing his drink and pouring another.

"Mmmm," said Colin. "Maybe."

They spent the rest of the night listening to music and drinking beer and toward dawn, they fell into a companionable sleep, their limbs brushed close against each other in Michael's bed.

*****

On Monday, they met early at the gates of Trinity College and walked the short distance to Leinster Lane. It was a bright, clear morning, the pavements washed clean from rain the night before.

As they came near the entrance, a woman in a long flowing scarf was floating down the steps.

"Aaah, new boys?" she said.

They nodded.

"I know you," she said to Colin. "You're that Paul Henry chap from the beach."

She lowered her voice. "Beware the Ides of March," she said conspiratorially. "Too much tuition can *kill* a good artist. So, don't let them ruin you and turn you into something you're not." She gave a nod.

They stared.

With that she was gone in a curl of silk.

"Who the hell was that?" said Michael.

"That's that woman from the beach," said Colin.

"That's Adeline Bell," said the porter, opening the door. "Lady Adeline Bell. She's often blowing about," he said, shaking his head.

"Why?" said Michael.

"Passionate about art," said the porter with a sigh. "And some of the tutors," he added under his breath.

"Well, well," said Michael as they walked to class.

"I'm telling you," said Colin, "I met her on the beach."

"Beware the Ides of March," said Michael, laughing, wriggling his fingers in the air.

*****

But there was a nervous anticipation trickling through the room as everyone started to arrive.

"This is when they tighten the screws," said Dearbhla McFadden, a painter from Roundwood in Wicklow. "Or so I've heard," she added, smiling at Colin and Michael.

After a life-drawing class in which they all seemed to draw hesitantly, like bicycle chains in need of oil, Stanley Fitzgerald walked in. His face was the color of a bruised plum, his wispy hair straying across his forehead like a matted cobweb.

"Jesus," muttered Michael, "has he been drinking?"

Colin sniggered, then coughed, and Dearbhla looked around and grinned. Sheila Mahon pinched Colin's arm and they rolled together at the back. "I bet you he has," Michael whispered.

"Now then," said Stanley. "I'm looking forward to seeing your work from the summer. All you great, young, budding artists. I hope you haven't been sitting on your arses dreaming great thoughts about masterpieces. I hope you've been hard at it, making an effort," he said. "I'm looking for meat and two veg. Work of substance and skill with something to say. If you've nothing to say, you've got no business here." He slapped the desk with his hand for emphasis.

The class shifted uncomfortably. Chairs scraped the floor.

"Right," he said. "You've all got your appointments with me during the week. Be on time and don't waste mine."

When he was gone, he left behind a curdled silence like sour milk in the room.

Then Helene, who was half French, stood up and said, "Phew, what an idiot he is."

And then the room came alive and people started talking again.

*****

Dearbhla was first in line that afternoon, but when she returned, her shoulders were cowed and her face was numb.

The class crowded around.

"Well?" said Michael.

"That man has just ruined everything," she said. "Here." She took out her folder, laying it open on the table. There was a really good series of pen and ink sketches of cats washing and stretching and prowling and eating and some close-up studies of Labradors staring from the pages with big, brown, round, sad eyes.

"And?" said Helene. "We all like these, what of them?"

"He said," she paused, her words forming slowly like rust covering metal, "they had about as much life in them as stuffed rabbits in a glass cabinet."

"Oh, for fuck's sake," said Michael.

"He said he didn't want to see this sort of rubbish again."

"He's just a *stupide* man," said Helene. "He's a wanker, phew."

"Yes," said Sheila. "But he's important. He's got influence, you know."

"Over whom?" said Colin.

"Over all of us," said Michael. "Come on, let's go for a drink."

And they went off to McDaid's then and settled for a while as a group before drifting away into the evening.

*****

It was the second week before it was Colin's turn. Everyone had been slated in some form or another, so he wasn't too concerned, although he did hate people criticizing his work almost as much as he was uncomfortable with people going on about it.

As far as Stanley was concerned, apart from Dearbhla and her cat drawings, which still filled him with indignation that she would try and pass them off as worthy of a summer's work, most of the others he could see were trying different styles, coming up with new ideas, and attempting to say something. The problem was most of them had nothing of consequence to say and those who had so far were failing miserably to be in any way convincing. Stanley sighed. He didn't know which was the hardest, becoming immune to the mediocre, dragged down by the sheer awfulness of some, or utterly frustrated with the promising ones who failed to deliver.

Colin Larkin knocked on the door.

Stanley was standing by the window when he came in.

"I heard about you sketching in Sandymount," he said without looking around. "A lady called Adeline Bell spotted you. She likes your work. Do you know who I mean?" He peered at Colin like a judge cross-examining from the bench.

"Well, I've met her," said Colin.

"Influential," said Stanley. "If she likes you, that's a good sign. Well, a good start, now what have you got for me?"

Colin laid out his notebooks and canvases. "They're mostly clouds," he said self-consciously. "And studies of the light on the beach."

Stanley flicked through them grunting under his breath. "They'll do," he said. "Good, solid technical work. Now what about the year ahead?"

Colin cleared his throat and began to tell him about Port Sunlight. Stanley walked around him like a dog circling a lamppost. Colin began to falter but kept on going, eventually trickling to a stop.

There was a dusty silence in the room.

"Finished?" asked Stanley.

"I think so," said Colin.

"No," said Stanley, turning around with a wild-eyed glare. "No. No. No," he said slamming his hand down on the table. The notebooks shook in their jackets under the force.

Colin was taken aback. "But ..."

"No," said Stanley. "No. Don't be ridiculous. You go to some posh bit of a gallery in England and come back with a whole load of trumped-up nonsense about a bunch of Victorian painters and you think that's the way forward ..."

"Well, I—"

"Well, it's not. It's going backward. Backward in time. Back to the past. You're wasting your time. And mine if you think I'm going to agree to it. Paintings like those are called illustrations, these days.

Illustrations," he said, pulling the word out of his mouth like something unpleasant he had swallowed.

"But Henry Moore—"

"Yes. Yes. Yes, I know who he is. All good and well. *All terribly admirable, my dear fellow*," he said, for some reason adopting an accent.

Colin looked on bewildered.

"Look, Colin," he said, "how do I explain this to you? Well, no." He sighed. "I'm not going to explain it to you. You're just going to have to work it out for yourself." He paused. "Right, I'll say three things," he said sitting down, slicing the air with his hand for emphasis.

"First, Moore and all that lot are all jolly lovely, all jolly good technically, and all jolly bloody well out of date."

Colin looked at him.

"They have nothing to say, Colin," he said in a slightly quieter tone.

Colin's head was bowed, all his ideas kicked about like sandcastles on the beach.

"Second, you have a penchant for Paul Henry. Well and good," said Stanley. "Learn from his abstraction of the landscape. Learn how he was able to distill the essence of a landscape into a pure expression of form. Learn from his pared down shape and color. Study it and do something with it. Something that's bloody well *new*."

Colin looked up from his shoes.

"Third," said Stanley, "go to the Hugh Lane and look for a painting called *Hy Brasil* by a talented chap called Patrick Collins. Stare at it and stare at it and when you understand it, come back to me."

Colin didn't know what he was talking about and gathered up his things quickly, feeling forlorn like a dog after rain.

"That painting is a gateway to another world," said Stanley, looking directly at him.

Colin sighed in frustration. "What world?" he said in a sulk.

"Just let it speak to you," said Stanley.

Colin raised his eyes to heaven.

"You're the man for that painting," said Stanley. "Not everyone is but you are. Now go."

5

Colin paused midair, the knife suspended between finger and thumb.

Rain was rattling the window behind him, but he remained utterly still. The evening light had drained from the room leaving a grey film behind. He couldn't see properly but this wasn't the first time he had painted past the point of no return. Leaning forward, he hovered above the canvas, drew back, then swung in again in a slow pendulous movement. Knife touched canvas. Hand held steady.

Thumb gave a flick and the knife dragged paint like jam across toast.

His hand came away with a flourish. He stood back and looked. Stop.

He put the knife down.

Done.

He turned his back and looked out at the pouring rain. He must have performed that final maneuver about twenty times. And twenty times he hadn't been happy. So each time, he did it again. And again.

Now he was. Job done.

He began to clean up.

*****

Two weeks to dry. A few days to get framed. A new painting to sell. The gallery on Molesworth Street had begun to show his work.

Despite the wet summer, he had sold more than he expected. More than the gallery had expected. The sales had given him a boost he wasn't getting from the college. The people who bought his paintings all went away smiling and that was a new feeling for Colin, which he preferred to Stanley's scowls.

One evening at the gallery's summer exhibition, the lady with six dogs arrived. She tied the dogs to a lamppost where they yapped for a bit, then fell silent, their eyes trained on the windows, watching her every move inside. Richard, the owner of the gallery, went to fetch Colin.

"Come and meet Lady Bell," he said. "She's been asking after your work."

"The boy from the beach," she pronounced as if it were an accolade of sorts. "I thought it might be you, from what Richard said."

"Yes, I remember," said Colin, pleased to see her.

"Adeline Bell." She stuck out her hand and gave a firm handshake.

Colin brought her over to see his paintings.

She looked at them intently. "Oh," she sighed. "These just make me want to go and swim in the sea right *now*," she said. "*But* I'm going to wait for one more year. One more year," she said loudly to the room. "And I'll tell you why," she said, looking directly at him, "because I think it will be *more* than worth the wait."

With that, she was away through the crowd, chatting to people here and there. She seemed to know everyone. Then she was gone as abruptly as she had come, in a hullabaloo of dogs.

Richard was impressed. "There you go," he said. "There you go."

Her comments had cheered Colin up. His second year had been a less than happy affair, contrary to his early ideas and plans. Stanley's dismissal of Port Sunlight had been deflating and Colin felt the barometer of expectation had been set unreasonably high. His confidence had been bruised and he wore his feelings plainly for all to see, like a T-shirt stained with mud.

*****

He had gone to see the painting *Hy Brasil* and found it initially to his disliking.

Then he found himself returning many times as if working out the courage to ask it to dance. Eventually he found himself slipping into its warm embrace as comfortably as a lover returns to his mistress.

The painting was almost void.

A narrow band of rock emerging from a swathe of grey nothingness.

A veiled swirl of nothingness.

A fairy fog. A mist.

A thin finger of land scratched delicately through the haze.

The mythical island of Hy Brasil. Said to lie off the west coast of Ireland, only visible once every seven years. Visible through the mist of the Otherworld.

But this was not a landscape painting.

This was a landscape of the mind.

And although it fascinated Colin, he felt overwhelmed by it.

Almost afraid of it. Afraid of its heady perfume.

It was haunting, ethereal, challenging. Too challenging. He didn't know what to do with it. He told Stanley he would need more time. To let it sink in.

But he was taken with the color. The veil of ethereal color. The color of a dream in the sea.

It was the abstraction he was not ready for. That would have to come to him later.

Michael made a face when he took him to see it.

"Don't know what you're worrying about. It's a mad blur of a mess," he said, dragging Colin away to McDaid's for a pint.

*****

The week before Christmas it began to snow. Delicately at first, like flecks of paint sprayed from a brush. Then swirling in waves until the streets were fringed with scarves of white, the entire city blanketed with a reverential hush. Colin watched, intrigued by the monochrome shift in color, the snow glimmering like dust in the low dusk of evening.

The snow left a lasting impression. In the new year, he began to experiment with a distilled, almost monastic use of color. Paul Henry had been known for his pared back shades, and Colin felt a strange exhilaration, a new freedom in limiting himself now to a stripped-down palette. His work began to tone down, the chords calming and coming to roost with the stillness of vespers, the mountains and rocks and waterscapes all layered with a sense of murk and haze.

It was a beginning. A start.

A start on the road to somewhere. Stanley seemed to soften his attitude a little, but Colin still felt like he was out on a limb, a monkey on a branch by himself.

But he painted on.

Smearing layers of tonal shades in drifts across the canvas. The paintings began to take on a new look, but he wondered was he breaking new ground or just cloaking his work in disguise. An answer to Stanley's gauntlet thrown down in September.

Perhaps.

But only half an answer.

A halfway house.

*****

"Progress," said Stanley, his lower lip protruding like a ledge from a cliff. "Slow, slow progress," he muttered, walking away, his hands behind his back, his head shaking from side to side.

"I think they're beautiful," said Dearbhla.

"Maybe you've gone too far," said Michael.

"What do you mean?" said Colin.

Michael made a face. "Are they a bit muddy-looking? Like you haven't cleaned your brushes or something."

Colin glared at him. For the first time a tension now stretched between them like a tightrope. Colin stroked his hand through his hair. The rope wobbled. His face was like stone. Michael withdrew and walked out.

"You can't always have everything your own way," Michael said later in the pub.

"I'm not even sure myself what I'm doing," Colin said, shrugging.

"I do like them," Michael said, giving him a push. "But some of your wildness has gone."

Colin looked at him. "Mmmm," he said slowly.

"I think for that sort of color to work you need to liven it up a bit," said Michael, "lash into it more with some wild strokes, the way you used to. They've gone too sober. That's it," he said, reaching for his pint with a grin. "Give them a drink. Give the bloody paintings a drink."

Colin laughed. "Sometimes," he said, "you can actually make some sense."

*****

The year dawdled to a close. In the summer, Michael went home to Kinsale and Colin started back in the gallery. They asked him to bring in a few paintings. Pleased to be asked, he brought in some of the earlier ones. When they sold and the gallery asked for more, he decided to return to his old ways. The new stuff would have to wait. On his days off, he went out to Howth and the sands at Malahide. He painted new pictures in the brightening wind that made him feel sunny and young again unburdened by Stanley's expectations. But at night he would dream.

Of an island far out in the ocean.

The island of Hy Brasil.

A vale of shadows in his mind. Cascades of spray and water streaming past. He would turn and twist in a world of sea and sand and foam. The song of seabirds encroaching through a fog. Sea haze, a surge of white, a broken line upon the page like an eyelash in the eye. His vision blurred like rain through mist. An island shawled in sea and jagged rocks where the fish go round. Where the fish go round and round through sea and sand and foam. And he would turn and toss in his sleep and moan and dream. Of an island in the sea. Merging and submerging through sea and sand and foam, where the fish go round. Where the fish go round and round ...

But in the mornings, he couldn't make any sense of it.

The mysterious Hy Brasil. The landscape of the mind.

"When you understand the painting, come back to me," Stanley had said. But he couldn't find the key. He couldn't solve the mystery.

And so, he let it lie.

To focus on brighter work. Work that was selling.

And that in itself was no small thing.

*****

Stanley tended to give final year students more space. As far as he was concerned, they should know what they were about by year three. And if they didn't, then in his view they probably never would.

"I wouldn't let that gallery go to your head," he snapped at Colin in the autumn term. "Selling *postcards* is not why you're here, but I think you know that," he said brusquely before walking away, leaving Colin feeling as if he'd just been pickpocketed. The one thing that had kept him going over the summer snatched straight out of his hands now like a chimpanzee swiping a banana.

"That man makes my blood boil," Colin said to Michael that evening.

"I wouldn't worry about him. Just do your own thing."

"Yeah, whatever that is."

"You shouldn't let him get to you," said Michael.

"He didn't like Port Sunlight. He doesn't like what I'm selling in the gallery. He doesn't like my monochrome stuff either. I don't know what he wants."

"For God's sake, it's not what he wants," said Michael, "it's what you want."

"I don't know what that is either," said Colin glumly.

Michael groaned. Ever since he'd come back from Kinsale, Colin had been glum and preoccupied. There was no getting through to him. He was as sensitive as ever and Michael could see that Stanley had really rattled him. It was a shame, but Michael was distracted too. He had met a girl in Kinsale and was up and down on the train every other month to see her. He worked in a bar the rest of the time at weekends. Colin did Saturdays in the gallery and painted most Sundays, and they were seeing a lot less of each other than in previous years.

Michael knew he didn't have Colin's talent. His style was more limited but so were his ambitions. Overall, he was just more laid back about their graduation, and going up and down on the train to Cork to see this girl was a diversion and an escape from the small, enclosed art world of campus.

*****

By Easter, Colin was waning. He hadn't made the breakthrough that had been expected. And he was starting to panic now with the end of year show looming on the horizon.

Walking home one night past the tall houses of Wilton Terrace, he stopped abruptly. Many of the windows had lights on, patterning the buildings like illuminated stamps. But there was one window that had caught his eye. A chandelier was glowing and there were tall brass lamps on either end of a mantelpiece. It was a painting facing the window that he was staring at. It had called to him like a telegraph wire connecting across the lawn.

Then came a straining, pulling sound and paws patterning the pavement. The panting of breath. Dogs. He looked around.

"Not you again!"

He grinned. "Is this is your house?"

"Well, who else do you think it belongs to?"

"The painting in the window …" He stopped.

"Oh, come in and see it properly," she said walking ahead, the dogs scrambling up the path.

He followed her in.

She let the dogs off in the hall and they scattered down the back. "Din-dins for the boys," she shouted after them. "Din-dins in the kitchen with Cook." She threw open a door.

"Like a drink?" she said, moving to a side table.

Colin headed over to the picture. "Yes, thanks," he said absently.

Almost immediately she produced two large vodkas with lemon. "*Dawn, Killary Harbour.* Spectacular, isn't it?"

Colin was staring at it. He hadn't seen a Paul Henry like this so close up before.

"No cottages, no bogs, just pared down shapes," she said.

A creamy, ethereal sky, the hills angled in shadow, the water magically light as if a fairy mist had just lifted.

"The paint is as thick as butter," he said.

She had moved to the other side of the room and put a record on. A fusion of haunting soprano voices seeped through the air like a dawn chorus coming from the painting itself.

"What's that music?" said Colin, still looking at the canvas.

"Hildegard von Bingen."

He shook his head, the name meant nothing to him.

"Medieval German nun. Mystic and poet. Listen to it," she commanded, throwing her arm out wide. "Don't you just feel you're in heaven?"

Colin nodded in agreement.

"Especially, when you're looking at that," she said, gesturing to the painting. "That is one bloody good dawn," she said, staring at it for a moment, then flung herself down on a sofa.

Colin sat on the armchair opposite.

"How are you getting on at the college?" she inquired.

"Not great." He made a face. "They're a bit down on me at the moment." He looked up. "Isn't that …"

"Yes," she said, following his gaze. "A Frank McKelvey."

"I love him," he said.

"Portrush, I think," she said. "Somewhere up there anyway." She waved a hand.

He moved to another picture close to it.

"Humbert Craig," she said.

"God, you do collect them," he said, bewildered.

"Yes, I do," she said, smiling. "I'll show you my modern room sometime."

"So, you like modern art too?" he asked, sitting down.

"Absolutely, although so much of what passes for modern these days is all fur coats and no knickers."

Colin laughed. "But surely——"

"No buts." She held out her hand flat in the air. "I don't want to fork out a small fortune for some paint splattered canvas which I then have to spend the rest of my life trying to figure out what on earth it's supposed to mean."

"But art should provoke and make you ask questions," said Colin.

"Oh, I quite agree," she said. "But a lot of the time there are no satisfactory answers."

"Mmmm," he said.

"Now, *you*," she said, looking directly at him, "*can* actually paint. You have your own voice. And that in my opinion is what counts. You're not trying to copy or mimic or shock. You're your own man. *Colin Larkin*." She unfolded the vowels slowly, like a rug on the lawn. "That's a compliment by the way."

"The college says I'm old-fashioned, out of date."

"How could you be out of date? You're barely out of the pram. Look," she said, "Paul Henry may be out of fashion, but one day, that," she said, pointing at the painting, "will be worth a lot of money."

"And then you'll sell it?"

"Never," she replied. "That's not the point. Fashions come and go, but do you know something?" She leaned forward.

He shook his head.

"Beauty lasts. Truth lasts. So be true to yourself."

"How do you mean?"

"Paul Henry went to Achill and fell in love with it." She settled back against the cushions. "So, go beyond. Go west. Find somewhere you can call your own. Find a blasted rock in the Atlantic if you like and write your name on it. Just for heaven's sake, *do* it. Then come back and surprise them. Surprise all of us. Surprise yourself." She paused.

"Mmmm," said Colin.

"I mean it," she said. "That *Dawn at Killary Harbour* didn't paint itself, you know."

"Mmmm," he said again, finishing his drink.

"Food for thought," she said as she smiled and rose. "Like another?"

"No, no, no, I have to think," he said, rising from his chair.

She took his arm and walked him to the door.

"Stay true to this," she said, thumping her heart. "This is the beating heart. Lose this and you lose everything."

He walked down the steps, the evening, the paintings, the drink, her words gushing through him like a stream racing over rocks.

He walked home bemused, kicking leaves along the path. Her words had made more sense than all his talks with Stanley. The next morning, he went straight to the library. There was something she had said. And something he had seen before. And the two strands of thought were embedded in his head like a puzzle he had to solve. But first there was something he needed to look up. Then he would know what to do.

The librarian looked at him over her glasses. "I'll just take a look for you," she said, and went away to check the card index. He stayed at the counter. She seemed a long time.

"Follow me," she said returning. "I think we may have something. Let's have a look."

She pulled a large hard-backed book off a shelf and handed it to him. "There we are," she said pushing her glasses back up on her nose.

Colin sat down at a table and passed his palm over the cover.

The Lighthouses of Ireland.

On the front, the majestic lighthouse on Fastnet Rock, towering above a cascade of spray.

Mmmm, thought Colin, looking at the jagged, cutthroat rocks, the most southerly point of Ireland. He had heard of it, Fastnet Rock, the last glimpse of Ireland that passengers to America would see as their ships passed out to the ocean.

He stopped daydreaming. No way. He'd be swallowed up by the elements.

He opened the book and started to search. He needed to find it. The place inside him. That world of Hy Brasil. He had to find it. A rock. An island. A lighthouse. A point in the ocean.

He turned the pages.

He wanted to find some distant point. Where he could disappear.

"Find a blasted rock in the Atlantic and write your name on it," said Lady Adeline Bell in his ear.

A place of sea and sky. Somewhere, way out there.

Then he stopped reading and looked up. "Mmmm," he said.

"Mmmm," he said again, cracking his fingers, then took out his pen and began to write.

He had found it.

The island of Inishtrahull.

6

Like liquid spilling from a giant cauldron, a torrent of waves sluiced Tor Beg rock, invisible in the darkness to the captain on board. The Cambria plunged on, cabin lights flashing like gemstones in the rain. When iron gashed rock, the ripping sound came like a hammered nail, then amplified upward like a detonated bomb. Water poured through, ransacking the hull and quenching the fires in the engine room. The ship was swaying like a drunken sailor, the cries of her passengers haunting the night. The lighthouse keeper at Inishtrahull gripped his lantern in the sway of the gale. Shielding his eyes from the rain, he could see the lights of the ship shining like stars on the water. He could hear the passengers' voices calling to God in the wind. And as he watched, the lights went out as if turned off by some invisible hand. And through the storm, he heard the terrible roar as the sea opened wide and swallowed her prey.

*****

Colin's first glimpse of the island from Malin Head was serene.

The sea was like a baby blue blanket unfurling into the distance where, if he squinted his eyes, he could just about see where it fused with the horizon.

He had never been so far north.

Here at the place of the storm. But there was barely a breath of wind today.

Not the merest hint or trace or sense of the *Cambria*. The steamer had sunk on the night of October 19th, 1870. And ever since he had read the contemporary accounts, he had been fascinated. The lighthouse keeper standing alone with his lantern, powerless to help across the divide of water from Inishtrahull to Tor Beg.

Of the one hundred and seventy-nine passengers, just one survivor.

Picked up the next day, drifting about in a boat with a lady in black silk who had Colin drowned.

So here Colin lay.

Stretched out on the grass like a rabbit gazing out to the island.

He could see the lighthouse at the farthest end rising up like a church spire. The island of Inishtrahull, the most northerly end of Ireland. The most distant point.

Finally, he had come.

And next, he would go out there. Join the seals and the gulls. The lost souls of the dead. And the ghost of the lighthouse keeper.

He would go to Inishtrahull.

And stand like the keeper, some dark night looking out at the rock of Tor Beg. That dangerous last outcrop of Ireland.

He would have to find someone to take him.

But for now, just for now it was good to soak it all in, to lie in the sun a few minutes. The island within grasp.

He blinked. He couldn't believe he was here.

*****

"You're out of your mind," Stanley had said. "You do know there's only five weeks left to the show?"

Colin had nodded. "Yes," he said, "I know. That's why I want to do this now. I've just about got enough time."

"You've had nearly three years," said Stanley, staring at him wide eyed.

"It's to do with Hy Brasil," said Colin, trying to explain.

"Hy Brasil, my arse," said Stanley. "I sent you to look at that years ago, much good it did you then."

"But you said …" Colin spoke slowly as if Stanley were deaf or thick or both, "that when I understood it to come back to you."

"Well, I didn't mean a couple of years later," said Stanley. "I mean, my God, man, you could have been to the North Pole and back more than once in that length of time."

"Well, this is important," said Colin.

"Fine." Stanley held up both his hands like he was under arrest. "Fine, go, I can't stop you anyway. But I can't see how tearing off to Donegal and some fecking rut of an island is going to be much use at this late stage in the game. But," he said, tired from his never-ending standoff with this young man, "I admire your sheer fucking pluck."

"Oh," said Colin and then stopped as if he'd just been jolted by an electric fence.

"But I don't know what you're going to do with all the rest of your work," said Stanley. "Sheer bloody waste of time and effort, if you ask me."

"I can sell it," said Colin boldly.

"Oh, yes," said Stanley puckering his face, "I forgot, you're a best-selling artist."

Even Michael was hostile. "Jesus, Colin," he said, "have you lost the bloody plot?"

"Why?" said Colin. "What's wrong with the idea?"

"What's wrong with the idea?" said Michael. "God, I need another drink. You do know you're completely off your trolley?"

"What did Stanley say?" he asked, coming back from the bar.

"The usual," said Colin, shrugging.

Michael laughed. "Well, if it gets up his nose, then all well and good," he said, raising his glass. "Here, good luck," he said, "'cause you're going to bloody well need it."

For the first time since the library, Colin felt uneasy, with a queer, sick feeling crawling into his stomach. If Michael was lukewarm, then maybe he was an eejit.

He told his mother he was going to Donegal. He didn't tell her about Inishtrahull.

She looked at him quizzically, suspecting something was up. His tone was too bright, too forced, too cheery.

"Have you fallen out with Michael or something?" she asked with a frown.

"Of course not," said Colin. "Sure I saw him last night in the pub."

Eileen left it at that. The next morning when he left, she packed him sandwiches. "I still don't know why you're going all the way up to Donegal," she said. "You don't even know anyone up there."

Colin smiled and sighed. "I just need somewhere fresh," was all he said.

Eileen snorted. "Well, I don't know what's wrong with the mountains in Wicklow," she said. Then they hugged and he left, and he was walking out the gate and down the road before he knew it. His mother watched him go. It took her a long time to close the door.

*****

Colin found a pub with rooms by the quay. The woman behind the bar raised her eyebrows when he asked about the island.

She shook her head. "I doubt if anyone's going to take you over there," she said. "Frank!" She called her husband out from the back room. "This young fella says he wants to know will someone take him to Inishtrahull."

"Why?" said Frank, peering at him. "What would he want to be going out there for?"

"He says he's a painter," she said.

"A painter?" said Frank as if he had never heard of the word. "Well, I don't know," he said, scratching his head.

"Are you having your dinner here tonight?" she asked turning back to Colin.

He nodded.

"We'll ask around for you," she said. "A lot of the men will be here by then."

Colin was back by seven for a meal of chicken and mash. He wasn't expecting to have much to eat for the next few days, and he needed a good meal now. But there were no offers to take him to the island.

"Too dangerous to land," said one. "No place to be," said another. "You couldn't be up to the weather," said a third. A row of heads in caps began to nod. Smoke drifted about.

Colin was thinking he would have to change his plans. He swore under his breath. He'd only just arrived after the arguments in college and now he was going to fall at the first hurdle. Perhaps he was just a stupid, stubborn idiot after all. *I should never have come*, he thought. *I'll never live this down if I go back with nothing to show.* He bit his lip. *I'll just bloody well have to do the best I can from here*, he decided. *At least I'll be able to see the island, which is better than nothing.* He swore again quietly, feeling utterly frustrated.

The woman came and cleared his plate. "Come up to the bar," she said, cocking her head. A young man with a freckled, weathered face and a five o'clock stubble was leaning on the counter. "Daniel O'Malley," he said, offering his hand. Colin shook it gladly. "I'll take you," he said. Colin grinned at him. "I hear you paint the sea," said Daniel, looking at him. "Are you any good?"

"Not bad," said Colin.

"Well if you promise me a painting, I'll take you in the morning. By the way," he said, looking directly at Colin, "you do know the sea around here can be brutal?"

*****

But Colin was down on the quay by seven. Daniel was already there. "Mind the steps," he called. Colin threw him down his rucksack and tent. The steps were greasy, but he jumped aboard in one go. Daniel fiddled about with ropes and moorings and in a few minutes, they were off. It was a small fishing boat and they sped out to sea quickly, the wind picking up in their faces.

The island was six miles out from Ballyhillin Quay. Although it had felt quite calm on land, there was a swell to the water. The boat began to rock and ride the waves, up and down, over, up and down, over. Colin held on to the handrail and braced himself against the slap of the wind and the bursts of spray landing on board. The mainland had receded, and was now small in the distance. The boat was completely hemmed in by water and dwarfed under the vastness of sky. Daniel grinned at him. He thought Colin was mad, but then he had heard all artists were mad. Inishtrahull began to loom close and Colin watched as the detail of rocks and birds and hills all swung into view as Daniel slowed the engine. The landing port was around to the northeast so the boat had to navigate the jagged coast, but Daniel had grown up on the water and he knew the way like the back of his hand.

"Well, you're on your own now," he said, "apart from Jimmy Murphy and the boys in the lighthouse and they'll not bother you." He helped Colin out with his things and looked up at the sky. "The weather's set to turn. I'll be back the day after tomorrow."

"But I'm going to need at least three days," said Colin.

"I'll delay it as long as I can," said Daniel, "but trust me, I'll be back at the latest by noon on Thursday."

"But—" said Colin.

"Well fine," said Daniel, "have it your own way. If I don't come back, you'll be stranded here for a week."

"Alright," said Colin. "Alright."

"And be ready to come," said Daniel, "because I won't want to be hanging around." He churned the engine then and Colin watched the boat slipping away.

He watched until the boat disappeared around the crags. The wind whistled all around him and for a moment he felt completely alone. But then he remembered the men in the lighthouse. He took a deep breath and pushed up from the shore, clambering onto the grass. This was what he had wanted. Time was short. Food was short. He had brought bread and water and biscuits, some apples and cheese and chocolate. And one flask of coffee. He would have to make it all last. But he wasn't here on a holiday. First, he had to find somewhere to camp.

The island was rocky and ridged and hilly. The wind tore around corners and subsided in hollows. There was a graveyard and an old school with a plaque from 1901. And the ruins of crumbling stone cottages. The islanders had been evacuated years ago and the ruins were well collapsed now. But he found a sheltered place for the tent, in between by the stone walls.

He decided to eat early. The boat trip and getting the tent sorted had made him hungry. He hunkered down with the loaf of bread and the cheese. He was intending to spend all his time working but he just needed for a moment to draw breath. After an apple, he felt ready and gathered up his things. He hadn't brought his easel. He knew it would have been useless in the wind. He wanted to make as many studies as he could of the changing light. There were loose ideas in his head, but he would need to try them out. Atmosphere. That's why he was here. To capture the atmosphere of this strange, distant place. Although sitting where he was in the lee of the ruins, it was hard to believe he was somewhere so wild and remote. The sun had come out and he was tempted to lie back and fall asleep. Not a chance. He stood up.

It was time to explore. To the west of the island at its highest point was the lighthouse. Its whiteness pierced the sky with a man-made defiance he found oddly comforting. He skirted past it, heading straight for the cliffs and the northerly drop to the ocean. Straight ahead lay the rock of Tor Beg. A dizzying moment. The most northerly point. The end of Ireland.

He stood gazing out to sea. Out to the rock of Tor Beg.

Out across the rock. Out across the ocean. Out to the horizon.

To the line between sky and water.

Then he gazed up at the sky and drew back, his eyes wincing from the light. The sky was even more vast here than the sea, stretching out like a mammoth umbrella every other way. The clouds seemed to be moving toward him at a fierce rate. Rushing in. The sky was moving. The sea was moving. Everything was churning. His heart began to pound. This was the moment to start.

He settled himself on the rough grass and watched the birds dipping and swooping in and out of the rock face. He could see how much even they were buffeted by the wind, which seemed to come from all angles. Then he bent his head and began.

*****

A shadow loomed across the page like a cloud.

"You're too close to the edge."

He looked up.

"Come back a bit if you want to stay safe."

Colin stood up.

"Jimmy Murphy." The keeper shook his hand. "We've been watching you. Had you down as a birdwatcher. Looks like you're a painter," he said with a smile.

"Daniel O'Malley dropped me off," Colin said.

"I know," said Jimmy. "I know everything here."

Colin laughed. "I'm only here till Thursday," he said. "I won't be any bother."

"Aye," said Jimmy, "Daniel will need to fetch you alright, there's a front coming in. Look, I'll leave you be," he said. "But watch yourself out here. And stop by for a cup of tea later," he added with a brusque nod of his head.

Colin grinned. "I'd like that," he said.

*****

All afternoon, he moved around finding different angles, better vantage points. Getting to know the terrain. Trying to catch up with the rapidly shifting light. Today, he just wanted to get the color and tone and the feel of the place right. In this open-air studio up over the ocean. Halfway to heaven. Tomorrow, he would begin to abstract. Find a new way to convey what he saw. He wasn't here for conventional work. He hadn't gone to these lengths to go home with the usual canvases.

He was here for a landscape of the mind.

This was meant to be *his* Hy Brasil.

But he still wasn't sure what he was going to come up with.

The evening was long, but the light was changing. And Colin continued for hours, absorbed in capturing the skeins of tinted light now flooding the sky from the west. And as he worked, he realized it was the light of dawn and the light of dusk which held him the most and would be the best to focus on. And he would need to be up early tomorrow to start. To capture the dawn.

So he stopped.

*****

When he knocked on the door of the lighthouse, his knock seemed to get lost in the wind, but after a few minutes, he was let in. "I'll show you around," said Jimmy. "We don't often get visitors here." He laughed.

Both of the other men were younger than Jimmy and both were working in the engine room, but said hello and seemed friendly enough, but shy. The stairs in the lighthouse wound round and round like a snail.

"Twenty-three meters high," said Jimmy. Colin was inside the lighthouse that had been inside his head since Port Sunlight. It was like a private pilgrimage. A hermit cell.

"Nineteen feet high," said Jimmy, showing him the lantern. It towered over their heads into the night sky. It was like being inside a

hollow diamond. "Every twenty seconds," he said as the light began
to blind. Colin blinked. They began to descend.

"A range of twenty miles," said Jimmy.

"Wasn't it the last bit of Ireland people going on ships from
Belfast to America could see?" asked Colin.

"The light of Inishtrahull, yes, still is," said Jimmy. "But there was
an older lighthouse back at that time on the other side of the island.
This one is only about eight years old, built back in '57."

They had a cup of tea which was welcome after the wind of the day.

"Well, at least you won't need a light back to your tent." Jimmy
laughed, opening the door for him. He watched Colin head across
the jutted terrain. He smiled to himself and shook his head. It wasn't
every day they had a visitor, apart from the occasional official on
inspection. The young lad had been really interested in the tour. He
sighed. He had liked watching his face brighten up but now it was
back to the routine of work. He enjoyed being the keeper, but it was
a lonely old job. He closed the door.

*****

Colin slept soundly. The flashing lantern from the lighthouse didn't
protrude much where he was camped. Walking back to the tent had
been like walking on another planet, the stony ground lit up every
few steps with the extraterrestrial beacon.

Morning came and he rubbed his eyes. There were rabbits darting
between the ruined cottages. He watched them bouncing about.
They seemed oblivious to his presence.

It was very early, but he made his way eastward, where the light
was rushing in, skimming the sea with a sheen like a silvery mirror.
Until breakfast, he worked on the dawn color, so different to the dusk
of evening. After some bread and cold coffee, an apple and a bar of
chocolate, he was ready again.

He wanted to produce a rapid series of sketches which he could transform into larger, finished works when he got back. He started by fusing the bands of color from the dawn. Then he added some strokes which were rocks. But they could have been the sail of a yacht. Or the hull of a trawler. Or they could have been a mountain in the mist protruding up from the deep. He was suggesting now rather than recording and was deeply absorbed. He did the same with the colors from the evening before. And from a spot farther up on the cliff. The series of strokes could have been seals or the wings of birds or the curve of a fishing boat out on the water. He worked all day, taking a break for an apple and a packet of biscuits which he munched in one go. Then he turned his attention to the sky. The sense of the sky like a glass bowl above him, all spangled with light and shade and cloud.

The wind today had quietened down. He saw no trace of the front Daniel had mentioned. It was a shame he would have to cut things short. But if anything, it made him work with a greater intensity. And now for the first time in his life, he understood the tension of deadline. By evening he had filled an entire notebook and started another. The final pieces to the jigsaw were assembling. The pictures were exciting because at first glance there was nothing there. But then on inspection there was an island. Or what appeared to be an island. And there was a lighthouse. Or what appeared to be a lighthouse. Take a step back and the image disappeared. Take a step closer and the image began to metamorphose out from the blurring of colors and shapes and tones.

But they still were only sketches.

The real work would come later.

It was a clear, calm evening. The light had dipped away to the west like a curtain dropping on a scene from a play.

Boy on island. Boy all alone on island.

Boy paints sea and clouds on island.

The End.

It had been a short play.

But the drama. The set. The colors.

He sat on for hours gazing out to Tor Beg. It was too dark to work anymore. He might get a bit more done in the morning but for now, this was everything.

The hissing of the wind; the blue, thin horizon; the pewter clouds hanging from the sky.

Here at the end of the line.

*****

There was no chance of more work in the morning. The rain was coming down. He was going to get soaked getting back on the boat. He packed up the sketchbooks, away from the wet. Then he struggled in the wind to collapse the tent which was wringing wet and flapping about like a fish on a line. Inishtrahull was a different place this morning. The sense of the *Cambria* was here now.

The drownings at sea. The shipwrecks across the years.

The lonely island, the gravestones, the ruins, the ragged mountain tracks.

The last bit of Ireland.

When he came over the hill, the wind nearly knocked him over.

He struggled down to the harbor to wait for the boat and stood hugging his elbows close to his chest, the rain dripping down his hood.

He hadn't wanted to leave the island. It had seeped into his soul. But now he wished the boat would come. He was already sopping wet and he was worried about the sketchbooks. There was no sign. He couldn't have missed it. Daniel had told him to be on the alert. He looked over his shoulder. The sky was darkening. It was going to get worse. When he looked back, the boat had rounded the rocks and was shaking from side to side. Then it slowed and slid toward him out of the rain. Daniel beckoned to him. There was no option but to wade through the water hauling the tent and rucksack with him. Daniel pulled him up on board. "Best get in the cabin," he shouted.

"Told you it'd be rough." Colin slipped and slid on his way to the cabin. His thigh hurt and he was wet through as he made it inside. Daniel turned the wheel and they were away. Colin looked back. The island was fading. The window was steaming. He brushed the glass. The island reappeared. The glass fogged again. The island began to disappear. He did it again. And the island came and went.

Just like his sketches. He smiled.

The island of Inishtrahull.

They passed out to open sea.

He looked back in the rain, but the island was gone.

*****

Arriving back into Dublin the next evening, his head was like straw and his throat was aching. He had been cold and shivering after the boat and spent the night in a rug with a brandy trying to warm up. The rain was still coming down in the morning but he knew he had to get on the road. He left a small watercolor behind in the pub for Daniel. He would have liked to have seen him again but he had to keep an eye on the time.

Eileen brought him a bowl of chicken broth in bed.

"If you get any worse, I'll have to get the doctor," she said.

Colin groaned. He was losing time every day. "I'll be fine," he whispered.

"I don't know what possessed you to go haring off up there in the first place," she said.

He just smiled and fell back on the pillows.

Then he slept.

And the fish swam round ...

... and the fish swam round and round ...

... and his fever raged ...

His mother nursed him for two days with hot drinks and soup.

By the third day his head was beginning to clear. The wind on the sea subsiding, his throat now calming, the howl in his ears receding.

He came downstairs for some lunch and spent the afternoon sorting out canvases. But he was in no state to go back to college. He would have to work from home. Which suited him fine. He wasn't ready to share the island. Yet.

But there were only three weeks to go.

He worked in Aine's old room. She had moved out over the winter to a flat. The room was perfect. Spacious, south facing, overlooking the garden. Pure, natural light. He had decided to go large and primed a mixed bunch of canvases. The largest was five feet by six. He had ordered it a year ago, but hadn't done anything with it.

"Are you sure you know what you're up to?" said Eileen. But Colin had that faraway look in his eye and there was no reaching him now. She left him alone in Aine's room and he spent hours up there like a rabbit in his burrow only coming out for meals.

By the end of the week, he had two paintings underway. Two small paintings.

Dawn and Dusk.

But he was picking up speed now that he was working in oil and the island was taking on forms he had only imagined. His blood was beginning to pulse. The brushes and knives were sweeping again freely like extensions to his hand. Eileen didn't know what to make of what she saw. These weren't the sort of pictures she was used to seeing him produce. She wasn't sure about them. But now was not the time. He began to work later and later into the night until the light had vanished behind the trees and the birds had gone to sleep. He was immersed in the work and the paint was coming thick and fast.

The canvases were beginning to mount up.

At the close of each day he would stand and stare at his work.

The shadow of Tor Beg rock. That might have been a seal or a boat or the hull of a ship.

The wing of a bird that might have been a bird or the curl of a cloud in the wind.

And the feeling of a squall of rain about to fall.

And he would smile. Because that was all that mattered.

Not seeing it.

Feeling it.

*****

The following week, Michael came to see him and watched him work, his eyes widening.

"You do know Stanley is having kittens?"

Colin put his palette knife down. "I was in bed for three days," he said. "There was no way I could have gone in."

"And the college knows that?"

"I phoned in," said Colin. "Whether they told Stanley or not is their concern."

"Have you got much more to do?" Michael asked.

Colin laughed. "How long is a piece of string?"

"There'll be war," said Michael.

"Nah," said Colin. "There won't."

But there was less than a week to go now.

And two paintings still to do.

First *Sky* and then the final one. The one he hoped would define him.

So, *Sky* first.

And he remembered it. The sky soaring over the cliffs. Soaring way up overhead. The clouds gushing past. The dizziness of it all.

And he painted as if in free fall so that the feeling was like that of a kaleidoscope, where the clouds seemed to surge before the eye.

And the effect was like falling from a great height. From a cliff.

It was time for the last painting.

But his mind had begun to panic. He didn't know whether he could get it finished. And even if he did, it wouldn't be dry. He had no way to transport it either.

"Leave it with me," said Eileen, aware he was agitated. "Just concentrate on the painting. Doesn't matter if it's not fully dry," she said. "It's more important you show up and the tutors and that Stanley fellow have something to look at."

So he left it with his mother and went back to work. The exhibition was Friday.

It was now Wednesday evening.

The canvases so far had been up close and intimate.

Now he pulled back.

Far back across the water to when he had first seen the island from Malin Head. That day when the sea had shone with a shimmering tinge and the island had seemed like a mirage in the haze.

He laid out the tones in the evening in undercoats of faintly changing color.

He was up early the next morning and working by eight.

From a veil of blue, he created the sense of the sea.

And out of the sea, he conjured the finger of land scratched across the ocean. The thin line of crag and rock and shadow that might or might not be land.

And on the island, the fleck, like the hint of a pin or the line of a shell, the lighthouse.

The lighthouse of Inishtrahull.

A pillar of white in the mist. Stand back and it was gone.

He had covered every inch of the canvas with paint layered like foam to create a viscous, luminous feeling.

He laid down his knife and stood back.

The effect was elegiac.

*****

Thursday. The end of the road.

His mother called him from downstairs. He stuck his head over the bannisters. "I have Frank Delaney here," she said. "He'll take you in his van." Colin grinned at him. Between them, they managed to get the paintings downstairs and out through the door. "We'll have to come back for the last one," said Frank. Eileen waved them off. But Colin was tense in the back with the canvases, his face thin and drawn, with dark pools under the sockets. He was nervous about returning to college.

*****

"Where the hell have you been?"

The voice cut the back off Colin like a blunted razor blade.

He turned around. "What the hell sort of time do you call this?" said Stanley, his voice bruising the walls.

"I was sick," said Colin.

"You were sick," said Stanley.

"I phoned in," said Colin.

"You phoned in," said Stanley. "You phoned in. Oh, get out of my way," he said, brushing past. "In all my time here, you really do take the biscuit."

Colin coughed.

"What is it now?" said Stanley, his voice rising like a whistle from a kettle.

"Be careful," Colin said. "Some of the paintings are still a bit wet."

"God almighty's sake," muttered Stanley, "still fucking wet." And he walked away heaving in tweed and corduroy.

For the rest of the afternoon, Colin focused on getting the pictures hung.

But he had run out of space. There was no room left.

In the end, he had to get permission to hang some of them in the corridor and he wasn't very happy about it. *Dusk* and *Dawn* on either side of the door. The large one at the end of the hall.

He went home feeling down, staring out of the bus at the crowds milling around like an army of ants. Aine's room looked forlorn with the sheets covering everything, the paintbrushes and knives all in jars. The tools of the job laid to rest. He drifted away to bed, his mind heavy with disappointment. His cargo lost in the corridor, separated from everyone else's.

*****

The exhibition opened at six, but Colin hadn't gone. His mother had left in an emerald green dress, telling him to get a move on.

He had freshened up with aftershave and put on a new blue shirt, but he was dreading it. He didn't want to go.

Meeting Stanley had pulled the rug out from under him. Hanging the pictures in the corridor where they were all separated was like hanging out your washing from a window. It would be seen as either looking for attention or worse as having been excluded from the main room. Stuck out in the corridor, the pictures hanging like posters in a primary school. Either way, a damp squib. A dull end.

But by seven he was on his way. Three years of hard graft and his mother in a new emerald dress. It would be far worse to stay at home. And childish and stupid and sad. So he went. Eyes down and morose. His face in a scowl on the bus.

There was chatter coming from the open windows as he approached across the cobbles. He could hear it rising and falling in the evening sun. Like a river running over stones. And he stopped to listen and he could make out the sound of laughter. And he could hear Adeline Bell's laugh crackling over the tide. And then he froze, one foot in front of the other.

He could hear it.

The laughing sound of ridicule. Blowing like hot air from a vent.

He listened and he could hear it.

The laughter. He couldn't bring himself to go in.

Into the sniggering.

The toe-curling ignominy of failure. The embarrassing shame.

His paintings on their own in the hall and people laughing at them. Laughing at him and his stupid ego-filled head of ground-breaking ideas. He turned to go.

Michael was coming down the steps and saw him.

"I'm heading over to the station," he called.

Colin nodded. Michael had told him his friend was coming up from Kinsale.

"You're dead late," said Michael. "Would you ever get yourself in there?"

Colin stared after him, tempted to follow.

Then he thought of his mother checking her watch, and he went up the steps.

He stood for a moment inside the door, his eyes blinking after the glare of sun.

He was trying to get his bearings. To spot someone he knew. But there was just a mass of heads staring at him. And then a rippling sound came.

Ricocheting off the walls and tiles like Ping-Pong balls. And he recognized the sound.

He began to see through the blur of faces and the indistinct murmuring. It was a clapping sound that had spread like a pack of cards falling. People were looking at him and clapping. Colin paused and walked into the crowd.

There was only one subject on everyone's lips.

Inishtrahull. The painting at the end of the hall.

They had gathered around it like seals on a rock. People were drawn to it before they had even gone into the exhibition. Hardly anyone had even heard of the place. But the spell of the mist was working.

People leaned in and stepped back and the mirage came and went.

Adeline Bell sought him out. He wasn't hard to find. In his pale shirt and fair hair.

"I see you found that rock," she said loudly, so that everyone heard.

Colin grinned broadly.

"I knew you could do it," she said. "I knew it. I just bloody well knew it."

It was that sort of a strange mingled evening. Everyone talking to everyone. Everyone coming and going. Michael was still not back. Perhaps the train had been delayed. But there were so many new people to meet tonight. Adeline Bell kept sending over fresh bunches of faces to chat with him. She was talking about him to everyone.

The evening swept on.

He was deep in conversation with some people he didn't know when he noticed Michael's head by the door.

They say the wind can change direction at the drop of a hat.

And the sea is warmer than land.

The people he was talking too were all smiles and laughter, but he wasn't following what they were saying.

And when a zephyr blows in, all thoughts turn to spring.

And the awakening of blossom and bud.

He was sipping a drink when he saw her. Then he lost her again in the crowd.

The people he didn't know were blocking the room like heads in a cinema. The crowd was parting and closing. He could see Michael coming toward him, the figures all around him moving apart like poppies in a field in the breeze.

And then he saw her. Again.

Red hair tumbling in curls as she moved through the crowd.

Slowly like a swan through the water.

Gliding across the room.

And he watched her advance.

She was walking ahead of Michael, a colored shawl draped around her shoulders, her eyes looking straight toward Colin. She was smiling when she settled in front of him.

"The artist," she said with a confident allure in her voice. "I've been hearing all about you," and she held out her arms, the shawl opening wide like a patterned silken fan of butterfly wings.

"Hello," she said, "I'm Aisling."

… Aisling, she said …

… Aisling …

… "I'm Aisling," she said …

Her words swinging in like the first peals of a bell that would ring all around him for years ……

II
camera

The day has been hung out to dry in the sun. A light, gentle breeze is flapping about. It is just after ten, but they have not appeared yet. She is sitting with a coffee outside the Lobster Pot. The sky is washed clean and is flung across the sea like a ceiling of azurite crystal. There are bees humming in montbretia and a donkey standing on the verge, twitching from midges. He moves his head like a pendulum and stares out to sea. Waves whistle far out in the distance. The tide is out, the sand moist and mauve with fringes of cream like a Japanese silk screen. Then they come.

The lame, whiskey-colored dog on the path, the man hunched with hands in coat pockets. She watches them navigate the stones to the beach. The dog moves gingerly, stops and looks up. The man bends down and lifts him onto the sands. He puts the dog down and the dog skips about, then slows to a trot. They are heading down to the shore. To the same spot as yesterday. They diminish in the distance, a child's drawing in her eye. She gets up and sets down her cup on the bench and follows. She is like a pencil sketching after them on the sand. Tracing their footprints and paw prints across the page.

But as she draws near, she pulls back, leaving them to the ritual.

She dawdles away to the rocks. The man stands like a lighthouse in silhouette. The dog stands four paws square, then wobbles on his bad leg and sits down on his haunches, his snout like a fisherman testing the breeze. *They are like a memorial sculpture*, she thinks, and turns her head to the seaweed draped over the rocks. When she turns, they have moved, and the moment is gone like a cloud dissolved by sun. They are ambling along when she curves in to meet them.

"Hello," she says, her voice breaking across the sand. The man is momentarily startled. The dog does a dance then runs to her, barking, his head thrown back with his eyes focused on her. The man is smaller up close, with fair, white hair like silk in the sun. But his eyes give nothing away. They sweep over her quickly like a searchlight. She fidgets.

"Ah," he says slowly, "a photographer." He has spotted the zoom lens camera strung across her chest. "You are a photographer," he says.

"I'm Laura," she says, touching the camera. "Yes, a photographer," she says as an afterthought. "I've seen you a few mornings with your lovely dog. He looks like a fox. What's his name?"

"Mozart," he says. "Yes, this is Mozart. Shush, you, shush." And the dog looks at him and sits for a bit, then comes over and nuzzles her hand.

"Why do you call him Mozart?" she asks.

"Because there is more genius in his eyes than most people will ever understand," he says simply.

She nods. It seems a logical reply. They are walking in unison now. Man and dog and photographer. Two are now three.

"Would you mind if I photographed you?" she asks.

"Ah," he says, "you don't just mean taking a picture. You mean photographs. Are you any good?"

She nods. "I'm freelance," she says, "always on the lookout. I'm meant to be on holiday, but I saw you on the beach and I thought ..."

"You thought we would make a good print," he says with a laugh. "Do you hear that Mozart?"

She shrugs. "I thought I would come and ask you."

He bends down and lifts Mozart up and steps across the stones to the path. "Car accident," he says, before she asks. "Years ago. Broken hip. Can't feel his paw in that leg."

"I'm sorry," she says with a grimace.

He looks at her. His eyes take her in.

They have a faraway look to them, she thinks.

"I don't even know your name," she says as she holds out her hand.

"Come back with me for a cup of tea," he says abruptly, ignoring what she has said, but shaking her hand.

She hesitates, not wishing to impose.

"If you want those photographs, that is," he says.

She accepts with a smile.

"My house is over there." He points along the ridge of the hill. "The last one," he says. "The last one on the island," he adds proudly.

She follows his gaze. There is a white cottage just visible at the turn of the crag. The whitewash glints in the sunshine. It is an inviting vision. Mozart is waiting for them, sniffing in bracken around a stone wall. They walk on.

"You must love it here," she says.

"I do." He is a man of few words.

The path curves upward into the hill where the view of the sea catches her breath. The air is warm up here. There are hedgerows of fuchsia and loosestrife ditches.

"Why do you stand and look out at the sea?" she asks, turning to him.

"Because I paint," he says simply, as if it should be entirely obvious. She wants to ask more, but he has closed the curtains on the sentence.

There is a garden around the house filled with color. Valerian, daisies, geraniums. The door is low; the porch, cool in shadow. The room is blue. There are blue candlesticks and blue cups and saucers on a dresser. The cushions and curtains and napkins are blue. It is peaceful and restful, like being in a cabin on a boat. There is a blue jug of wildflowers on the windowsill which is painted white.

"Have a seat." He gestures to a chair. Mozart wags his tail and licks her hand then flops on the rug, panting and eyeing her like a laughing fox. He offers tea and boils the kettle. There is a picture of a blue mountain above the fireplace. She can't help staring at it. He follows her gaze. "The magic mountain," he says softly. "My mother gave it to me when I was a boy." He hands her a cup on a saucer and a plate. She likes his formality. She takes a cookie from the plate. His mother is all around him. In the flowers in the garden, in the neatness of the house, in the painting on the wall, and in the napkin he offers her as well.

"And you say you paint?" she queries, wondering why only a Paul Henry poster is framed on the wall.

He pauses and rises from his chair. Mozart gets up in unison. He jerks his head and motions to her to come. "I'll show you," he says.

He opens the door into what once would have been a bedroom. But he opens the door into the sea. The room has been extended and has walls of glass framing the sea on two sides. There are canvases stacked around the edges, two easels, a table with tubes of paint, bottles and jars of knives and brushes. A cocktail of oil paint, turpentine, and linseed oil assails the senses. It is the smell of the artist at work. The mysterious smell of the conjuror. She recognizes the style of the canvases, but takes a moment to reassure herself, then bends down to check the name. He says nothing. "You're ..." She straightens up.

"Yes, I'm Colin Larkin," he says and shrugs.

The paintings have an aura of enchantment and seeing them unframed, just stacked against the walls, somehow makes them even more special than in a gallery. Here, in this room, in this space it is as if they have emerged from the sea. Ethereal, illusory, and gentle, as if borne on an onshore breeze. As she turns from one to the other, he watches her. She is enrapt. It is akin to an angel playing a violin in the room. She has the desire to clap.

"So why Inishbofin, then?" she asks, curious about his choice of this island.

"Bofin," he says, "is like a lantern in the fog."

She smiles but wants more.

"The island was floating in the mist," he says. "One day, two fishermen came across it in the fog. They sheltered and lit a fire and the fog began to lift. Then they realized it was a fairy mist and they saw an old woman driving a white cow. She hit the cow with her stick and the cow turned to rock and the island became real. The island came out of the mist." He stops.

She smiles.

He shrugs. "That's why," he says. He moves back to the front room.

She does not think it is the whole answer. She does not think it is the reason. But she does not press any further.

He has moved to the window and opens the sash frame. He is looking at the garden. But she cannot see what he is looking at. There is a butterfly fluttering through the flowers and bees hovering and humming over petals. The song of birds rises in the air. He is silent, listening to the last chords of summer and watching the painted wings caught by the light. The butterfly dances through the air. The butterfly is dancing in his head. And he emits an involuntary shudder like a crab in a cobweb. She points the lens of the camera. He turns his head slightly. The light catches his brow and his silver and white hair. She snaps. He is lit like a Vermeer.

butterfly

"A solitary turf cutter was mechanically throwing up lump after lump of the rich purple turf … the only sounds were the sough of the brown grass, the soft fall of the turf as it fell in irregular heaps, and now and then, the harsh discordant cry of a raven."

—Paul Henry
"A Connemara Dinner"

1

The October rain spat in Colin's face as he came out of the station. Traffic splashed past in the lamp-lit night, needles of rain piercing his collar. He had an address and was dragging his bag like an unkempt tramp peering at gateposts and doors for numbers, but most of the houses didn't have numbers. Many were dark and the rest all divided into flats, uninviting with weeds on the steps and bins by the gates. So far, Bayswater was a desultory introduction to London. It was a foreign place, alien to his nature, which was part of the reason why he had come. A desire to break his mold, like a baby chick cracking through eggshell.

He had boarded the boat with a queer sense of dread and adventure. He had stood for a long while on deck watching Ireland disappear in the palm of evening light. Then darkness closed in and the ship began to lurch. He went in and found himself a seat for the night. And he had stayed there until Holyhead, content with the cine film of the summer in his head. The exhibition seemed a lifetime ago. It had changed his view of himself. Made him more confident in his work, in his voice as a painter, in his visual decisions. His introduction to Aisling had been brief but memorable and she had left an impression that had lasted all summer. But it was a transitory feeling, like daffodils lit by the sun in spring. After the exhibition, they had repaired to a bar, the lights along the Liffey dipping like ice-pops into the river.

Aisling had gone to the ladies and Michael had said, "Well?" Colin had grinned and raised an eyebrow and said, "Mmmm."

"Told you," said Michael. "Told you she was a catch." But he had made it seem like a lucky find of flotsam on the beach. A bit of cargo from a ship that he had seized upon. Colin had the impression that first night that Michael hadn't really taken Aisling in fully. A bit like looking at the *Mona Lisa* and remarking on the frame. It was just a feeling Colin had. Aisling had come back and squeezed in between and the three of them drank and laughed until closing time. It had been like sitting beside a gypsy queen. With her curls and her earrings and her perfume and her laugh.

"Do you know?" she said when they were leaving that night, "I think I'll call you Island Man."

"Why?" he asked.

"With your Inishtrahull and your pale blue shirt and your quiet ways, you are an island man." He had laughed. "And island men tell no lies," she whispered. They had all laughed together and then they waved; she had winked, and Michael and Aisling were gone. And that was the last he saw of them. They had gone to London for the summer. She had asked him to promise to come.

But she was right, he was quiet and singular in his ways.

They say still waters run deep.

But no man is a fathomless pool.

He went to Offaly in search of the countryside of his father. To the ancient ruins of Clonmacnoise on the banks of the Shannon. And he had looked out across the mirrored river, across the flat plains of meadows and wondered long thoughts about his past and his future.

Drop a pebble in a pond and watch the ripples take effect.

He cycled along back roads his father would have known as a boy and stayed in the village with the stone bridge where his father had grown up. He walked the fields of his father in golden sun and turned hay in meadows with distant cousins. And all the time, the nagging idea of London dragged on. He fell asleep against haystacks, sunburnt in the sun, his hair bleached white like a Scandinavian and on cool, quiet mornings he painted soft, pale canvases of the river, the haze of early light on the water like the imprint of milk in a glass. Paintings of a hidden fairyland, where every bank and stream and hedgerow seemed to harbor some sense of pagan magic. The gallery had liked these paintings. They were a soft follow-up to the drama of Inishtrahull. But it had been good to get away from the sea, to get out from under the shadow his success might have cast. It had been a new spin of the wheel. But the dream of London frightened him. That would be a different throw of the dice. He felt he would be traveling in the opposite direction to where he should be going. But the thrall of distant lands drew him on. And after a day of slow fishing in August, he made up his mind.

*****

Number 128 was hard to read in the rain because the eight was broken and could have been a three. But he pushed up the steps and rang the bell. There was a faint strain of music bubbling like a pot on the stove. A shriek of laughter, then footsteps running downstairs. The door was scraped back. He realized he was dripping like a fisherman on the porch. And he realized she was staring at him without speaking. Their eyes met.

"You're wet," she said. "What a dirty old night you've chosen to come."

"Is it alright?" he asked, unsure.

"Alright? Oh, my God, of course it's alright." She pulled back the door. "It's so good to see you again."

He lifted his bags and stepped inside.

"The island man," she said, observing him. She was wearing embroidered mauve with lavender gems dangling from her neck.

Then she kissed him on the cheek. "Welcome to London," she said. "Well, Bayswater." She laughed. "Michael's upstairs in our humble abode."

He found Michael sprawled on a sofa with a brocade rug. There were candles on the table and the smell of chicken in the kitchen. His eyes were closed, his fingers drumming to the rhythms of Bob Dylan.

"We're having a chicken pie," she announced.

Michael jumped up and gave him a great big hug. Aisling set an extra place at the red cloth table. She came up behind him and pulled off his jacket.

"Oh, you're wet through," she said, dismayed.

"Have a drink," said Michael.

They both lit cigarettes and looked at him. Colin sat down in the twilight of the room, the aroma of chicken wafting in. Aisling got him a bottle of beer and they settled down, Michael on the sofa, Aisling on the arm of the armchair, and Colin cross-legged on the floor.

It was a night of chicken and beer and cigarettes and candles. Aisling brushed about, serving up the meal, clearing up, tousling Michael's hair and every now and then patting Colin on the shoulders, her fingers once or twice just catching his neck. They worked in Covent Garden in a bar and were having a couple of days off. Talk crisscrossed the summer.

*****

Colin slept on the sofa with the sound of traffic coming through the makeshift drapes from early morning on. Aisling cooked him scrambled eggs when he got up, the plates and ashtrays all washed and cleared away from the night before. Colin had the feeling she was more than capable. More than just a pile of red curls and gems. Michael was still asleep.

"I like food," she said simply, when he complimented her. "I like entertaining. I like art." She paused.

"And Michael?" Colin added.

"And Michael," she said. But it sounded like an afterthought posted late.

She poured a hot drop of coffee into his cup. "And I like your paintings," she said, and sat down.

Colin felt drawn to her and they talked in the kitchen late into the morning, past noon, when Michael appeared bleary eyed in a dressing gown.

"I'm taking Colin to the British Museum," she said. "Do you want to come?"

"God, no," said Michael, "that old warhorse of a place. No, you two go," he said, yawning, pouring black coffee. "I'm going to read the papers in the park."

*****

The Egyptian room held a queer fascination for them both. It was like an alien mausoleum.

"I don't know if they should be here," said Colin. "Is it right to take them out of the pyramids?"

"Then you wouldn't see them," said Aisling.

"Which is worse," asked Colin, "to be embalmed like this behind glass or entombed at the bottom of the sea?" And he told her about the *Cambria* and the lady in black silk who had drowned. Aisling wrapped her arm in his and shuddered. "Behind glass," she said, "I couldn't bear the thought of water."

"You can't swim?" asked Colin.

"God, no." She laughed. "The bath is as far as I go. A long hot bath," and she laughed again.

"You can't swim and you're from Kinsale," said Colin, shaking his head.

"There are worse things in life," she said quickly, walking on.

In the evening, the three of them went to a pub called the Mouse and Dragon and had fish and chips. Michael admitted he hadn't done any art over the summer.

"He's hopeless," said Aisling making a face.

"But," said Michael, "I *have* been applying for things."

"You're out of practice, Michael Murtagh," said Aisling, taking one of his chips.

"Like riding a bicycle," said Michael. "You never forget how to draw."

"If I didn't paint for a while," said Colin, "I think I would get really restless."

"See," said Aisling. "So speaks Island Man."

"Yeah, yeah, yeah," said Michael.

A few mornings later, an envelope arrived.

"Bloody hell," said Michael when he read it, "if I get this, I'll be well set up."

"Get what?" said Aisling, swiping it from his hand.

"God, I'm going to have to pack," Michael said to Colin. "I've got an interview."

"For what?" asked Colin.

"Illustrator," said Aisling, "with the tourist board," and handed him the letter.

The following evening, Michael was gone back to Dublin.

"Look after her," he said to Colin, giving him a hug. "Wish me luck." Then he kissed Aisling on the cheek and took his bag. They watched him go down the street.

London suddenly seemed very big.

Michael was a pillar from home. The house seemed instantly very still. They went back upstairs together, both quiet and aware of the changed dimension to the room. Both circling each other like cats, not quite sure where the new boundaries lay.

But Aisling was working that night so there was no time to dwell. "I'll be back after midnight," she said. "What will you do?"

"Wander about, I don't know." He shrugged.

"Island Man ... all at sea ... in the city." She spoke the words slowly, like a poem. "Well, don't talk to strangers. See you later."

He raised his hand in a wave.

It was odd. To be here. On his own. A few days ago, the room had seemed so different with candles and beer, the three of them locked in conversation. He went out into the night and walked along the strange streets. Dull roads turned into posh roads of white stucco houses with multipaned windows and high-ceilinged rooms. And he thought of Adeline Bell and his paintings. But he was not here a week yet. Time had stretched onto a different plane. He was glad he had come. But Aisling was right with her poem. He did feel exposed with Michael gone, in a city that rushed past every corner and with a girl he barely knew. But as he retraced his steps to the flat, he told himself to just go with the flow. Time enough later for worrying about money and paintings and making a living. He had never been anywhere like this and it was a curious feeling like being in a library full of books he'd never read. He pulled up his collar. It was beginning to rain. Even in London, the rain never seemed far away.

*****

"What will you do?" he asked Aisling at breakfast.

"What do you mean?" she said, buttering toast.

"If Michael gets that job, will you join him back home?"

"Oh, I see," she said, sitting back, munching. Her eyes looked out the window.

He followed her gaze. There was a pelargonium with serrated leaves on the sill. The leaves were imprinted in shadow on the wall like a scrap of chinoiserie.

"I don't know," she said hesitating. "It hasn't fully occurred to me. Let's see if he gets it first."

"You mean …"

"I like London," she said quickly. "Ireland is such a parish."

"It's not that small."

"Oh, you always bump into someone. Even in Dublin, there's someone who knows where you're from. I like it over here, away from Kinsale."

"But surely you must miss …"

She shook her head. "Not really. I like the *idea* of home," she said. "But London is like a garden filled with flowers. There is so much to see." She buttered another slice of toast. "And do," she added. "Speaking of which, what are you going to do?"

"Stay on for a bit?" said Colin. "I'm not in a great rush."

"Why don't you take Michael's job?" she said. "They need someone." She shrugged. "And if he doesn't come back," she paused, "I'm either going to have to get someone to share this place or find a bedsit."

"Michael's job? I'd be useless," he said.

"Think about it," she said. "There's a party on tonight at the owner's house. You can mingle. Oh, come to the party," she said, "it will be fun. You can think about the job."

"Mmmm," said Colin.

"I finish at nine tonight, so meet me at the bar. We'll have a ball."

*****

He was wearing his pale blue shirt when she came out. "You smell nice," she said. She had added extra color to her eyes and changed into a short purple dress. She grabbed his hand and started running. They ran through Covent Garden, through the crowds and people scattered in front of them. "Why are we running?" he shouted, the air rushing past his cheeks. "Because we can," she shouted back. "Because it's London. Because I'm off work and we're going to a party." She slowed down and they came panting to a halt, laughing and catching their breath.

"You're mad," he said.

"I know," she said, "what's wrong with that?" Then she pulled him by the arm and they jumped on a bus to Kensington.

But when they arrived at the party, Aisling seemed to vanish. She was swept away into the melee, a feather in the wind of the night. He hesitated and hovered for a bit. *Oh, sod it*, he thought buckling his nerves around him.

Then he stepped in.

The party gushed about him like a Gustav Klimt. In a swarm of cigar and tobacco, cologne and perfume, and a chap in a hat playing bongo drums with a lady singing jazz above the din. He swiveled and turned and took it all in.

Short skirts and long legs, high heels and sling backs. Rouged cheeks, painted lips, and black lashes. Men in tight shirts and ties with high cheekbones, shaved faces, and some men in turbans with trim beards and moustaches. Saucer shaped glasses with cherries and limes and hors d'oeuvres of baked ham with pineapple on sticks. Nibbles and fancy bits, chocolates, eclairs and meringues oozing cream. A haze of smoke rising from cigarettes and incense in burners and candles on wrought iron holders. He was drinking something mint green like absinthe, tasting of licorice, and he stopped by a window looking onto a terrace of stone lions, box plants, and anemones in front of dark hedges. A woman in a turban walked past the window and leant in and beckoned to him with her finger. "I couldn't find the bathroom," she said confidentially, "so I had a look in the garden. I couldn't find it there either." Their eyes met. Her eyes were glassy like marbles. Then her hands slithered down the sill and she disappeared. He looked over the ledge. She was sprawled on the grass. The man beside him looked out and said, "Oh, Maisie, she always does that," and walked away. Colin's own drink was nearly gone so he went and fetched another. The green liquid thing was getting inside his head, but he quite liked it. He bumped into Aisling on and off who smiled and squeezed his hand and said, "Darling." She was usually surrounded by people. She seemed to know everyone and blew smoke in circles while she talked, and they listened. The bongo drums were still banging on, the chap in the hat with a smile fixed on his face that showed a gleaming set of white teeth. The lady singing jazz had taken off her shawl and her arms were silky and smooth and waved like tree branches to the tunes as she swayed. Colin found himself in a deck chair on the lawn at midnight discussing the merits of the mountains in the moon with a couple from Maryland who didn't know anyone and who had wandered in off the street attracted by the noise and the glamour and stayed. They too had been drinking the green cocktail thing. So, they sat in an arc of three and discussed the ridges on the moon. After a while, the couple from Maryland drifted away like debris into space and Colin stayed where he was, happily talking to himself.

Sometime long after, in the middle of the night, Aisling and Colin found their way home. They veered up the steps to the front door and nearly fell down, but fell instead into the hall in a pile of giggles and groans. The next morning, Colin felt dead and couldn't move. If he moved, the green cocktail thing came back. He had to lie very still, otherwise the room swam around. The drapes lay closed. His forehead hurt like someone was trying to pull it off him. It was his first taste of London by night. London with Aisling.

"Never again," he said when he surfaced a day later. Aisling was back at work. He admired her stamina. "Oh, I just love the buzz," she said. "I don't bother much with the drinking. Sure, you'd never last if you did that all the time."

"So now you tell me," he said.

"Well, no one forced it down you," she said.

"I never want to see that green thing again," he said, shuddering with the horror of it.

She laughed at him. "A couple of beers and you'll be fine. Are you coming on Friday?"

"To what?"

"Another party," she said.

"Mmmm," he said.

So it went. A party every weekend. Some intimate and small, some bigger like the first one in Kensington filled with color and music and all sorts of cocktails with strange sorts of names.

Michael had got the job. He phoned a few times, but Aisling always said it was a bad line, that she couldn't hear him. He wrote a few letters instead, but Aisling only sent him back postcards. So, the letters dwindled. Colin had started work in the bar. He thought he might as well stay until Christmas, and he needed the money. The first day he was a disaster, mixed up orders, forgot change, forgot where the customers were sitting, spilled drinks, dropped a tray, and got the prices wrong. But he looked good, was eager, and tried hard to please. The manager liked his attitude and said he would try him for a week. A month later, he was still there. And part of the reason for his success was Aisling. He was happy. They became close one night on their own in the flat. No party. No music. No beer. Just them. They spent a long time together on the sofa, then they went to Aisling's room. The one where Michael had been. But it seemed natural. It wasn't planned. It had been in the air like rain on the wind, but it had taken a while for the cloud to burst. And when it did, they found themselves drenched in a closeness neither had expected and only dreamt of. *Perhaps deep down*, Colin thought, *this is the inkling that I had all those months ago, in the midlands, dreaming of London.* It had started out as a curious fascination and grown into something more lasting, deep rooted. Both of them instantly felt it and both of them felt it would last.

Sunday mornings were precious. The streets silent behind the closed curtains. They would lie late in bed with the radio on, dozing, mumbling, talking, sleeping. Aisling talked little about Kinsale. She had been brought up by her aunt, both her parents dead from TB. The aunt was called Nora and ran a guesthouse. She had taught Aisling how to cook. Aisling wrote postcards to her every other week and bought earrings and scarves and sent them by post in brown parcels. Nora liked the finer things in life, but as Aisling pointed out she was stuck on a farm up a hill. It answered a lot for Colin about Aisling and her attraction to the lights of London.

He told her about his father and she liked hearing him talk about his own paintings as well, about the sea and the sky and the light in the clouds and the water. "I can't paint, and I can't draw, but I can cook, and I love it. The chopping, the herbs, making the sauces, the smells from the oven." Sunday breakfast was midday, poached eggs with potato cakes and bacon. Sometimes, she made hollandaise sauce, perfectly smooth and creamy, whisking it over a bowl of steamed water. Colin could make sandwiches and bake a potato. He could boil an egg and grill a pork chop and tomatoes, but he wasn't a chef and had no inclination to be anything other than a rudimentary cook. But he loved her meals and he loved watching her work. He was missing his paintings but winter had set in, the city shivering in a cold east wind and lit with Christmas lights, and he intended to wait until the spring. He wondered about painting in London. He wondered about bringing Aisling back to Dublin, but said nothing about either for now. When she asked him about his plans, he remained vague on the details and she sensed it was best to leave him be.

On a Sunday afternoon, when they were watching an old Hollywood film, he asked her about coming home for Christmas.

"Oh, I'll be fine," she said, "you go. It's too soon to meet your mother."

"She's not going to take a bite out of you," said Colin.

She snuggled in against him. "Too soon," she said. "Too soon."

"But when?" he said.

She closed her eyes as the credits rose. "Soon," she said. "Soon. Maybe in the spring."

"And what will you do here at Christmas?" he asked.

"Oh, I've been invited over to Grainne's in Hammersmith," she said. "I'll help her cook dinner for Eddie and the boys."

"She needs help?" said Colin.

"Grainne doesn't know one end of a chicken from the other," she said, laughing. "God knows what she'd do with a turkey. Don't you worry," she said. "I'll be fine. I'll be busy and I like being busy."

Colin said nothing, his fingers stroking her hair, and he let it lie.

*****

He finished early on Tuesdays, so on the Tuesday afternoon before Christmas he caught the bus home. He had gone shopping in Oxford Street and had bags. It was dark and cold and wet and everyone was bundled up in scarves. He was pleased with his purchases and wanted to get home to wrap Aisling's presents before she got in. She was due back at six. But when he walked down the street, he could see the lights in the flat were already on. He would have to hide the bags.

He pushed the door open. "You're home early," he called, peeling off his scarf and setting the bags at the back of the coat-stand. He checked the kitchen. She wasn't there. He put his keys in the drawer and nipped into the sitting room with the bags. Empty. *Perfect*, he thought, shoving them down behind the sofa. He realized he was humming. Well, there was only a week to go now. He unbuttoned his coat and pushed open the bedroom door, about to speak. He stopped in his tracks.

Michael was sitting on the bed.

He stopped humming.

Michael looked up at him under hooded eyelids.

"Oh ..." said Colin. "... I thought you were Aisling."

"What exactly is going on?" said Michael, in a voice like a cloud threatening rain.

"What do you mean?" said Colin. Christmas suddenly seemed a long way away.

"You know damn well what I mean. What exactly have you two been playing at?"

"Look, it's not what it looks like," said Colin.

"Not what it looks like?" said Michael. "Well, it bloody well looks like a lot to me. All your stuff in here. You're in my bloody bed, for Jesus's sake."

"It's ... not your ... bed," said Colin. He realized he was speaking in short, shallow breaths.

Michael had a face on him. His eyes were wide and staring at Colin.

"Of course it's my bloody bed," said Michael. "I go home to Dublin to get a decent job. To make something of myself. I don't hear a word from you and what do you do when I'm gone? Move in on my girl. That's what. Jesus, how long did it take you? Did you even wait till I got on the bus, never mind the blasted boat?"

"Look, Michael," said Colin, "it wasn't like that. Believe me, it just happened. Look, we can talk about this."

"We are talking," said Michael. "And I'm listening. I'm all ears, I can tell you, but I'm not fucking hearing anything, am I?"

"I was going to come and see you at Christmas," said Colin quietly, thinking maybe he should have written. But he hadn't. Because it wasn't the sort of thing to write in a letter.

"Oh, right," said Michael. "At Christmas. Well, you're going to need these then, aren't you?" he said, picking up a pair of Colin's shoes and hurling them at him. "And these," he said, pulling open a drawer and flinging socks and underwear across the room.

"Look, Michael," Colin shouted, backing away, "I didn't hear a word from you either, you know."

"Why should you have?" said Michael. "I was writing to Aisling, not you." He had opened the wardrobe and was tearing Colin's shirts off the hangers and slicing them one after the other through the air. The carpet was littered with clothes at Colin's feet.

"Well, she wrote back to you, didn't she?" said Colin.

"Postcards," said Michael. "I should have guessed something was up, but why would I with Aisling? Little did I realize you were stealing my girl."

"I didn't steal her," snapped Colin. "You can't steal someone. She's got a mind of her own, you know."

"Yes, you did."

"No, I didn't."

"Of course you fucking well did," Michael shouted at him. "Do you know why I came back here, do you? No, you don't, because you're so wrapped up in yourself as usual. Well, if it's of any interest, I came back with a ring."

"What, an *engagement* ring?" said Colin, confused. "But surely ..."

"But surely, what?" said Michael. "I can't afford one? Well no, I can't as a matter of fact. Not yet. Not that I see it's any of your business. And you know ... maybe I should have guessed something was up. But I didn't, alright? Now, you can take your gear and get out of my room and get out of here." He shoved Colin backward. "Go on," he said. "Get, get. Get the hell out."

"Will you lay off me?" said Colin. "There's no need for all this."

"Well, you should have thought about that before you got into my bed," said Michael, shoving him out the door. Colin fell back in a heap.

*****

Aisling found them like that. Michael standing over him on the landing, the bedroom door open, the clothes sprawled about.

"For God's sake," she said. "What on earth has been going on?" She knelt down to Colin. "Are you alright?"

"Yes," he said through gritted teeth.

"Aisling, can we talk please?" said Michael.

"No, we can't," said Aisling. "You're a disgrace."

"Now," he said. "Kitchen," and pointed.

"Two minutes," she said. "You've got two minutes."

They faced each other. Michael's hackles were raised, his eyes open and wide. He had a small, black box in his hand. "It's not the full shilling," he said, holding it out, "but it was all I could afford. I can get you a proper ring next year." He spilled the words out like grit from a bucket, gravelly, uneven, and hoarse. He coughed.

She took it and opened it. Imitation sapphire on gold. It winked back at her. "I can't," she said.

"Two months ago, you could," he said.

"Two months can be a long time," she said.

"What is it? What happened?" he said.

"Us," she said. "We didn't happen."

He looked at her.

"Did we," she said "happen?"

"You never said," he replied.

"You never asked," she said firmly.

"Aisling." He reached out to touch her.

"Don't," she said.

"Is this it then?" he asked. "Well, is it?"

She looked at him, her eyes glistening. "Don't do this."

He stood stock-still. "Keep the ring," he said.

"No, I couldn't."

He stared at her. "Then give it to someone," he said, and walked out. He grabbed his bag and brushed past Colin still sitting on the landing. His steps pounded down the stairs.

Aisling ran after him. "Michael," she called. "Michael, where are you going? It's pouring rain out there."

"Does it matter?" he yelled back. The front door was yanked open. "Michael," she cried. The sound of rain lashing down floated in. The door shut with a bang. Colin hung his head in his hands. Aisling was standing halfway down the stairs, her fingernails clawing the bannister rail. She stayed like that for some time, unable to move. Then she came back up the stairs to the landing. To the mess of clothes on the floor. The flash of sapphire in the kitchen. And Colin, who was staring into space.

Neither of them spoke. The only sound was the rain on the window.

2

"The extraordinary thing about studying law," said David, "is that you can never really get to the bottom of it. It's like emptying the sea with a bucket. There's just too much of it." He paused, looking at Colin's face, who was miles away. "Knock, knock," he said.

"Oh," said Colin. "The sea, yes, I see what you mean."

"You seem very down," said David. "Do you want to talk about it?"

"Not really," said Colin. "It's just I've met a girl, that's all."

"Well, that's the oldest story in the book," said David. "I never meet anyone."

"That's because you've had your head stuck in books all your life," said Colin. "If you get me another one of these though," he said, handing him his glass, "I'll tell you about it." He watched David go to the bar. Everything about his old school-friend always seemed so straightforward. Classic and reliable, like a grandfather clock. *The total opposite to me*, he thought. But it was a diversion to see him again. In the week between Christmas and New Year.

Johnny Fox's pub was high up on a mountain in Wicklow, and David had borrowed his dad's car. The air was pure, the Milky Way dusting the sky like iced powder, and Colin felt completely at home. Here in the dark on the mountain, the lights of the pub shining like embers in coal, he felt a world away from the parties of London, the smoke of the bars, and the Bayswater flat.

Things had been tense between himself and Aisling until he left for Christmas. The episode had left them both feeling sick, like they had been burgled. Both blamed Michael but both in some way blamed the other as well. Colin was upset. Aisling was upset. Both had hated the scene. Both desperately missed Michael. But it was over. He was gone. There had been no further contact. And Colin realized now there probably wouldn't be. The year was dying and a brand new one full of new possibilities lay ahead. And so, for now, he settled back in his seat and chatted with David. Fox's was a cozy place, with smoldering turf fires and rickety tables and chairs. David let him talk and he listened late into the evening. Colin seemed oblivious to the time.

"The way I see it," David said in the car on their way back, "the most important thing is your painting."

"But I wasn't talking about painting," said Colin, looking out the window.

"That's what I mean," said David. "That's what was missing." Then he slammed on the brakes and the car began to skid.

Colin gripped the door handle.

The car swayed with a jerk to a halt. They both held their breath. A deer was crossing the road in the Glen of the Downs. It lifted its head and stared at the windshield the antlers and eyes outlined clear as day. There was a quick turn of the neck, then the deer bucked and was gone. They let out their breath in one gasp.

"Like something from another world," David said. Colin nodded. The moment was still there inside him. They drove on.

The deer and David's words resounding in his head.

*****

"Lost in clouds," read his mother aloud. She was standing by the fireplace after breakfast reading Christmas cards. "Colin," she called, "who is this Aisling person who's lost in clouds?"

He came in and took the card out of her hand. "A girl from Kinsale," he said.

"And you've been seeing her in London, is that it?"

"Yes," he said, "in London."

"It's a funny thing to write all the same," said his mother walking out, shaking her head. "Lost in clouds." He could hear her repeating it all the way down the hall.

He looked at the card. She had signed it *Yours always, Aisling, lost in clouds*. He grinned.

"Oh, by the way," said his mother, popping her head around the door, "the gallery phoned before Christmas, wondering where you were and whether you had any new work for them?" She looked at him and raised her eyebrows, then disappeared again. She had delivered the message. She knew well he wasn't painting. But he would have to find his own way back to it. Her role was backstage. He was his own man, just like his father. You couldn't talk to him.

*****

There was a family lunch arranged for New Year's Eve. They were having pork. Finnegan's meat was always a cut above, and Eileen had made Bramley applesauce. Aine was bringing Cathal. Eileen suspected they had an announcement. She was right. Just after dessert, Aine, her face blushed with a smile, told them Cathal had asked her last night. She held out her hand, a crown of diamonds on her finger. Peadar and Mick cheered and slapped Cathal on the back. There was a toast and Eileen went out to make coffee. Colin was happy for them. They had been seeing each other for years. Cathal was steady and worked in the bank. His mother approved of him. *Aine's always had her head screwed on right*, was how she described her daughter. Colin admired the ring, shook Cathal's hand, and promised them a painting. But the ring and the moment were such a contrast to that night in London. And he left the room early to go for a walk. He doubted whether either of them would approve of his lifestyle in London. And he wondered could he ever see Aisling fitting in with his family. He walked on in the freezing cold of New Year's Eve, his hands thrust deep in his pockets. Just wandering about and thinking. He slipped back before twelve for some sparkling wine and the blast of the foghorn at midnight. The wine cheered him up and he began to smile and join in. He had a couple of days left before leaving and he knew what he wanted to do.

*****

"I've missed you sitting there, you know," she called, her words almost lost in the wind.

He was wrapped in multiple layers, a woolen hat, and thick socks but he was sitting in the same place as before. The sand was blowing in gusts as the wind whipped in from the sea. He was working in oil pastel. It was too blustery for painting in oil and he had just come to feel the tug of the wind and water around him. The feel of the sea once again. This was his old haunt and he was here to soak it up. Refueling on the adrenaline of the place to bring back with him, when he was in need of remembering in London. He had needed to come because this was the start of his first year without college and he was aware now of how much the school had anchored him, defined him, and given him boundaries to break. But he was on his own now and it was like trying to find his own way without a map.

He looked up.

Adeline Bell was bundled up like an Eskimo in a fur hat and gloves. The six dogs all had red tartan coats. She glanced at his work in progress.

"Not bad for a storm," she shouted. "Will you be much longer?"

He shook his head. "I can barely think straight in the wind," he shouted back. He wasn't sure if she had heard him.

"Stop by for a drink, when you're done," she yelled, the dogs pulling her away.

He was pleased to have met her again. He watched her disappear like a Russian princess with her wolves.

*****

Her drawing room was just how he remembered it, except now there was a garland of spruce and pine cones on the mantelpiece and extra bottles of brandy, malt whiskey, and port on the sideboard. This time, she let the dogs in and they scattered themselves around the room like cushions on a sofa.

"Been meaning to get in touch," she said, handing him a hot whiskey. "I kept it for you somewhere," she said, rummaging in a drawer. "I was asking about you in the gallery, but they didn't seem to know where you were. Here we are." She handed him a folded newspaper page.

"Mmmm," he said, looking up after reading it.

"Right up your street," she said.

"Oh, I don't know," he said, "do you think?"

"They're still accepting works," she said. "If you get a move on, you can still make it, you know. The exhibition coincides with the commemorations."

"I don't know," he said "1916 was all bullets and gunfire and blood. It's not really my thing."

"Oh," she said, "just treat it as a bit of a storm. You know, the storm that launched a nation." She waved her hand in the air like a singer onstage. "Look, it's a commemorative thing," she said, "at the Hugh Lane. They're not asking you to paint soldiers and rebels, although of course everybody will. But that," she said, rising from her seat, "is where you come in. Where you will stand out."

"Mmmm," he said. "But I'm meant to be heading back to London."

"What for?" she said. "Trust me, this is your chance to shine. You can take it or leave it." She shrugged.

He took it.

Dashed off a letter to Aisling. She wrote back. Not a postcard. A letter. She was longing to see him. She would wait. She understood and signed herself *lost in clouds, Caitlin Ni Houlihan.* He smiled but had no idea where to begin.

He walked around Dublin, retracing the steps of the rising, scouting for inspiration.

The January weather was bright, and Dublin looked starched and smart, like it was a wearing a new suit. A thousand years away from fifty years ago, when the rebels had fired their guns and flown the flag. Adeline Bell and her gauntlet. He groaned. But he had the bit between his teeth and that look in his eye. The faraway look had come back again.

He took himself out of the city and up the steep hill of Howth.

Out to the country in search of the city. In search of the past. He hadn't thought about it in those terms before. He thought of the landscape as just always being there. And walking up Howth, it occurred to him that the hill had changed little if at all in that time. The sea was the same sea. The wind, the same wind. The view, the same view. And the air, he breathed it in. Ireland. The same air as the rebels. An unnerving feeling. Somehow, he had assumed, it would have been different in history but of course it wouldn't have been. The elements were entirely the same and somehow that made it all the more real. Like being able to reach out and touch it. And smell it and breathe it.

And he stood in the wind and scanned the horizon.

The sky touched the water like an altar cloth from heaven. The air was fused with a feathery haze and he began to think.

Slowly, like clouds forming shapes in his mind.

Then coming down the hill, the island appeared.

Ireland's Eye.

The lonely uninhabited rock with the remains of a Martello tower and an old abandoned church.

And a murder. There was said to have been a murder on the island. Bloodshed. A woman killed by her husband. Although some said she had drowned. From the harbor, the island was clearly visible. A rock torn out of the sea. Nothing but seals and wild birds circling around. Old stones and ruins and bloodshed in its history. And then he knew what to do.

He did the sketches first.

O'Connell Street at dawn, when it was quiet. The GPO. The bleeding heart. There were still bullet holes denting the pillars like blackened scars. And as the early morning crowds trickled in and filled the scene with color, it was like watching an old photograph come alive. A giant waking from slumber. A battleship in the wind, masts and rigging and all.

His mother knew to leave him alone. He was back in his zone like a boxer in the ring and she was glad to see it. Two weeks later, he came out of his room and smiled for the first time since Christmas. She went in. It was a large canvas and it stared back and held her and she couldn't move, she just stood there looking at it.

He stayed a few extra days but then he was gone.

The painting haunted the house. He left instructions with his mother about the framing and said he would be back in time for Easter and the opening. He had called around to Adeline Bell but she was away down in Kerry, so he left a note. He left in the early hours before the light of day had crept through the house. His mother heard him close the door and listened to his footsteps on the path, then the clang of the gate and he was away. The house was quiet without him, like a school closed for the holidays with no one but the caretaker about. Even when he was painting, the walls seemed to resonate with his presence. He spread color throughout the house like a watercolor wash across the page.

*****

Aisling was out when he got back. He could smell her perfume in the flat, on the cushions and throws. There was a vase of carnations on the table and a note. She was working and would be late. He ate a sandwich by the window in the kitchen watching the streetlamps cast a glow like silkworms in the trees. He wondered how the trees managed to grow in the pavements. He sighed at the thought. The freshness of Howth had stayed with him on the boat and the train. But there had been a palpable frisson in the air when he arrived into Euston and stepped on the tube. And now in the darkening kitchen, there remained that quivering sense of the unknown beckoning and he was glad he was back. When Aisling came home, they did not speak at first, but just held each other in a Rodin hug.

"At first I thought I had lost you," she said. "But you're here. You're real again."

"I missed you," he said. "I missed you."

"Did you see Michael?" she asked.

He shook his head. "Sure, he would have been back home in Kinsale for Christmas."

She nodded.

"You're not still thinking about all of that, are you?" he asked.

"I've moved on," she said. "But you. You and Michael were best friends."

"I know we were," he said. "And maybe it'll come good again. But, Aisling, you know we didn't set out to hurt Michael. You know we didn't." He took her hand. "I feel terrible about it. I really do but let's just leave it for now."

They didn't talk about it again.

Not for years.

And Michael faded and became a ghost.

But sometimes in the night, he would visit one or both in their dreams. Neither ever commented on these nocturnal scenes. And so, Michael remained with them. An unmentioned presence. Sometimes real and strong like he had just walked into the room. Sometimes faint and barely there like the trace of a scent in the air.

The bar took him back. They were always short of staff. February slipped by in a matter of weeks. Crocuses coloring the grass in Hyde Park.

Evening light seeping across the city skyline. The mornings brightening and the buds starting to ripen again. Dublin seemed a long way away. But with the light emerging from the winter sky, his thoughts were turning to painting. At first, he contented himself with visits to galleries. There were plenty to choose from. And after a spell in the National with Aisling, he brought up the subject. She hemmed and hawed. And made a face.

"I don't know," she said. "Dublin? But why, when we're just starting to explore over here? Why would we leave here?"

"Mountains?" said Colin. "Sea?"

"Oh, they have those here," she said.

"In London?" said Colin.

"Well, roundabout," she said. "England. Wales. Around."

"But sure, you can see Ireland from Wales," he said. "You can almost reach out and touch it. What would be the point in that when you could be home?"

She sighed. "You'd miss London," she said. "You know you would."

"I love it," he said. "I love it here but I'm a fish out of water, and this is about my painting. Why can't you just consider it?"

"Because next," she said, "you'll have me back in Kinsale."

They laughed, but the topic remained unresolved and kept pawing at the window like a cat wanting in from the rain.

His mother wrote.

The painting had been framed and accepted. She hoped he was well and said she was looking forward to seeing him. She said the painting looked very well framed but had been heavy to lift and she had to get Frank Delaney and his son to take it to the gallery. She said Aine had bought her wedding dress and was busy making plans. She said the weather was wet and the crocuses flattened with wind, but the daffodils were coming up.

But Aisling wouldn't go with him, even just for a visit. She shook her head.

"I thought you liked a crowd and a fuss," he said.

"If I go with you now," she said, "you'll only hold me there."

"But this is important," he said.

"Fine," she said. "Go. Lose your job again. Then what happens? We lose this place. You decide not to come back. I'll be stuck in a bedsit. Is that what you want? Is it, Colin?" she said, her eyes welling up. "Because that's what will happen."

"You're just being ridiculous."

"No," she said. "It'll be a week, then a fortnight. A month. And if Adeline Bell gets her claws into you, it'll be the summer. Or longer. I know you, Colin," she said. "You'll be away like a hare. I won't stand a chance. And I won't see you for dust."

He went silent.

Thought about it. Kicked it around in his head like a soccer ball against a wall.

Endlessly.

*****

"I mean you've done the painting," she said a few days later. "Why do you actually have to be there?"

"Because I'd like to be," he said.

"Yes," she replied, "but there aren't a whole load of dead artists hanging around the National Gallery, are there? I mean people can still look at their paintings and admire them without them being there. Think about it," she said.

He looked at her. She had her own kind of logic.

"You can have the best of both worlds, Colin," she said. "You can paint here. But you can have fun at the same time. Don't you see what an advantage that could be? How you could really grow as a painter if you widen your horizons." She looked at him and raised an eyebrow and smiled a quizzical smile. "Don't you think?"

And there they left it like a half-opened package on the table.

His mother wrote again.

He read the letter on the bus. He could see her writing it at the desk in the sitting room, with the screen of wild horses in front of the fireplace. He could tell she was enjoying the stretch in the evenings and looking forward to his visit. She seemed to take it for granted he'd be coming. Her last line was about how his father would be proud. He stared out the window at the mention of his father and he nearly forgot to get off. He shoved the letter in his pocket and just made it before the doors closed. The sun was shining in Covent Garden. The place buzzed about him, people flying around like dancers in a musical. He felt a tug-of-war going on inside him. He was proud of the painting but felt pressured by the exhibition. He ducked through the door into the cavernous dark of the bar and had visions of himself catching the boat in a midnight flit.

But they spent March taking day trips, taking his mind off things. Bus fares were cheap. They went to parks with woodlands and lakes. They went to the zoo and had a picnic by the Serpentine. London was opening up like a box of chocolates. And he unwrapped each new experience with care. He brought his sketchbooks with him everywhere, making studies of colors and clouds and skylines. Changes in the weather patterns. "I'm just getting to know the terrain," he told Aisling. "Then I'll start again properly soon."

Easter was looming now and Colin became more subdued as the date drew near. He phoned home a few times but his mother was out, and in the end, he just left it. He didn't really know what to say anyway and shoved it to the back of his mind.

"You don't believe me," said Aisling, eyeing him over coffee one morning. His eyes had the glazed look that said he was somewhere far away.

"When I promised you the sea, you didn't really believe me," she said, clearing up.

"Well, I don't see any," he said, looking around, "do you?"

"How about we go to a desert island?" she said. "You'd believe me then."

He looked at her, his eyebrows raised.

"I was going to wait until it was warmer," she said, "when you could swim in the sea. But I think judging by your face, it's a good time to go."

He looked at her, shaking his head.

"You'll see," she said. "We'll go in a few days."

*****

His mother aired his room and bought a leg of Finnegan's pork. She made applesauce and stuffed the pork with breadcrumbs and onions and herbs and sealed it and placed it in the fridge. She set the table and ironed napkins and rolled down his bed. She placed flowers in the hall and made an extra loaf of bread and an apple tart as well. And then she waited.

But the evening drifted out like the tide and she realized she was sitting in the dark and hadn't turned the lamps on. She went to bed and tried to read. In the morning, it rained then stopped and the sun came out and she listened for his footsteps and the clang of the gate. But he didn't come. And she knew he wasn't coming. He would have been here before now.

She put on a blue dress with a jacket and a choker of pearls, sprayed some eau de parfum, did her lips, then she gathered up her bag and her scarf and waited for the bus. She spent the journey gazing out the window for company. And as she walked the last stretch to the gallery, she felt lonely and sad but proud as well. And for the first time in a long time, she really missed Jim and she thought of her young son holding her hand.

*****

The train shuddered out of King's Cross.

Aisling hadn't told Colin where they were going. It was early and half the city was still in bed. The windows were dirty and the sky a low-lying grey. Colin fell asleep and she was quiet. The train rocked from side to side.

The landscape was changing.

*****

The crowd had gathered like seagulls on a pier.

Eileen felt self-conscious at first on her own but there was a friendly whir of voices circling about. She began to relax. The lord mayor gave a speech about how the artists, many of them young and unknown, had managed to bring the past back to life. He said it was a journey of the imagination and one to be applauded. He said it was an honor and a privilege to be in the company of so many gifted people. After the speech, Eileen drifted to the sidelines and watched the crowd circulate. There were paintings of gunfire and guns and strained faces and arms holding flags. There were scenes of explosions and smoke and bloodstains. The paintings had exotic names like *The Valour of the Irish* and *I am the Blood of the Serf*. Colin's painting was just labeled *Storm*.

*****

The buildings had disappeared. Fields of khaki and ochre stretched away from the windows like a patchwork eiderdown. The sky was a bowl of watery blue with a few stray wisps of clouds. Colin was awake and watching. Aisling was looking at him, watching.

There wasn't far to go now.

*****

The people were moving in circles of eight.

Around the bronze sculptures, up and down past the pictures. They moved and came together like sheep on a hill and they moved as one across the room to the painting on the wall. And the painting drew them in as Eileen watched. She watched, one hand clasped in a knot by her side, the other holding a glass, the liquid swaying at an angle. And she held her breath as she heard the low murmuring.

There were no bullets in the picture.

No flags and no soldiers, no firepower. Just the hulk of the thing.

Rising up out of the mist like the rock of Tor Beg from the ocean. A great big wretched rock of a thing puncturing the canvas, battered and bruised, blackened and blue through the smoke. Like an injured beast about to topple, a cliff about to crack, and a temple about to fall with its veil ripped in two. The GPO rising up.

Up out of the swirl of smoke and shadow and mist. As if shaking off a tidal wave of fear and oppression. The rock in the sea of O'Connell Street. The general post office headquarters stormed and held by the Irish volunteers and then hammered with the bullets and cannons of the British. Ripped out of the waves of smoke. The spectre of the past, haunting the mind. The ghosts of the place all around.

Dreamt. Suggested. Etched.

And Eileen listened as the crowd began to chatter.

*****

The bus was following the thread of the coast from King's Lynn.

The seats rattled and shook on the country roads. There were few cars about in this part of Norfolk. Colin's face had come alive. The sea had appeared, and the light was suffused with a soft-focus glow.

*****

"Your son is a genius and a fool not to have come," Adeline Bell, said appearing like a figure from the past, her hair coiled around her head in a plait.

Eileen stiffened.

"He wasn't feeling very well," she said. "He just wasn't able to make it, that's all," she said, speaking slowly and unevenly. She wasn't accustomed to women like Adeline Bell.

"If I had painted that painting," said Adeline Bell, "I would have waded through thick fog and deep water to get here, no matter how ill I was. But no matter," she said, drawing her fur around her shoulders, the Celtic brooch catching the light, "all artists are a law onto themselves."

"And," she said, clasping Eileen's arm, "we just have to accept it." Her voice had softened like someone whispering in a concert hall and she looked Eileen in the eye and squeezed her arm. The two women stared at each other.

"But I think you already know that," said Adeline quietly. Then she nodded and left.

Eileen stood watching her go.

*****

The wind took their breath away. A flat wind.

Flapping in over the endless expanse of sea under sky. The island lay stretched out like the backbone of a whale in the water. The tide was curling in across the damp, wrinkled sands, the water flushing every gully and rivulet as if through wide open floodgates.

They would have to wait for the ferry.

*****

Eileen was walking down O'Connell Street. The buildings were bathed in a heavenly light. And a lone tear strayed down her cheek with pride. And she walked down the street through the golden light. The painting in her head.

One word on her mind.

Storm.

Her son in her thoughts. And she wondered.

And she walked and she walked. And as she walked, he was once again holding her hand, skipping along by her side, his fingers holding her fingers tightly.

*****

But Colin had found a new world.

They were walking across powdery sand. The ferry had dropped them off and they had just a few hours. After that the tide would circle back in. Cut them off. Cut it off.

The island of sand.

Scolt Head Island.

Salt marsh and sand dune and shingle. A desert island. Just one of a kind.

The dunes were high and brushed with blue grass. They could feel the sun warm all about, the heat baking back from the sand.

They crossed to the far side and gazed out across the bay.

Across the wide-open canvas of Holkham Bay.

The surface crackled like foil into the distance. Then the sea became chiffon and disappeared beyond their vision.

There was no land about.

There was only sea and sky. Transfused with a strange sort of light.

No mountains, no rocks, and no crags. A new place.

A place of serenity and calm.

And Colin took Aisling's hand and they walked on into the light.

3

His voice was like a wild bird, rising in a screech across the marsh.

"Where are you? Where are you? Where are you?" he was crying out in his sleep.

The sound pierced the night like a spear thrown at random. Aisling sat up in bed.

"Colin! Colin!" She tried to wake him.

But his eyes were closed, and he was still crying out. She turned the light on. It was three o'clock in the morning.

"Where are you? Where are you?" His head was rolling from side to side.

"Colin, you'll wake the place up." She shook his shoulders.

He opened his eyes and let out a yell. He stared at her.

And she saw the fright and strange fear in his bulging white eyes.

In the morning, he was quiet and had no appetite.

"It was horrible," he said. "I was in a boat. There was no land at all, just water, water, water. You weren't there. The boat was drifting. The engine was broken. You weren't there. Something had happened and I couldn't get back. I couldn't get back. I couldn't get back to land." He stared at her. "It was like a premonition," he said.

"It was a nightmare," she said.

But he looked at her without speaking.

"I'm fine," she said. "We're fine." She put her arm around him and held him close. She had never seen him like that before. Like a terrified young child with frightened, vacant, staring eyes.

Their room was a doll's room. A bolt-hole in the attic of the pub. The White Horse.

The island was meant to have been a day trip. Then an overnight stay. But the place had greeted them like a dream in the sea. The White Horse needed help in the kitchen and Aisling had talked her way into it. They went back to London and packed up and left without a backward glance. To Aisling, Scolt Head was not so much remote, but more a gateway to a lot of new places. And that gave it added color and texture.

Winters were cold with a cruel wind from the north, spring slow to come but the summer full of sun from the east. On days off they would trundle along in their secondhand Morris Minor to bigger seaside places like Great Yarmouth and Lowestoft. Driving through Norfolk with the radio jangling and Aisling singing loudly out of tune and guffawing with laughter. A picnic basket packed in the trunk with sandwiches of cold cuts and mustard, a thermos flask and a rug for the beach. And after lazy days bathing and paddling, driving home in the evening with halfway stops at old pubs for fish and chips, peas, and warm beer, the journeys ending with the car rolling up to the White Horse and the sun burning red in the west. Colin's summer paintings began to exude a new happiness. An impressionistic sea light like Kroyer interwoven in multiple colors like a textile cloth stretched on a loom. Autumn was a palette of fading light with tinted, smoldering colors. They were a curiosity of sorts, the girl from Kinsale and the fair-haired painter. But after six months they were accepted. They had settled in.

The sea stretched invitingly north. To the far distant waves of Viking seas.

To Ultima Thule. That far distant point.

Beyond the known visible world.

And others came. At Easter and in summer, other artists came and set up and painted with Colin. Young men and women from Cambridge and Sweden and an old man from the Zuider Zee. Summer nights filled up with their laughter and talk in the pub. They seemed to find something special together in their passion for painting the water. But they were gone by September and he painted on alone through the autumns and winters. And after three years, Aisling and Colin had become a fixture.

Then the letter came.

Colin was shaving.

The wind was dying down from an autumn gale and the land lay clean like a face rinsed with water. But when a razor shaves skin, the blade can draw blood like a blotch in the sink. He came out of the bathroom and picked up the letter and opened it before the kettle boiled. He scanned the short lines quickly. It was a rejection. He stared out the window. The sea was like a plate of grey soup.

A rejection from the Royal Academy.

For his painting *Invasion*.

From a mackerel haze of sea and cloud, a Viking hull. Heading for shore.

Faint to left and faint to right, spanning out. A flotilla of hulls. Advancing.

Advancing to shore. Coming out of the sea.

From the north.

Invasion.

Rejection.

The word cracked against his teeth. He spat it out like a piece of broken glass.

It was an ugly word. Rejection.

Aisling was already at work in the kitchen. He went out for a walk by himself on the beach.

That was the night the nightmare came.

*****

"No," said Aisling when he mentioned Ireland.

"I don't know why you're so dead against it," he said frowning, but didn't persist. He was in no mood to argue and Aine's wedding had not exactly been an encouraging start.

It had been an April wedding.

Colin and Aisling had stayed for a week. He could tell she was nervous. He wasn't sure why. She seemed at times all buttoned up and at other times shrill and loud. He couldn't understand why she was trying so hard.

"It's a pity it's going to rain on your parade," she said to Aine on the morning of the wedding. "Your train will get wet. You'll be like a mermaid," she said, cackling with laughter.

Aine gave a watery smile and turned away.

"Doesn't Colin scrub up well?" she said to Eileen. "You'd never think he was a painter," she said with a wink. Eileen made a faint sound in her throat.

It rained.

The heavens opened and it came down in buckets. But the photographs showed Aine like a ballerina under black Renoir umbrellas. It was Aisling who looked smeared and bedraggled in her lopsided hat and red shoes.

"What do you make of her?" Aine said to her mother.

"Now is not the time," Eileen said, waving the question away, but their eyes met and they knew.

"I don't know what he sees in her," said Aine under her breath. "She seems very …" and she paused, searching for a word like the right shade of lipstick, "… *common*."

"Aine!" Her mother said, frowning.

Aisling was watching from across the room and she settled the strap of her dress across her shoulder and wished she had never come.

*****

Scolt Head had been an unexpected dream.

The disappearing tides, the white breakers like silent sea horses far out on the horizon. The tides circling in and the mist and the fog. The disappearing island. The seabirds singing like an invisible choir and in summer the sense of a Caribbean blue sea and the sun twinkling on water. The paintings had all done well in local galleries and in London in a new gallery that Adeline Bell had found him on Cork Street.

She had written a short note with the name. Wrote, *If you're going to stay over there, you're going to need this.* She said to mention her name. They would know her. Colin had laughed when he read it. Of course they would. Adeline Bell presumed everyone knew her.

But the gallery was enamored with his work and gave him his first exhibition.

He called it *SkyWater.*

Gilbert, the owner of the gallery, was very precise about the important things; hanging arrangements and prices. He was invariably dressed in pinstripes and brogues and spoke with a drawl in slow honeyed tones. "Oh, I should think we can easily pop another fifty onto all of these lovely fellows," he said as Colin showed him the paintings. "These are what you might call rare specimens indeed. Ravishing pictures, *ravishing,*" he said, hovering over the word and rolling his r's.

Stanley arrived on the opening night out of the blue.

"How the hell did you end up in Norfolk?" he said, scrunching up his eyes into tight little balls.

Colin groaned and gave him a drink.

"I've been rattling around London all summer," said Stanley, "and I heard about this, so I just had to come and see for myself." He was wearing a linen suit that made him look like a crumpled handkerchief pottering about.

"I like them," he said, clapping Colin on the back. "But next time," he said, "I'll be looking for a bit more of that third dimension."

Colin winced.

"You do know what I mean?" said Stanley.

"Mmmm," said Colin. "You mean some more mystery and depth?"

"That's it," said Stanley. "The spiritual. The sense of something intangible, that sense of something else out there, something you can't even see. You with me?"

It was like the hands of a clock were swinging back in time.

"The third dimension," said Stanley, tapping the side of his nose. "You're nearly there." Then he nodded and coughed and was gone, his words draping the air like a mist at sea.

Colin bit his lip and turned away. The exhibition looked dull now and drab all around him, the paintings overworked and pretentious and he was feeling chastised like a child. All he wanted was to get away from the crowd, to get back to the sea and start again.

*****

But in the end the Scolt Head dream was like a Russian doll.

It had disappeared into itself until nothing was left. Perhaps *Invasion* had just been a step too far. Colin had thought it would get through and he felt cheated and confused when it hadn't. It was hard to feel the same about the place anymore, to see it fresh like he had when he'd first come with Aisling. Perhaps he'd just run himself dry. Inside he knew it was time to start again, to forget all about it and move on. Move away. Go home. Go west.

"How about south?" said Aisling.

"Mmmm," said Colin.

"Some beach looking out to France," she said.

*****

In comparison to the attic of the White Horse, the house on Camelford Street seemed more than spacious, even though it was a only a box house, with one room on four floors. The sea was at the end of the street. But there were pubs and places to eat, fish and chips on the beach, seaside hotels and trains, visitors, neighbors, and artists, and the piers diving out like iron fish in the sea.

Brighton.

A stony beach and children with candy floss and people and dogs swimming in the sea.

But that was at weekends. On most mornings, the place was deserted, and Colin had the beach to himself.

They filled the house with salvaged scraps and sticks of furniture. Upturned crates and deck chairs, secondhand electrics and yards of frayed fabric for curtains. Money was tight. The *SkyWater* money had dried up and Colin took a part-time job teaching. He hated it. Felt unsure of himself in front of strangers with memories of college like low hanging clouds in his mind.

And his own ideas were intermittent and hesitant. He felt all dried up. But after the silence and flat wind of Scolt Head, the battered old cruise ship of Brighton was a distraction. He painted happily enough on his days off, allowing the canvases to fill up with colors long absent from his work. The seaside colors of beach balls and Windbreakers and kites and beach huts. But he was really only passing the time. The change in direction was good for him and the paintings were doing well locally, and that in itself for now was enough.

"We need the money," said Aisling. "All that fancy work in Norfolk was all well and good, but just look how you felt when you didn't get into that academy place."

"Mmmm," he said. But as far as he was concerned, this was still just a holiday.

Yet Aisling was thriving in the seaside town. She had found her new London by the sea. With a job as a cook in the Lion and the Lamb, she was occupied, unperturbed by the long hours, and making friends all the time. Their next-door neighbor was called Madge and had a greyhound called Rose. Madge and the greyhound liked to come in at all hours for a chat. Aisling kept an open house. There was usually somebody drifting about, but Colin didn't mind as long as he had the upstairs to himself. Aisling went to all the new plays around town and the house seemed to swell in the evenings with new friends like Hilda and Edmund and Jill. Aisling drew people in with her easy ways and infectious laugh. She was the girl that stood out in a crowd. "Oh, Colin's the clever one," he could hear her saying downstairs. "Colin's the artist. I'm just a country girl from Kinsale."

After a few summers, the paintings began to evolve. He took to going out with the fishing boats, observing the sea at close quarters. Way out in the middle of the waves, the sun flashed down, igniting the water with a dazzling glare that bounced back, hurting his eyes. And that was how he got the idea. "The third dimension," Stanley had called it. The man had a habit of saying things that lingered. Things that got under Colin's skin.

On the boats, eyesight was accentuated by the reflected light. Smell was brine and freshly caught fish. Sound was an array of echoes spliced together, timber puddling water, the creak of chains hauled, and the rolling of ropes with the shouts of the fishermen punching the air. Taste was the flaky fish roasted on the beach in the evening with a packet of hot chips washed down with cold beer.

And he began to try to convey these sensations. These were different days now to Inishtrahull years ago where the sky had dipped into the sea, the cliffs had fallen steep down to the white of the waves, and the birds had circled in jabs on the wind as the light came flooding in. And there was a new kind of energy here to Scolt Head. He started using new vivid, bold colors in thick sweeping impasto like Jack B. Yeats. If he was going to be in Brighton, he was going to rebel. A reaction to the overworked *Invasion*. And the paintings began to swing with the sights and sounds of the seaside town. And he was reveling in the change of mood. The canvases were singing with a new energetic brightness. A flock of seagulls bursting through the air, beaches littered with bright towels and deck chairs, flip-flops, and fishing nets. And the paintings came one after the other in waves.

Paintings that captured the sense of the seaside. The feeling of just being there.

He called them *Sea Senses*.

*****

"Ah," said Gilbert, eyeing them up. "These are rather good, these are. Yes, rather good, old boy. Rather rip-roaring good, indeed."

The exhibition sold out.

Colin Larkin was becoming better known. Making a bit of a name for himself. And he didn't really care if he was cheapening his soul. He had some money in his pocket. And he went out and bought a ring.

The house was empty when he got back.

He bumped into Madge walking Rose. Madge inclined her head toward the sea, when he asked. He found them on the beach.

Aisling with Hilda and Edmund and Jill around a fire with bottles of beer and bags of chips. Their faces were glowing. Aisling looked up and held out her arm. "Come and have a chip," she said. "We're all having ships in a bottle." And the four of them fell about dying with laughter.

Colin beckoned to her gently.

Aisling stood up. He was smiling at her. The waves roared and pulled back. She took his hand and they walked down to the water's edge, Hilda and Edmund and Jill gazing after them.

Colin opened his hand. The ring glinted in his palm.

"Island … Man," Aisling said, wrapping her arms around him and they stood close together while the water lapped in.

"My shoes are getting wet," Colin whispered.

"Come on," she said taking his hand and they started running. Running up the slope of the beach like running through Covent Garden on their way to a party.

They found Hilda and Edmund and Jill still smiling and laughing. Aisling and Colin sank down and the chips and beer got passed around and they stayed on the beach like that until the fire had dwindled and the cold had crept in from the sea.

They settled on the following June.

"When the nights are long and the sea is blue," Colin said.

"But let's do it quietly," said Aisling, "let's just disappear." She winked.

Autumn came and Colin was busy working, trying to make the most of the light before the evenings closed in. Aisling was spending more time with Madge. She found her comforting, like a mother from home, and she needed someone to confide in.

"I don't know," said Aisling over tea. "I just got that impression."

"But what makes you think that?" said Madge, opening a packet of cigarettes.

Aisling made a face. "I only really met them at Aine's wedding," she said. "But the mother is like a hen around Colin. You know the type I mean? He'll always be the little boy to her and I'll always be the girl that took him away. They just don't think I'm good enough, that's all," she said, pouring more tea. Her eyes were unusually dark and broody.

"But sure, what does it matter anyway?" said Madge. "Aren't you over here? It's not as if you're going to see very much of them."

"I suppose," said Aisling with a frown. "But I do like to be liked, you know."

"You're being daft," said Madge, laughing. "Everyone likes you."

"Everyone here likes me," said Aisling. "That's not the same thing."

"And Colin hasn't told them yet?" said Madge.

Aisling shook her head.

"Do you really think that's wise?" said Madge. "You know, getting off on the wrong foot."

Aisling made a face. "Well, as far as I know, Aine's meant to be going to America anyway. And the two brothers are in Australia. So, that leaves only his mother, really."

"Well, that's what I mean," said Madge. "Cutting off your nose to spite your face. I mean that would be like one of the royals not inviting the queen."

Aisling giggled and sighed. "I don't know," she said. "She wouldn't approve anyway and inviting her isn't going to make her change her mind."

"No," said Madge, "but it might break the ice."

Colin hadn't told his mother.

But he didn't intend not saying anything. He didn't particularly want a hole-in-the-wall affair either. But nor did he want a fuss. For now, he was focused on painting and when he was painting, he thought of little else. He had bought the ring and asked the question. The date was still a good way off and as far as he was concerned that was enough.

*****

The seaside in autumn brought different sounds.

Rising winds, high tides, and bigger waves. The brass bands of summer had departed and the promenade was taken up by walkers in raincoats with dogs on leads. Rain on umbrellas and the sound of rain prickling the water. The freshening sounds of autumn, the seasons changing gear. The sun still came out on most days but hung lower in the sky and had turned a paler shade of gold, as if diluted by water.

He had started work on autumnal vignettes and was trying to get enough done for a new small exhibition. On colder nights, he passed the time with a painting couple whose work he rather liked. It was like a more grown-up version of the old days in college. And the companionship was helping him regain a sense of self-worth. Tony Martin painted large surrealist canvases and Nicola Martin was well known for her portraits. They all liked the fact that each of them did something different. Sea Senses had been great fun and a good seller but Colin didn't want to get carried away. And spending time with other painters like this was helping.

*****

Madge was turning fifty in November and was planning a party.

"I'm like a sack of old bones," she said. "Even Rose can hear my knees crack. They're worse than hers if you can imagine that."

"There's life in you yet, you spring chicken," said Aisling.

"Not if I smoke any more of these," said Madge, stubbing out her cigarette. "But," she said, getting up from her chair and beckoning to her dog, Rose, "there's a grave waiting somewhere for all of us."

Aisling shook her head. "You sound like an old woman of the roads."

"Just mouthing off as usual. Don't mind me. And you're sure you're both coming next week?"

"Of course," said Aisling. "We wouldn't miss it for the world."

*****

The morning of the party, a thick fog had crawled out of the sea.

The houses on Camelford Street were blurred in the creeping damp, the lights in the windows like smugglers' lanterns. Aisling had left the house early to be at work by seven. Colin was preparing to head down to the pier. At the farthest point, he would be suspended over the sea like a bird in the eye of the fog. One of his ideal conditions.

He was taking the milk bottles in before he left when he paused. A hole had appeared in the veil of fog. There was a man standing across the road.

In a black coat with dark hair. As if he was waiting for a bus. But there was no bus on Camelford Street.

The man was a stranger to Colin. He had his collar turned up and his hands in his pockets. Colin wouldn't have paid much attention except he had the impression the man was looking at the house.

Staring at the windows upstairs.

The fog closed and then drifted and thinned. Colin looked again. The man was gone.

A few minutes later he headed down to the pier with his easel and bags. The man on the road was nowhere to be seen. Colin shrugged and thought nothing more about it. There was nothing but sea and fog on his mind.

By four o'clock, the light was fading, and he packed up his things. The day had been worth it but now he felt chilled to the bone. He went home for a bath and to get changed for the party. He was looking forward to it.

The Old Boat Inn was a dark, faded pub just a few streets away. It had a reputation for good fish and folk music. Madge's choice.

Aisling and Colin had bought her a new bed for Rose and a patchwork quilt Aisling had found in The Lanes. They arrived early but the party was already in full swing. A band from Cornwall was playing. The music was fast then slow. Fast then slow and haunting. A girl was singing. She had a ragged beauty to her voice.

The place was filling up. Hilda and Edmund and Jill were already there. After the fog of the day, the warmth and the chatter and singing and beer were welcome distractions.

"I never realized I knew so many people," said Madge.

"Here's to your next fifty," said Aisling, kissing her.

"Jesus, no thanks," said Madge, blowing smoke. "I'd be like a worn-out doll. You couldn't give me away."

It was getting quite crowded and hot.

People were squeezed in all over the place like passengers on a train. The band had struck up a new tune and the crowd was joining in like a rowdy choir. Their voices rose and swooped and fell.

I found my love by the gasworks croft,
Dreamed a dream by the old canal

Madge was singing along with everyone. She loved a good song.

Kissed my girl by the factory wall

The crowd hit the chorus.

Dirty old town, dirty old town

The bar was packed. Everyone was singing now.

Clouds a-drifting across the moon
Cats a-prowling on their beat

Then Colin saw him.

Spring's a girl in the street at night

The face came and went and the crowd sang on. For a moment, Colin wasn't sure.

Dirty old town, dirty old town

Then he saw him again. And this time he knew.
The man was staring at Aisling.
He was on the other side of the room. He seemed to be on his own. Just a face in the crowd. The perfect disguise.
Colin tapped Aisling on the arm. "Do you know that man?" he said, jerking his head.
Aisling looked over and back. A strange look had come into her eyes.

Saw a train set the night on fire

"Well, do you?" said Colin.
"No, I don't," Aisling said, shaking her head.

Smelled the spring on the smoky wind

"Are you sure?"

"I said no, didn't I? Why do you keep asking me?"

"He was standing outside our house this morning," Colin hissed. "That's why."

"Are you sure?" said Aisling, staring at him.

"Yes, of course I'm sure," Colin said. He looked over to where the man was standing. The man was gone.

"He's not there now," said Colin.

Aisling looked around, her eyes scanning the room. Scanning every shadow that moved. No one. She fidgeted for the next hour. There was more singing, but she couldn't settle.

"Take me home," she said to Colin. "I need some air."

It had begun to rain as they were leaving, the rain hitting the ground like a shower of bullets. They stood on the porch buttoning up their coats.

The voice spoke from the shadows.

"Hello, Deirdre."

She turned her head. Colin's arm was around her shoulders. The man was leaning against the wall, half in and half out of the rain.

"I think you've got the wrong person," said Colin. "Her name's not Deirdre."

"Her name's not Aisling either," said the man. "Tell him, Deirdre."

"Get me out of here," she said to Colin.

"Leave her alone," he said to the man. "D'you hear me?" And he pulled Aisling with him out into the rain.

They hurried back the few streets to Camelford. The rain gushed down like gunfire and they didn't speak. They could hear the man's footsteps following. Then the footsteps seemed to grow fainter and disappear. They got home, alone.

"What on earth is going on?" said Colin when they got in. "Why was he calling you Deirdre?"

"I don't know who he is, I told you," said Aisling. "I don't know why. I don't know."

But her voice had tightened like a cockle in its shell.

The knock came after midnight. Banging on the door. Bang, bang, bang. Then a pause. Then it started again. Bang and bang and bang.

"Don't go down." Aisling caught Colin's arm.

Colin pulled the window open and looked out.

"Deirdre! Deirdre!" The man had been drinking. He was shouting and swaying about.

"Deirdre, will you get down here to me now, please. I'm losing patience with you."

"I'm phoning the police right now, if you don't feck off," Colin shouted back.

Aisling was sitting up in the sheets, not moving. Her forehead was moist with beads of sweat.

The police arrived swiftly. The man was still banging on the door.

Colin and Aisling looked down from the window. Some lights had come on in the other houses.

"Your name's not Aisling," he was shouting. "Tell them, Deirdre."

"You'd better calm down, sir," said the constable.

"Take your fucking hands off me," said the man. "For fuck's sake, Deirdre, will you not come down to me? Can't you see they won't leave me alone?"

"Look, whatever your relationship is with this young woman, you're coming with us now," said one of the police.

The man swung a punch. "She's my daughter," he shouted. "Can't you just leave us alone?"

"Is this man your father?" said the constable, looking up to the window at Aisling.

She shook her head. "I've never seen him before in my life."

The constable nodded and pulled the man away. They dragged him across the street, bundling him into the van, slamming the door. The van skidded away in the dark.

Colin closed the window and stared at her.

"What in the name of Jesus is going on?" he said. "I thought your father was dead. Who the hell was he?"

She stared at him.

"And who exactly are you?" he said.

"You know who I am," she said. "I'm Aisling and we're getting married to each other. That's all there is to it."

"No," said Colin. "No, that's not all there is to it. Why the hell was he calling you Deirdre?"

"I told you I don't know him," Aisling shouted.

"But—" said Colin.

"There are no buts," she said, her voice slow now and steady and firm.

Colin let out a sigh and sat down. "Christ," he said, "what a fucking awful night."

"Well, there's one other thing," she said, pausing. "I think now is the time to tell you."

He looked up at her, his head cupped in his hands.

"I'm pregnant," she said.

4

The wind was tearing across the cliff.

Tearing at his eyes, moistening the rims like rain. He was bent into the wind. Fighting it, clinging to the path, embracing the wind as if the storm could blow his mind clean. He couldn't think at all here and that was the whole point. He didn't want to think about anything. He just wanted to forget.

*****

Madge had been in a like a shot the next morning.

They say some days can stretch like a year in a day.

The two women had talked in the kitchen behind the closed door. All morning.

And then into the afternoon.

Colin had gone down to the beach and wandered about on the shore, just waiting and wondering.

But they say you can never really tell what another person is thinking.

It was the next morning before she was ready to talk.

And now he had come up here. To the top of Beachy Head. To get away and let it sink in. Digest it.

"Yes, I know him," she said. "Yes, he is my father. Was my father once," she corrected herself. "It's all in the past. I've spent years trying to forget." She paused, looking out the window then turned back to Colin. "And yes, my name is Deirdre. Was Deirdre," she corrected herself again.

Colin took a deep breath.

She went on before he could say anything.

"It's a sad name," she said, "and it made me very … very … sad."

"Why?" he asked softly.

So, she told him. In low, hushed, hesitant tones. Sometimes, her voice barely over a whisper.

About how it was only her mother who had died of TB when she was young. Not her father. He had taken to drink. And he had drunk like there was no tomorrow. About how the guards had to drag him out of pubs at all hours. About how he would come to her room at night looking for favors. About how she would hide behind the door, in the attic, in the shed. About how he would always find her and put his hand up her skirt.

"Come here to me now, Deirdre, till I lift up your skirt," she said, repeating the words slowly and coldly.

Like they were as much a part of her still as blood in a vein. Scratched across her soul like graffiti.

"That's how it began," she said, her voice trailing off. "He'd spend time in the sanatorium," she said. "The guards and the priest put him in it. And they'd let him out after a few months and things would stop for a while. He'd act like nothing had happened and buy presents and dresses. Then he'd start drinking again. Whiskey at first by the fire at night, with Jimmy Murphy from the farm up the road. That's how it would start. Then he'd be back in the pub and it would begin again. All over again."

Colin went to put his hand on her shoulder.

"Don't touch me," she said. "Sorry, I didn't mean it like that," she said. "Just let me finish."

He nodded and stepped back instantly. He couldn't speak. The room was listening.

"Then one time they took him away for good. That was when Nora took me in. She had to, really, there was no one else. But I was never able to tell her, although I think she suspected. I think she was responsible along with the guards for having him taken away."

"So, what happened?" said Colin.

"She brought me up. I never saw him again. Everything else you know. She taught me to cook. I helped out on the farm. She was very good to me, so she was," she said, wiping a tear at the edge of her eye. "But I always just wanted to get away. To get away from the fields, the rain, the memory of the place. Of him."

She stood up and walked to the window.

"I left as soon as I could make my own way. Met Michael in Kinsale, as you know. Told him I was called Aisling. It's my confirmation name anyway." She laughed. "I didn't make it up. Just switched names, that's all. Nora knew I preferred it."

"And so, you're not really from Kinsale either," said Colin gently.

"Ah, Nora's place is a good bit farther on than that," she said, laughing again. But her laugh sounded off key, as if forced.

"And so, to London," said Colin.

"And so, to London," she said. "I wanted out. I needed to get away. Like it had never happened."

"Does Michael know?" he asked.

"No," she said, shaking her head, "no one, only yourself and Madge."

*****

The wind was flapping about his head now, the noise tunneling inside his ears like a storm underground. The water was wild and scattered with white waves charging in. Clouds threatened rain overhead. He stood buffeted in the wind, calmed by the surge of the elements. Then he turned and headed back down the hill.

He had tried to persuade her but she wouldn't go.

She wouldn't go to the police with him.

She had said her piece. And when she had finished, she closed the lid on it like a trapdoor sealed tight. Colin couldn't get back in. She didn't want to talk about it further. She was tired with the shock and said all she wanted to do was sleep.

She placed his hands on her stomach. There was no real sign yet. Aisling said the baby was her first concern now. Their first concern. And so, he left her sleeping on the bed.

In the evening, she was up, a dressing gown around her shoulders. Her hair was tumbled up on her head with clips and she was standing by the window, her face lit by the streetlamps outside. She was fingering the curtains. He had never seen her look so beautiful, this Deirdre of the Sorrows, this Aisling, this Irish woman with his child in her belly. But when she turned to him, there was a look of rising panic in her eye. As if someone had switched something on in her head.

"What's wrong?" he said immediately.

"The Sluagh have come," she whispered, pressing a finger to her lips. Colin moved forward.

Aisling's eyes were scanning the sky as if she was looking for something. Then she pulled back to one side and drew the curtains quickly.

Colin looked at her.

"They wait until it's evening," she whispered.

"Who does?" he asked.

"The Sluagh," she said. "I used to hear Nora tell of them. When the sun has gone down, they fly in from the west. That's why we've got to keep all the windows closed and the curtains shut tight."

"Aisling, what are you talking about?" said Colin slowly.

"Shush," she said, "it's bad luck to talk of them. They're like a flock of birds," she whispered. "But they're not birds at all and they come when it's dark to steal away the souls from the dead."

"But we're not dead," he said.

"The baby's soul," she said. "They can come for that too."

"Come on down for something to eat," he said. "You've been dreaming."

He left it at that. But a change had come over her. She seemed distant and was obsessive about closing the windows and curtains. He put it down to the flood of distress that had flowed from that night in the pub.

The father. Her childhood. The baby. All playing on her mind.

*****

Colin stopped painting.

He couldn't settle on anything, except keeping an eye on her. He couldn't think of her as a Deirdre. She was an Aisling to him.

But she noticed him hovering and circling around her and she didn't like it. She said he was making her nervous and that wasn't good for her condition. She had taken time off work for a bit, for a break. He didn't like leaving her on her own in the house, but she was adamant. So, he went down to the beach and walked by the shore, the grey sea like a tonic for days and weeks.

Then it happened.

Again.

She saw the face at the window. In the morning. Across the street. This time there was no fog. But the face was there. The man was there. Her father had come.

She pulled back against the wall. Colin looked out. The man was there. Clear as day in the dawn. The soft light of morning glowing pink on the walls of the houses and the man standing still like an undertaker waiting for a hearse.

"That's fucking it," Colin swore loudly. "I told you that you needed to go to the police."

"Where are you going?" she asked, her eyes widening with fright.

"Downstairs to phone the police," he said. "I'm not having this. I'm putting a stop to this right now," and he pounded down the stairs, his footsteps thudding through the house.

Aisling could hear him on the phone, his voice persistent and urgent, like a different person. And she stayed by the window, glued to the spot.

He got a restraining order put in place and the police said they would keep an eye on the man. But even so, she was adamant.

"I'm not going anywhere," she said. "I'm not running out of Brighton. I'm not running away anymore."

In time, they were told that her father had left town. But Colin could tell from her eyes that she was away like a hare all the time. Running in her mind. Scanning the faces in every room. Always checking. Always running now. And Colin was unsure about what to do. Until the clocks swung to a sudden halt in January.

One of the first blue seas of the year. A cold sun was shining, and the water had turned from the grey shades of New Year to a bluebell bright sea.

Aisling had the curtains drawn and the house was getting on Colin's nerves. She had gone back to work part-time but had been unwell in the mornings and was struggling. Apart from work, she had taken to going nowhere except next door to Madge. She was avoiding the streets at night. He knew why but didn't say anything. Her father was one thing and he could understand that. The nightmare of being dragged back to Deirdre.

But now there were the Sluagh as well.

And she was convinced they were coming for her child. Coming at night in the dark, flying in a flock down the street. Swooping down from the sky. And that's why she was staying away from the streets, keeping herself and the baby safe.

He hadn't realized she would be this vulnerable.

The story of the Sluagh had followed her from Cork, from Nora and the people roundabout. And she seemed a long way now from the bright young girl he had known in London. In his mind, he still saw them running down the street. Running through Covent Garden, on their way to a party. Carefree and young. But he saw it all differently now. Aisling had always been running. He just hadn't known that before.

One morning he returned from his early walk on the beach. The bright blue sea had lifted his mood and he was thinking about getting back to painting.

The bathroom door was closed.

All the taps were on and there was the sound of retching. She was getting sick.

"Aisling?" He knocked on the door. He could hear her moaning.

He pushed it open. Her hair was matted across her face. She was leaning over the sink, wiping spittle from her mouth. There was blood on the floor and splotches of blood in the toilet.

"Pains," she mumbled, "... cramps. The baby, blood, I couldn't stop it ... kept coming out ... I ... I couldn't help it ... couldn't stop ..."

She began to sway.

"Aisling," he said, shaking her shoulders.

Her body was getting heavy. She was falling. They sank down together on the floor. She was gone. He couldn't reach her.

"Aisling ... Aisling ... Aisling." He kept saying her name.

She was moaning now, a kind of moan he had never heard before.

She had fainted stone cold. But she was coming back. It took some time before the moaning subsided.

"Stay with me, Aisling," he said, holding her head. Her forehead was wet with sweat. He tried to pat it with a towel. Then he got some old towels and a bowl and a glass of water. He got her to sit up and take a drink. She managed a few sips, then reached for the bowl and got sick. She felt sick from the queer sensation of her insides flowing out of her. Sick at the feeling of the baby disintegrating. Flesh turning to liquid. In front of her.

*****

The hospital said it was a common occurrence. It was just that people didn't talk about it much. The doctor performed a small routine procedure. But her mind was elsewhere.

"They took the baby," she said to Colin. "I told you they were coming for the baby. They took our baby."

He held her hand. But it was like he wasn't there.

Her eyes were open and staring at the hospital wall. Staring at the Sluagh flying back to the west. Flying back to the west with the baby's soul.

Madge helped to get her through. Kept her company through the long, lost, lonely evenings. Getting her to go with her on walks with Rose. Got her to go back to work.

"Help take your mind off things," said Madge.

And the kitchen was like a breath of fresh air. The cookers humming with heat, the orders shouted in from the pass. She tried to concentrate on the simple tasks in hand. But her first day back was unnerving. Handling the succulent cooked skin of chicken, holding the moist flesh of fish between finger and thumb and the squirting of sauce on the dishes. She sent the first plates out and wiped away tears from her eyes.

The next order came in.

Two cod. One chicken. One steak.

She seared the steak, the skin tightening on the hot pan, the meat oozing juices of blood. She plucked it onto the plate with the tongs and poured the sauce on, the brown peppercorn sauce smearing the meat. The flesh, soft and pink and perfectly cooked. When they carried the plates out, she noticed her hands were shaking. And her apron was stained with splatters of grease and sauce like blood.

*****

His mother didn't come to the wedding.

Her hand tightened on the phone as Eileen listened to her son down the line.

"Well, if that's what you want," she said, keeping her words short and her feelings intact.

He hadn't told her about Aisling's father. He couldn't. He mentioned the miscarriage in passing. Her fingers tightened even more on the phone. It wasn't something she'd been expecting to hear. But she thought he was brave to bring it up. Her voice began to soften, and he knew she was concerned.

"She'll have to keep an eye on that in the future," she said. "You'll have to be alert to the signs. There are usually signs."

They were married in June in an office in Kensington. Aisling's mood had lightened somewhat since her long grey winter. And she looked well in a short lacy dress with a cream jacket and hat and a posy of orchids and ferns. Madge came and witnessed it for them. The girl with red curls and the boy with fair hair. People smiled as they walked through the streets. Aisling blossomed with the attention of strangers and smiled back at them as if she were famous. And people looked at the couple and could see what they saw in each other. Or so they imagined.

*****

She began to spend more time with Hilda and Edmund and Jill again. And Colin was glad to see her making an effort. But after the wedding an anticlimax had set in like a low-lying sky and most of her days seemed overcast now. She had moments of brightness like the sun breaking through. But they didn't last. And her moods swung high and low, unsteady and unsure. She gathered her friends around her more at home, going out a lot less than she used to. She disliked being left alone and grew restless when Colin started back painting.

"If you took more hours in the college," she said, "we'd have a lot more money and time together."

"But I haven't painted properly in ages," said Colin. "I'm not even painting properly at the moment. I'm finding it hard to concentrate."

"And that's my fault, I suppose?" she said.

"I never said that," he replied.

"Well, it's not as if you're doing anything new," she shot back. "You're just doing more of the same. And if you can't do those, then don't blame me," and she went out banging the door.

Colin swore under his breath. The lighter days of June seemed to have completely vanished now. He could hear her in the other room playing music rather loudly and he laid down his brush. *I'm just going to have to get through this*, he thought, and looked at the canvas. The canvas was a mess. He walked away and went out.

The beach was half deserted and he bumped into Tony walking his dog.

"How's the painting going?" Tony asked, pleased to see him.

Colin bent down to pet the dog. "I've been taken up with other stuff," he said. "I haven't been able to concentrate."

"It happens," said Tony. "There's nothing wrong, is there?"

"Nothing I hope can't be fixed," said Colin.

"You sound very down for a man who's just got married."

Colin straightened up. "I'm fine. Look I have to go, but we can catch up again," he said, slapping Tony on the back and heading off.

Tony stared after him.

"Get back painting," he shouted. "Don't leave it too long." But his voice scattered back in the wind. Colin walked on with his hands in his pockets and his head bent down with his shoes scuffing against the pebbles.

*****

They went home to Eileen for Christmas.

His mother gave Aisling a scarf and a necklace as presents.

"Oh," said Aisling, fingering the necklace. "Thank you," she said, fiddling with it in her hands.

"I wouldn't wear that in a million years," she said to Colin in their room. They were getting ready to visit his father's grave.

"What's wrong with it?" said Colin. "And what's got into you?"

"Nothing," she said, "it's just that it's like something a nun would wear."

The wind was gusting in all directions in the graveyard. Eileen had brought a wreath and the place was packed with people arriving and leaving. Scarves and skirts flapped about like wrapping paper in the wind. On their way back to the car, Aisling was walking ahead, her red hair in a swirl, her coat swinging open and her skirt blowing out like a flag. Colin was linking arms with his mother.

"What *does* she think she's wearing?" Eileen was murmuring. Colin didn't know what to say, so he said nothing.

But Aisling helped Eileen in the kitchen with the dinner, stuffing the turkey and making the soup and the gravy. And she insisted that Eileen go in and sit down with Colin and have a sherry, saying everything was under control. After dinner, she did all the washing up and set the table for the morning.

"But you're meant to be a guest," said Eileen, looking in at all the breakfast things perfectly laid out in the dining room.

"But sure, am I not part of the family now?" said Aisling with a smile.

"Come in by the fire with us," said Eileen warmly.

*****

Christmas faded and Easter came. And it happened again for the second time.

Although not quite as severe, it was still bad like an earthquake in her body. And afterward she struggled with the feelings in her mind. For a few days, Colin felt she would crumble but the waves subsided and her nerves returned to calm waters. She rallied and pulled through and he could see she was making an effort. He brought her trays of oddly cooked food which helped bring a smile to her face. But the house seemed empty to Aisling, as if guests who were expected hadn't arrived and she felt let down inside. No amount of cooking could cover up how she felt. As if she wasn't good enough.

Not suitable enough. Her body a reject. A failure. The war raged on in her head.

But the third time it happened a year and a half later was worse. She was twelve weeks in and complaining of pains in her back and struggling with cramps. For a week, she felt strange and unwell and alarmed at the increase in bleeding but refused to believe it. Colin was taking her to the doctor to make sure she was alright when it started to happen.

This time the pain was prolonged and intense, as if there was barbed wire inside. The current began to flow like a river gushing into the sea. And each time it subsided, it started again soon after. He got her to the hospital where the nurses took over and eventually calm was restored. Afterward, she lay staring at the ceiling as if it were the sky or a pathway to heaven. Then the tears came. They both cried together. There were no words for each other. No words to describe it.

She didn't sleep well for the rest of the winter and he'd find her staring out the windows, staring into an abyss of her own. He couldn't reach her now. And every day the house seemed more like a reminder, a reminder of a private tomb. It lay heavy with grief. Dark with no lamps on. Aisling on her own on the couch staring at the television. Sitting rigid and frowning through comedy shows.

*****

His paintings turned darker.

The Night Watch.

In twilight shades like Whistler on the Thames. Lonely bleak nocturnes at sea.

The crepuscular light of evening and the first pale rays of dawn. Blackened blue seas with barely a thread of light emanating. Dark, prowling waves in cold, angry seas. The piers painted like knives slashing water under skies, heavy, opaque, and oppressive.

Oddly, they sold.

He wondered who bought them. Obviously, there were other people out there with a taste for the lonelier edges of the soul.

His mother came for a visit in the summer.

She was shocked by the state of the house but said nothing. They went out to eat which told her something because normally, Aisling was only too happy to cook.

The next morning, Eileen and Colin walked on the beach. Aisling was still in bed with the curtains pulled.

"I suppose you're aware the house is a mess," she said, broaching the subject.

"Mmmm," said Colin.

The wind freshened around them, blowing ripples on the waves. A few swimmers glided by like seals through the water, their bathing caps bobbing in the sun.

"I mean you do realize how you're living?" she added, looking at him for a response. "What on earth are you going to do?" she asked. "You can't continue on here like this."

"She hasn't been well," said Colin.

"I know that," said Eileen. "She's been through an awful, awful time. But we all have to pull ourselves together, Colin. You of all people should know that."

"She'll come back to me," he said.

"Well, I don't know if she will," said Eileen.

They walked on through the wind. Drops of rain tried to fall then gave up.

"And look at your paintings," she added.

"What's wrong with them?" he asked.

"You know well what's wrong with them," she said. "You don't need me to tell you."

He let out a long sigh. He wasn't in disagreement with her. He was just clinging to the idea that things would get better. She was right. The house was a mess, the kitchen upside down, even though Aisling wasn't even bothered cooking in it much anymore. The rooms were stuffy, unaired, the windows closed, and the curtains drawn. He knew she was right.

"She will come back," said Colin. "She will." But he said it more as a prayer than as a statement of certainty.

They had reached the end of the pier now. The sea splashed about grey and green and foreboding, slopping against the ramparts.

"Look, I've never asked you this before," she said, "and I promise I never will again, but what in the name of heaven did you ever see in that girl?"

"Mum," he said, "how can you even say that after all she's been through?"

"I know well what she's been through," she said. "I went through it myself years ago."

Colin looked at her. "I didn't know that," he said.

"No," she said, "how would you? A lot of women go through it."

"I found her a breath of fresh air," he said after a pause.

"When she's on form, she's all fun and laughter ..." He stopped. "Used to be full of laughter. We used to laugh all the time. We used to have a lot of fun. She took me out of myself. Out of my work ..." He stopped again, his words faltering.

"I don't know what exactly," he said. "But I know that I love her and I always will."

"Well," said Eileen, "that may be, but I think the two of you should come home. Get yourselves sorted. You can't stay on here like this. And Ireland would do you both the power of good. Come home, Colin," she said, turning to him, "before it's too late."

"Maybe it's time," he said, dwelling on her words. "I don't know. I'm not sure."

"Well, what are you going to do?" she said. "You can't just do nothing."

"I'm going to take her on a holiday," he said. "She could do with a holiday. Then I'll know what to do."

They walked back the length of the pier. The rain had come down now and they walked with their collars turned up, through the grey, wet wind.

*****

Burgh Island rose out of the sea like a conch shell covered in lichen.

The tide was full in and the sea was glittering like the Mediterranean. Up above the sky was clear and inviting.

"Is that the hotel?" said Aisling, squinting at the white building snug in the hill.

"Aye," said the man loading the sea tractor, "that's her alright. There she is."

"It's like a little ship," she said with a laugh.

"Be a queer ship that," he replied, "moored up there on the hill."

The sea tractor was a sort of boat on big wheels, a wagon equipped to bring visitors across when the tide was in. When it was out, they could walk across the golden stretch of sand with the tractor just taking their bags.

Colin and Aisling had been driving along the Jurassic Coast for the past week, stopping off at small hotels on the way. Their journey had brought them now to South Devon, and here near the close of September, the weather was still perfection. So far, the trip had been worth it. Aisling had come in and out of herself like a flower opening and closing but that at least was an improvement on Brighton, and Colin was grateful to see it. Money was beginning to run low and this hotel would be a treat. Their two nights here would round off the trip, the art deco hotel their last extravagance. Then it would be straight back to Brighton and the autumn.

Dinner was served in an airy room with sea windows, the menu a mix of freshly caught fish and home baking. There weren't that many other guests around.

"Getting a little late in the season," said Johnny, the owner, with a smile of perfect white teeth. He was smartly turned out in a white shirt and cream slacks, and had a pretty wife called Imelda with dark hair and blue eyes.

"We could a run a place like this," mused Aisling. "We'd make the perfect charming couple."

"Yes," said Colin with a grin. "You could cook, and I could paint."

"But you'd have to entertain as well," said Aisling.

"Oh, we'd have staff for doing that," he said, laughing. "Sure, what would I be entertaining for when I could be painting all day long?" They laughed together. It was how they used to laugh.

"Speaking of which," he said, "you don't mind if I go off sketching tomorrow?"

"Oh, if it's sunny like today," she said, "I'll be fine."

And it was. Fine and sunny in the morning.

Aisling waved him off. The tide was out and she could see him mooching around the shore, switching between the rocks making sketches here and there. She was lying in a deck chair, with a pair of sunglasses on and a red hat shading her skin. The terrace was a suntrap and the morning stretched slowly to lunch.

She had a glass of white wine with her meal. It was a new thing to drink, and expensive, but she shrugged it off as a holiday treat. She waved to the other diners and an old man in a blazer came along and invited himself to her table.

"Malcolm Baldwin," he said, offering his hand. "How d'you do?"

Her lunch was simple, a bowl of mussels with crusty bread. The man was full of talk and had a moustache and a cravat. He had steak and chips and a couple of glasses of claret.

"Never married, never believed in it," he said. "Much prefer talking to pretty girls like you."

Aisling gave him a cold smile and put her sunglasses on.

Johnny asked them would they like coffee on the terrace but she asked for tea instead. She was developing a headache. A combination of the wine and Malcolm Baldwin. He was like a buzzing fly.

The man talked on.

Aisling wasn't really listening, but he didn't seem to notice.

The air was muggy now, the sky changing. She lay back with

her eyes closed. The wine was making her sleepy.

Johnny brought her tea and she sat up. He winked at her. The man was still rattling on.

Sipping her tea, she realized Colin had disappeared from view.

The sky to the west was changing color.

"... Yes ... so ... rather a good yarn in the end," the man was saying.

"What was?" she asked, realizing she was paying him no attention.

"The Christie book, the one I was telling you about," he said. "You know the one this island is in. This hotel that you're staying in."

She looked at him quizzically. "Which book is that then?"

"The one where they all die," he said, leaning forward, looking at her.

"What everyone?" she said, laughing thinly.

"Ten total strangers come to the island ..." And he began to tell it again. It seemed to be a staple story of his. As if he had written it himself.

She was intrigued at first. "Go on," she said, "what happens?"

"But it'll spoil it for you," he said.

"Oh, but I won't read it," she said.

"Ah well in that case ..." He settled back and continued.

"... And one by one ...... each and every one of them die ...... until in the end, you see ...... there were none."

The sky had turned a purple shade of blue.

"What do you mean none?" she said looking at him. "But how could that be? I don't understand."

And he started to explain it to her again, about the ending and the one who was dead who wasn't dead but seemed to be dead ... He was losing her in the intricacy of the thing ...

But her eyes were glazing over and her hand was rubbing her stomach ...

"So, in the end you see, there were none," he said. He seemed to keep saying it. "None, you see ... in the end there were none ... none in the end ... at all ..."

It had started to rain.

The man jumped up. "Spot and bother," he tutted, "rain on a day like this."

But the day had changed now.

The man went in.

"In the end there were none ...... in the end there were none ..."

She went across to the wall and looked over.

Where is Colin? Where is he? Where?

She scanned the beach. The tide was foaming in. She stood looking out to sea. There was a boat way out. She shielded her eyes. "Colin?"

The rain was coming down, but she didn't notice. She had to find Colin.

The terrace was glistening with rain. She ran back in through the hotel. There was no one around. People had gone to their rooms to change. She ran out the front door, down the steps, down the hill to the beach. Her hair, her arms, her dress were wet. There was rain in her eyes. "Colin? Colin?" She was calling his name, but it disappeared in the rain. The wind was whipping up.

There were rocks covered in shells and she clung to the rocks with her hands and the rocks began to tear her hands as she pulled herself along. The rain was in her eyes and she couldn't see through the rain. She couldn't see through the fog and the rain in her eyes. She was wading through water, her white dress clinging like a wet tissue, the water streaming down her back, her hat floating out to sea. The water was freezing cold, swirling under her feet, all around. Her hands thrashed the water, catching the jaws of hidden rocks in her fingers. Her hands began to bleed.

Colin ...... Colin ......
Colin ...... there was ...... no Colin ......
...... no baby ...... no babies ......
...... in the end ......
...... there were none ......
...... in the end ......
...... there was no one ......
...... at all ......

And they found her like that in the water. Still wading through the water, waist-high.

"No one. There's no one," she was screaming in the rain as they pulled her back onto the shore. Her hands were bleeding, her arms torn and scratched and her hair was wild and plastered to her head and she was terrified, cold, and shaking.

Colin came running up the steps. He could see her resting on a couch in the foyer. Johnny and Imelda were with her. A crowd hovered in the background like people at a funeral.

"I went out in a boat," he stuttered. "We got caught in the rain."

She stared at him.

"It was like that nightmare I had years ago, remember?"

But she wasn't following what he was saying. He gripped her hand and sank his head against her cheek. Her expression was numb.

Johnny spoke a few words in his ear.

"I'm taking you home," Colin said.

She looked at him with eyes that were tortured and wide and afraid.

"I'm taking you home," he said again, burying his head in her shoulder.

*****

Brighton seemed shabby and run-down when they got back, like an old threadbare theatre, with the curtains drawn and the audience gone. The house on Camelford Street felt dusty and dark, every room, every window a reminder of the past.

After a week of medication and rest, Aisling had settled a little but her eyes were shadowed, hollowing out her face like a cave at low tide. Her hands lay inert on the bedspread and her voice when it came was slow and monotone, as if someone was talking through her.

"Anywhere," she said. "Anywhere but here. I can't stay here."

Colin hesitated.

"Ireland," he said.

"Anywhere," she said. "I don't care."

"Are you sure?" he asked.

"Anywhere," she said, shaking her head from side to side. "I don't care anymore."

*****

Colin changed gear and the Ford Cortina groaned and coughed up the steep incline.

The sky was lilac blue and patterned with soft moving clouds and the sun was warm through the windshield. Aisling stared out at the passing rocks and blackberry bushes and ferns on the side of the road.

"You said a country drive," she said. "You didn't say a mountain drive. Where exactly are we?"

"Rocky Valley," he replied. "Nearly there now," he added, glancing at his map. Adeline Bell had drawn it for him. He swung the car to the left up a stony side road. They were very high now.

"I think we're here. Yes, I'm sure this must be it," he said, switching off the engine.

Aisling followed him over to the gate. There was a stone wall and some trees, a short pathway and a house tucked away from the world.

A low, white cottage.

"Why are we here?" Aisling asked. "Where is this?"

Colin was staring at the cottage.

"Carrigoona," he said softly.

Then he turned and looked at her. "Paul Henry's house."

"But he's dead," said Aisling.

"I know," said Colin. "I just wanted to see it."

Aisling sighed quietly.

"Come on," he said, pushing open the gate.

"But we can't go in," said Aisling. "People live here."

"Oh, they're away in France," he said. "Adeline Bell told me they wouldn't be here."

They walked up to the cottage. Low, white, traditional. All it needed was thatch.

They went around to the back and stopped in amazement.

The hill fell abruptly away as if someone had ripped it out and in its place scattered a vast postcard of mountains and clouds and a deep wide valley painted purple and green and gold.

"Now can you see why?" said Colin, taking her hand.

The mountains of Wicklow were shaded in the colors of evening and the hills were sliced with sun. A mass of clouds tumbled above in the sky and the vista stretched left and right and as far as the eye could see. The only sound was the drone of the bees and the swish of leaves in a hawthorn tree. Butterflies circled in the air and the sun burnt down stretching out their shadows like tree branches through the soft, brown grass.

"Carrigoona," said Colin in a drawn-out whisper.

They stood quietly in the secret silence.

And the mountains echoed back of enchanted paintings.

"Carrigoona," said Colin, "now I know I've come home."

5

The apple tree rustled in the wind and two small apples dropped to the ground. They sat on the grass like red, impressionist daubs in a painting. The scene from the window had caught his eye. Colin roused himself and checked his watch. It was almost time to leave. He had been thinking of that first glimpse of Carrigoona, five years ago. But now, his suitcases were in the hall and America beckoned. He just had to remember "wallet, passport, tickets." He repeated the words: "wallet, passport, tickets." He always forgot something.

"Are you sure you're going to be alright here on your own?" he called again.

Aisling came out of the bathroom, her hair wrapped up in a towel.

"Of course I'm sure. There's the garden, the cat, the restaurant. I won't have a minute to myself."

"Mmmm, I suppose," he said. "I still think you'd have been better off coming with me."

"Too late for that now," she said. "I'd only get in your way. You wouldn't want me."

"Mmmm," he said.

"Wallet, passport, tickets," she said, standing with her arms folded.

"Yes, one, two, three, got them." The taxi pulled up and he held out his arms.

Aisling gave him a light hug as if there was no strength or feeling in her limbs. "Go on," she said, "you'll be late."

He left in a fuss, double-checking for everything and stumbling out with his bags. When the taxi drove off, he rolled down the window and waved. She was standing in the porch of the cottage, the towel on her head, staring after the car, her arm raised in a limp, little wave as if the effort was just too much. The taxi turned the corner and she was gone. Colin turned his eyes to the wide sweep of sea. She was so distant these days. Like a sailboat far out on the water.

"Can you take the coast road?" he said to the driver, who nodded. They chatted for a bit about nothing, but Colin was only aware of the sea. From Greystones to Glasthule and Dun Laoghaire. After that they joined the main road and he lay back in the seat, satisfied. He would take the sea with him on the plane in his mind as he would the lone figure of Aisling in the porch in Greystones with her limp little wave. As if she just couldn't be bothered anymore.

*****

The mountains of Carrigoona had brought him back to life that day five years ago. He could still remember the freshness of that moment when they had rounded the corner of the cottage and seen the view. The scent of the countryside had stirred him that evening and he had left with a new appetite for painting. The mountains of Wicklow had spurred him on to find a new world he could make his own. And he had found that new world in Sandycove.

It had happened by chance.

His first visit to the Forty Foot, the well-known bathing spot in the sea. The natural pool was surrounded by sienna-colored rocks like something out of Sorrento. The rocks were warm to the touch as if baked in an oven and he had stripped off and plunged in, lured by the gently bobbing water. Afterward he had gone into the tower.

The James Joyce Tower.

With no purpose in mind except to wander around.

He had never really been able to make much sense of the multi-layered voices in *Ulysses*, but in many ways, they had left a lasting impression, and he had often wondered about trying something similar in painting, about finding a way to imbue his landscapes and seas with a greater, lingering, spiritual presence. His early work on Inishtrahull had been a first step in that direction.

The first two floors held a collection of photographs and note-books and artifacts. Then he went up to the room where the novel began. The bed and the chairs and the table and the shelf above the bed. The bed half made and a striped cotton dressing gown across the back of a chair as if waiting for Gogarty or Joyce to walk in. But it was only when he went up to the roof that the idea came. At first it was like a wind chime tinkling in the breeze. Then louder in his head like the bells from a church.

He was on his own on the roof.

In a helmet of sky. And encircled by land and water.

To the front, the sky folding into the sea in a ribbon of haze on the horizon. Closer in, the water shot with sunlight, clouds tearing overhead, and to the left, Howth like a giant whale, almost an island. Then the great sweep of the bay, and left again the blue sparkling water of Dun Laoghaire harbor and the tightly packed rooftops of Glasthule. He turned around to the mountains, their dark slopes ripping the sky and on past the sweep of their contours to Dalkey Village and the sudden steep height of Dalkey Hill and then out to the lighthouse and back out to the front with the sea disappearing far out in the sky.

And he turned around again and again. And the clouds kept moving. The light kept changing. The scenes kept evolving. In a circle of light.

The skies and the seas of the Sandycove *Ulysses* tower.

*****

"Oh, you'd need permission for something like that," said the lady at the desk.

"And so, who should I ask?" said Colin, leaning on the desk, his hair falling like a boy's across his brow. He pushed it back, grinning.

The lady had a perm and blue eyeshadow and a tightly buttoned blouse, and she rummaged in a drawer and found Colin some names. He took them quickly and gave her a wink. She blushed and stared after him.

On impulse, he drove straight into Dublin, to Wilton Terrace on the off chance. "Try the beach," the woman at her door had said. He pulled in at Sandymount and spotted her far out on the sands in a pink turban with a whole batch of new dogs.

"Are you completely deranged?" said Adeline Bell.

"No," he said. "Come on, you've got to see it."

"And the dogs?" she said. "Do the dogs want to see it?"

"Oh, pile them in," he said. "Trust me, it'll be an adventure."

They packed into the old, green Cortina then and Colin and Adeline talked all the way and the dogs stuck their heads out the windows and barked at everyone, then rolled in the back like unruly children.

He parked the car in the shade of a wall and the dogs fell quiet, their noses pressed against the window, watching Adeline's every movement as she walked away with Colin.

"Oh, my great aunt," said Adeline, from the top of the tower. "I see what you mean."

"I knew you'd be able to see it," he said.

"See it," she said, "I love it." Then she gave him a hug and her turban flew off in the wind and they watched it bobbing away in the breeze.

"I haven't painted anything yet," said Colin.

"But you will," she said. "You will."

*****

Access came easily and quickly and for the next three years, he visited regularly. The ladies at the desk got used to him arriving after his swim in the Forty Foot, with his hair still wet and carrying his easel and paints and bundle of sheets to protect the stonework. He even managed to get used to the visitors popping up and down to the roof like rabbits in and out of a burrow. They often watched him work and he didn't mind except when they talked. But most knew to leave him alone.

All of the finished canvases were done at home. The tower was where he could work en plein air making small-scale studies of the colors and tones and the feel of the place. He worked quickly using different shaped palette knives and a variety of filbert brushes in varying sizes. When he started first, he was tight, and the work was dull and meaningless and flat. One morning he began scraping the paint back off the canvas in order to start again, when he stopped and looked at it. The scraping had left an underlying ghostly impression formed by the paint that was left in between the tight weave of the canvas. The sky and the water now had the appearance of transparent gauze. He set it to one side to dry and started a fresh canvas and when he had it well covered, he scraped off the top layer. Again, the same effect came through, like an old faded watercolor exposed to the sun. He went home that night and thought about it and the next day when both canvases were touch dry, he went back to the tower and painted new sections over each of them, from the same scene again and then using the flat edge of his longest palette knife he scraped the paint off again and examined them. He had something now. The impression was there of another painting underneath, a feeling of shadows, of light, of something else there behind, a ghost of the place—and that's exactly what it was, the same scene painted in similar but different light conditions as the day before. It was time repeating time, recording the place, and he nodded to himself, pleased with the result. He made all the rest of the studies like this, in these scraped back multiple layers, until they all had the same feeling of faded fragility, illuminated from the layers underneath with a delicate, ethereal, threadbare light. Over time, these studies took on their own language of visual poetry as if they, like the rocks in the sea, had always just simply been there.

*****

He loved the drive every morning from Greystones. The fresh air and the sense of a new day ahead. The splash and dip in the Forty Foot and the rough towel-down with the feel of the sea in his blood. Then up to the tower and the ladies at the desk and up to the roof with his easel and paints and canvases and sheets. And in the evening back home along the coast road to the cottage. After Brighton, they had found a cottage in Greystones up a narrow side road from the sea. Four windows to the front and a porch with a rambling rose.

"Weeds and brambles," said Aisling, looking around the first time.

"You didn't have a garden in Brighton," he said.

"I'm not a patient," she snapped.

"I didn't mean—"

"I don't want to talk about it," she said.

"We could put an apple tree in," Colin said, "and get a dog."

"I don't like dogs," she said, screwing up her nose as if the garden was packed with them. "They smell. I think I'll get a cat."

What had happened in Brighton was a closed topic now. What had happened in Burgh Island was taboo. He tried a few times to bring the subject up but found he was only stirring bad feelings like a storm stirring waves in the sea.

"I don't know how I ever ended up in this place," she said once or twice, and then stopped.

"Because of what happened," he said.

"What happened?" she said.

"I had to rescue you," he said.

"From what?" she said.

"From yourself, from everything."

"To end up in a place like this," she said.

"You have a beautiful cottage and a view of the sea."

"I have a room with no view. I have my memories in my head, and I have you. Painting away at all hours, day and night. This is not somewhere I wanted to be."

"You gave up in Brighton."

"I caved in. That's not giving up."

"But we are here now."

"You are here. I am not. I am not here."

"Look at me."

"No, listen to me. I am not here. This cottage, this view, this dream, it's not me. It's all you. You. You. You. Just go and paint and … leave … me … alone. Just … leave … me … alone."

Her words fell away until they were barely audible.

Colin left it like that, but he knew they each felt betrayed.

The cottage was run-down and cheap but the location was great with a long garden front and back. Colin liked Greystones right from the start. It was next to the sea and close to the mountains, and as far as he was concerned not that far out from Dublin at all. And in the end, it was all they could afford. Aisling found a job as a cook with the Red Deer Hotel, the busiest place in the village and he was glad to see her back in a routine again, doing something she loved. And she got herself a cat. A black velvet cat with green eyes and claws that could draw blood. Colin was wary of it from the start. Aisling called it Poppet. Colin called it Lord Muck.

He called for her one day at the hotel and stood at the back kitchen door watching her work. She was oblivious to him and seemed like another person entirely. Twirling around with her ladles and spoons and dagger steel knives, joking with the other cooks, shouting when her order was ready. She was searing steaks on a hot grill, her face flushed, her hair up in a hat and her second arm stirring a sauce. Then she flicked the meat onto a plate, poured the sauce, added parsley with a flourish and a quick grind of pepper, and called for the waiter to come. Then she bent into the next order seamlessly and started all over again.

Yes, he thought, *yes, she is alive. She is still alive inside.*

But after a couple of summers, the novelty was wearing thin. Poppet kept her company on the long wintry nights with the sound of the waves crashing down the road and Colin preoccupied with his work. But Aisling had no time for his new ideas and little interest in Joyce or visual lyricism. Her nerves began to fragment and fray. And they began to row. And she began to develop a taste for wine. And for smoking. And banging doors. And going out. And when she did go out, staying out too late. And then not getting up in the mornings.

"Just as well I've got a decent wage," she said after dinner one night. "If it was up to you, we'd be living off bread and water."

"What do you mean?" he said. "I'm selling paintings all the time."

"Yes," she said, "selling them and where is the money? Most of it from what I can see goes back into framing and canvases and paints and brushes and oils and God knows what else."

"Look, this is a big project," he said.

"You can't eat a big project," she said. "Honestly, Colin, why can't you see reason and get a job teaching or something. I mean it's 1980, for God's sake. This isn't Inishtrahull, you know."

"Do you know," he said, "you're never, ever happy. You're being ridiculous and you're totally exaggerating. I bought that new garden shed for you for a start."

"And if it wasn't for me in the restaurant," she said, "we'd be living in it."

"For God's sake," he said, "will you stop all of this? You don't bring that much in yourself you know, and you spend money like there's no tomorrow. But do you hear me complaining?"

"Spend it on what?"

"On clothes and on cushions and food and wine and now all these blasted cigarettes."

"Well, why shouldn't I have a bit of luxury for myself? You're never around. You're always working in that room and there's nothing to do here in Greystones."

"And what is so awful about Greystones all of a sudden?"

"It's grey. It rains. It's cold and it's windy and that's just the summer," she said.

"Well, why don't you go up to Bray or somewhere for a day?" he said.

"That's even worse," she snapped. "Sure, everyone there is on the dole."

"Oh, and how would you know that?" he said. "Have you asked them?"

"I don't need to," she said. "You can tell by looking at them." Then she poured a glass of wine and lit a cigarette.

"Do you know," he said, "if you didn't drink so much and smoke all the time, you wouldn't have all this angst."

"No," she said, "I suppose I'd be a bloody saint like you."

He glared at her and picked up his coat.

"Where are you going?"

"Out."

"Down to the sea, I suppose," she said, starting to laugh.

He paused in the doorway.

"You do know that I know you get handouts from your mother and checks from that bloody awful Bell woman," she said, spitting the words across the room at him.

He banged the door and went out and walked down to the shore. The sea roared in his ears.

*****

The rows came and went. As the moods took her and as the seasons changed. She was better and brighter in spring and in summer. But she struggled with the darkness of winter and took on more evening shifts in the restaurant to offset the tedium of long nights in the cottage.

Sundays were their best day. Colin never painted on Sundays and visited his mother in the afternoons while Aisling cooked a roast for the evening. Sometimes his mother came for lunch instead and he would drive her back around six o'clock. Either way, they rarely fell out on Sundays, as if that day was somehow divorced from the rest of the week.

And the painting went on. And to bring money in, he painted a whole load of other scenes away from the tower, of the Sugar Loaf and Rocky Valley and Glendalough and Avoca. And Aisling was right to some extent. Adeline Bell had helped a bit along the way, but Adeline he knew believed in him and believed in what he was trying to do and he needed the freedom to focus and concentrate on his work. And the effort was paying off. He had twenty large canvases now in addition to the multiple smaller sketches and studies. Twenty large canvases. The title simple and factual. *Landscapes from a Tower.*

*****

The exhibition was held in the Georgian Gallery.

The title gave nothing away of the spirit of the work.

Over the past three years he had tried to capture the essence of the landscape, that illusory sense of place. He had tried to convey the feel of the wind and the rain, the warmth of the sun on the stone of the rocks, the grey falling drizzle and the damp in the air, the light from the sea and the shadows of the clouds moving slowly on the mountains, the intangible sense of the fresh salt air, of a past and a present, the feel of the place, the ghosts. He had painted all the sketches and studies in scraped back layers that left spectral images infused with light. But for the larger canvases he had wanted a greater depth of luminosity and finish and he did this by coloring each canvas first in a golden ochre ground and then building up the lighter areas like clouds and water and sunlight in bright, pale shades and working over these, enhancing their glow by applying a whole range of contrasting tones in a series of thin, transparent glazes. He used glazes as well for the shadow areas, enriching the dark and deepening the contrasts so that the overall effect of the finished paintings was one of almost insubstantiality, as if the land and sea were bathed in some light that came from another world. The paint had an added lustre and sheen as well because he had used traditional, high quality blending mediums made from balsam resin and stand oil and larch turpentine, which deepened the depth of the gloss. These were all slower techniques than he had used in the past, but he had managed to make them work for him and now when seen hanging together in the gallery, the paintings seemed to form a continuous tapestry of light. He had decided to show what he now called the "Whistler studies" as well in a separate room, so that it was almost like two exhibitions in one. He was pleased with the results and glad to be finished. He had started that first day in the tower with some vague ideas in his head around Paul Henry's magical *Early Morning on the Lake of the Glittering Sword* and Turner's shimmering sun-drenched skies, but had wound up at the end with a set of landscapes perhaps more directly inspired by le Brocquy's series of *Portrait Heads* of Beckett and Joyce and Yeats, in which those heads seemed to emanate an echoing sense of lingering spirit with their skulls shining through their skin.

The exhibition got good reviews in the papers and he did an interview on the radio about it. Adeline Bell was there virtually every night. Aisling came on the opening night in a black silk dress and wool crochet shawl and drank too much wine. His mother came and wandered around, invisible to the chattering crowd. And Bertha Frances Morgan came from New York.

"I told you," said Adeline Bell. "The man's a genius. Colin," she said, "come and meet Bertha."

Bertha's hair was jet black like a wig and she spoke in staccato-like questions, as if having crossed the Atlantic, she was still in a hurry to get somewhere else.

"You did these?" she said. "You did all these? How did you do them? You just made them up? You did? You did this? Oh, my word, look at this. Adeline, will you look at this over here. You see this? I am just absolutely going to have to have this, I really am."

"Hey," she said to Colin, "you can come over and see it. Stay in my hotel for a week, for a month. We'll put you up. You can see it. You can say hello and you can see it. Well, what do you say?"

In the end, she bought two.

She owned the Parnell, an old Irish hotel on Lexington Avenue. Adeline was a friend from years earlier and Bertha stayed the weekend in Wilton Terrace. Colin stayed clear for fear of a headache. But when she was leaving, she produced her card: *Bertha Frances Morgan, The Parnell Hotel, 650 Lexington Avenue* in stout manila, with a border of black like something from a funeral parlor, and ordered him to phone her, and let her know well in advance.

"Hey, you can see them again," she said. "I'm gonna put them in the lobby. We've got a great big lobby. They'll look real good there. Hey, and you can see New York too while you're at it. How about that for a deal?"

"Don't look a gift horse in the mouth," said Adeline Bell, sweeping past. She looked at him over her shoulder. "I mean it," she said. "She doesn't ask if she doesn't like. Trust me," she whispered, giving him a look.

*****

Colin felt free now but at the same time a little sad as the plane cleared Shannon and the coastline of Clare disappeared. He turned his neck to the window like a passenger passing Inishtrahull or Fastnet, but within minutes there was nothing but clouds. Ireland had disappeared. And momentarily he found that an odd feeling. The exhibition was over. Years of work just vanished behind him, gone. He sat back in his seat and closed his eyes and let his mind drift slowly away.

Aisling had never really bought into the tower project. She had come on the opening night but had been ill at ease when she saw just how many people were there singing his praises. Where once it would have excited her, he thought now that she must have just felt left out. But there was little he could do about it. She had given him enough grief over it in the first place and maybe he was foolish to wish she had come to New York. He had thought that perhaps it would have brought them closer together. But his image of her in the porch left little to be optimistic about. He thought he had tried to make things work. Perhaps when he got back, they could start again like in the old days in Norfolk, when they had been happy and bobbed along. Maybe, he thought, in the new year, they could go to Paris for a break and try again. New York was too much about him. His exhibition. His invite to the Parnell. His new friend Bertha Morgan. And his sister in Maine. *And yes,* he thought, *that was the other thing, she hadn't been very keen on seeing Aine again.*

*****

Clouds were gathering over Greystones. Aisling was in the garden turning compost with Poppet on the bench beside her, his paws dangling over the edge.

"I think it'll rain soon," she said to him, looking up at the clouds. It was strange thinking of Colin up above in the sky. On his way to Manhattan. Her hands were covered in dirt and muck and leaves. Poppet was watching her and purring in the sun. She was talking to him and his ears were alert.

"Turn the dead leaves and bury the past," she said, leaning on her fork and looking at the compost heap. She poked it again. "The past is dead," she said, stabbing the leaves. "The past is dead and we can bury the dead and some of the dead will go to hell. But that's their own lookout. People like my father," she said to Poppet. "His own lookout," she said, her lips pursed and tight. "But we can cover over the past, cover over the sins," she said, turning the compost again. "And out of death will come worms and all sorts of stuff and by this time next year," she said, stroking his head, "we'll have something new. Something fresh. The past," she said, "is always there. All we can

do is keep churning it down. Down. Down. Down. And then maybe
sometime," she said, holding Poppet on her knees, "we can move on."

*****

Manhattan was like some giant labyrinthine maze from Picasso's
mind. The buildings so long and tall it was as if they'd been dropped
from the sky. And the streets so straight, with no end in sight. A new
vista around every corner, like an unseen cubist painting. And people
hurrying about as if pursued by some invisible enemy. The noise
so loud, it felt like a drill in the head. Colin looked at the people
hurrying about. And he looked at them aghast and amazed and
bemused. And he thought of Inishtrahull and tried to imagine people
on it scurrying about with briefcases and sunglasses and trainers, and
he shuddered. And he thought of himself in the tower in Sandycove
turning around, just looking at the clouds. And suddenly he felt very
small, like an ant underneath someone's shoe.

St. Patrick's was a votive-candle lit oasis, one which he welcomed.
The Parnell was a plush, indulgent world with thick carpets and
velvet draped windows and deep-set burgundy chairs. But once in
through the glass doors, a beautiful, peaceful calm descended with
soft light emanating from large lamps on marble side tables.

The paintings were like strangers at first when he saw them again.
They were well lit and stood out and looked well but it was almost
as if someone else had painted them, and he felt almost shy looking
at them up there on their new posh walls looking down at him. They
were miles away from home and from the tower and from his studio
room in the cottage in Greystones where he'd painted them, but
after the first night, he got used to them again and glanced at them
and smiled every time that he walked through the lobby.

"Born to be here," said Bertha Frances Morgan. "Born to be
here. Both of them. Love them both. Love them both. They look
great, right? They both look great. Both look great. Our guests love
them. Told them all you were coming. Told them all. They all want

to meet you. All want to meet you." Bertha, he realized, verbalized her thoughts in a steady flow of entirely subjective assumptions and statements of half-truths and facts. She answered her own questions in conversations with herself but included you in them to the point where it felt like a discourse. But she was a more than generous hostess and he was glad of the distraction of her company and flattered with her interest in him. She took him to Brooks Brothers for shoes and silk ties and Delmonico's for lunch, the Frick for old masters, and the MoMA for Van Gogh's *Olive Trees* writhing on their canvas in that intense Mediterranean heat. At night, they went to *La Traviata* at the Met and he went by himself up the Empire State Building, the city emblazoned in the night air like a glittering comet that had fallen to earth. And after a week he was saturated with the city and longing for air. For the sea. For fresh air. He was going to Maine to see Aine, but he had another few days yet before his flight. He had to get out. And so, he inquired around.

*****

The journey to Montauk took him three hours by train. Way out to the tip of Long Island. He rented a bicycle and cycled five miles to the beach. And here he could breathe in the wind and Atlantic air. There was hardly anyone about. It was the perfect distant point. A white lighthouse. And seagulls circling over the sea, binding the sky and the water together as if with invisible thread.

Slipping off his shoes, he paddled in the water. The weave of the gulls pinning memories together. Always seawater and clouds in the sky And the memory of waves. And of the wave that day.

Holding on in the water.

To his father's hand. But the hand had slipped away underwater. And the memory of it was still there like a bruise in his mind. A lingering lunar eclipse.

He sat at the water's edge looking out to sea, the water slapping in, the wind freshening his face. And he realized that for so much of his life he had felt like he was underwater. Struggling to breathe. To escape. To find air. Trying to climb out of the waves. To paint the perfect picture. To overcome the sea with his dreams. Before he got dragged down again. But every dream, every picture, left nothing. Because in the end there was nothing, only memory.

The tower had had given him a new energy. The success of the paintings had lifted him and Manhattan had been out of this world, something he'd never experienced before, but he was feeling tired now and drained from it all. From all the work and excitement and effort. And that was why he just needed to be here. On his own with the sea. There would always be the sea rolling endlessly in. From that day in Wexford to this. Like a drug in his brain. And after everything else when all the noise had died down, there would always be just himself. Left alone on his own with his thoughts.

A white collie dog with a black eye crept out of the air and surprised him.

"Hello," said Colin. "Who are you?"

The dog licked his hand and looked at him with eyes like varnished chestnuts. The right eye in a circle of black.

"That's Wolfie," said a voice. The voice was young and well-mannered and apologetic.

Colin looked around. A tall, tanned boy with dark hair and brown eyes in a T-shirt and shorts was standing behind.

"Why Wolfie?" he asked.

The boy laughed. "Because he looks like a wolf."

"A pirate wolf," said Colin.

The boy laughed and sat down. "Hello," he said. "I'm Tom. Actually, it's because he likes it when I play the violin, he likes Mozart the best."

"Ah," said Colin, "a musician with a musical dog."

"Well, I'm a student," said Tom.

"Even so, lucky dog," said Colin.

Tom leaned over and petted the dog's head. "So am I," he said."

Colin could feel Tom's arm on his leg. Tom said nothing. Colin said nothing. They looked out to sea. And stayed like that for a while. Close together like shells on the sand. Then the dog scrambled onto Colin's lap and started licking his face. The moment was broken. Tom looked at Colin and they laughed, then he got up and chatted for a bit and called the dog and threw a ball. Wolfie raced away like a whippet in the wind. Colin watched them, his hand shielding his eyes from the sun. Then the boy turned and looked around. Colin held up his arm and waved. The boy waved back. It was a strange feeling waving to a boy on the beach in Montauk. The boy and the dog diminished into the distance. The encounter was over.

Colin looked down at his hands. He could still smell Wolfie on his palms. The sand was all creased where Tom had been sitting. He sat gazing out across the sea. It was time to go but he let the moment linger.

He was in a tent on a beach again a long time ago.

Michael's body close to him, skin against skin in the warm, humid night. He was in the attic in Norfolk, Aisling's body languid and sleepy beside him, her breasts soft and warm, her legs wrapped around him like smooth, silky stockings. He closed his eyes. For a moment, he was with Tom on a bed in Montauk. He roused himself and opened his eyes. He thought of London that time and the shouting and the stairs. He thought of Aisling, her face like a drowned rat in Burgh Island. Her cat and her garden in Greystones. And he wondered how the present became the past. How moments became memory. Because after all the moments, the laughter, the rows, and the closeness of limbs, that's all there was left. Memory.

He rubbed his hand along the sand where Tom had been sitting, erasing the creases, like crumpled sheets on a bed. Seagulls were weaving the clouds in the sky, hemming them into a patchwork of shadows. The shadows fell over the sand.

And he was once again Lal.

The sun was going in. The seagulls were swooping and soaring, stitching the sky and the water together. The day was changing. It was beginning to rain. And he got up to go and glanced out to sea. Lal was jigging about like a plane in the flashing rain. His arms twirling around like an octopus. And he watched the boy dance in the rain. Like a plane coming in to land. Through the slanting tinsel drops of rain.

*****

Aisling was humming to herself, cutting roses in the garden. The sun had brightened the day and the sky was a rich petrol blue.

"Three vases. Three roses. One for each vase."

"One, two, three," she said to Poppet. "They are all I had," she said. "And now they're gone. Three babies," she said. "They never even became proper babies," she said. "But you are a proper cat. Oh yes, you are. Oh yes, you are. You are a proper little cat. A proper little Poppet. And I know you like it here, but you can't stay here forever, you know. No, you can't. Can't stay here forever. I'm just going to have to sort something out. Yes, I am. I am. Just going to have to sort something out."

Then, she went in and made a phone call. The number rang for a while and when it was answered she sat down on the sofa, leaning back against the cushions. Poppet jumped up and settled in beside her. And he began to purr to the sound of her voice on the phone.

*****

The island in Maine was a breath of fresh air. Like a Winslow Homer canvas. A boulder of churning foam. The waves rushing in like a flood of ice cream splashing against the rocks.

He had enjoyed a wonderful week of good food and wine with Aine and Cathal and they had suggested it. He'd changed the date of his flight and made his way to the island and stayed for nearly two weeks, making sketches of the seascape. An American island like Achill with Paul Henry clouds. He worked freely and quickly, his palette knife sweeping and scraping the paint in the wind. Buoyed by the holiday, he was enjoying painting again just for the sheer pleasure of it. And he knew when he finished them a bit more when he got home, they would do very well.

The island hotel served a seafood chowder which he ordered nearly every night after windblown days on the hills and the shore. Sunsets came flaming in like the end of an era and Colin watched them from the deck of the hotel with a glass of red wine after dinner. It was, he mused, a place he could happily stay in forever. Far away from everything. From galleries and exhibitions and troubles back home in Greystones. But the days ticked away with alarming frequency and soon it was time to leave. And he vowed he would come back with Aisling. They would stay here together and sit on the deck watching the glorious sun go down. Like on his last night when the sky turned vermillion like a linen cloth stained with wine.

He returned to Aine's house for a week. A low barn of a building which Aine and Cathal had restored by themselves. A kitchen with rafters and copper pans hanging from hooks. Old benches with cushions, glass lanterns for lamps, and a dresser with hand-painted Delph.

"And how are you and Aisling?" Aine asked over breakfast.

"Why do you ask?"

"She didn't come," she said simply.

"No, she didn't," he replied, toying with a blueberry muffin. "I suppose you've been hearing stuff from Mum."

Aine shrugged. "I think she's concerned about you both," she said.

"Mmmm," said Colin. "It's been a rough few years. But I think she's on the mend."

"Mum doesn't think she likes Greystones," said Aine.

Colin paused. "She loves her job," he said.

"What did she make of the exhibition?" Aine asked.

"She was glad it went well," said Colin, pushing his plate away. He took a sip of coffee and sat back.

Aine looked at him.

"Don't," he said.

"Don't what?" she said.

"Don't look at me like that."

"I just don't think Aisling fully appreciates your work," she said. Colin stared at his cup and sighed.

"I just don't think she really gets it," said Aine.

"What would you know about it?" said Colin. "You're never ever there. And anyway, what are you suggesting?"

"I'm not suggesting anything," said Aine. "Look, forget I brought it up," she said, and took his hand across the table and held it.

His eyes strayed out to the garden and he nodded his head. Aine could tell he was upset.

They didn't talk about Aisling again and spent the rest of the week sightseeing in Maine.

*****

The day before his return, Aisling made a casserole. A beef casserole with Guinness and garlic and mushroom. One of his favorites. It would last for a few decent meals. Poppet devoured the scraps from the diced cubes of meat and spent the evening licking himself on the sofa. Aisling was busy tidying and dusting and plumping cushions. She had made a fresh loaf of bread and an apple tart, and now they had cooled, she wrapped them in cloth and put the casserole in the fridge. Then she made a phone call and went to bed early.

*****

It was raining when the plane took off from Boston.

The jet cleared the runway in a downpour of rain, the lights of the airport laid out below like a diamante dress in the dark. America had been an escape and a tonic. And he couldn't believe he was back on the plane. Ireland seemed ages ago now. Somehow unreal and small and old-fashioned. He could understand how Aine loved Maine. He could see why Bertha Morgan loved Manhattan. And he could see why he had loved Montauk. And the island in Maine. But now it was time for home. Aine had taken him to a Shaker village on his last day and he had bought a tablecloth for Aisling. And just before boarding he had bought her some perfume in duty-free. He was all set. After the meal, he fell asleep.

*****

Aisling woke early. Five o'clock in the morning. It was still dark and the room had that middle-of-the-night blue tinge. She yawned and got up. Poppet was curled up asleep and murmured when she pulled back the bedclothes. Downstairs, she made a cup of tea and checked her watch. Colin's plane was due in at eight. And she still had a lot to get done.

*****

Colin was slumped in his seat, dozing when the lights came on. It was time to freshen up. Coffee and orange juice were being served. He stirred and stretched. The engines started to whir. They were beginning to descend.

*****

Aisling set a tray on the counter table. Then she took the bread and the apple tart out of the cupboard and left them beside it. She washed out her cup and put it away and went upstairs and got dressed. She made the bed and pulled the curtains back. The sun was breaking through. It was going to be a lovely day. And she sighed and picked the cat up and went downstairs and fed him. She looked around. Everything was ready. She checked her watch and looked out the front window. It was five minutes to eight. Then she put the cat in his cage. Poppet stared at her in horror and began to wail. But Aisling had turned her back and was looking out the window.

*****

The plane had broken through the clouds and Dublin lay spread out below like a village on a map. Colin could see the mountains in the window as the plane curved through the air.

*****

Aisling put the cage on the backseat and gave the taxi driver an address. Then she climbed in the back. The man tried to make conversation about cats and vets but he saw the expression in her eyes and gave up. Within minutes, the car was speeding along the dual carriageway to Dublin.

*****

The plane had swung across the sea and was turning past Howth. The pictures came and went in the window as the plane dipped and swerved. Colin could see cars and buses down below on the roads. The plane sank through the air. A moment later the wheels bounced off the ground.

*****

"It's just around to the left," Aisling said. The car pulled in at the curb. She paid the fare quickly and got out. Poppet was still making noises in his cage. She carried him up the steps to the door and set him down. Then she rang the bell.

*****

The first thing Colin noticed when he got home was the smell of furniture polish.

The house smelled like a highly polished church. He smiled when he saw the tray and the bread and the tart. He went upstairs and rinsed his face in cold water and washed his teeth. He felt worn out and crumpled from the flight, like an old shirt for the laundry. The cold water helped. Then he went down and boiled the kettle and read Aisling's note about the casserole in the fridge. The water was ready, and he made a cafetière and cut some bread. He opened the cupboard for marmalade and smiled, remembering the muffins in Aine's kitchen. That was only yesterday. Or was it today? He shrugged and turned around.

And then he saw it.

The second note.

Folded. Propped against the lamp.

His name in Aisling's handwriting. He paused and looked about. He didn't know what he was looking for. Then he noticed the cat's bowl was missing. He poured the coffee as if delaying for time. The kitchen felt eerily quiet.

He took the coffee into the sitting room and sat down.

Then he opened the note.

He read it through in a glance. Then he drank some coffee and read it again. He paused and took another sip. He went over to the window for better light, as if he might have misread it. But he hadn't. The apple tree was shaking slightly in the breeze, its boughs laden low with red apples. He watched one drop to the ground. Then he turned and flung the note across the room. It fluttered in the air like a paper butterfly, then slowly fell to the floor.

He went back to the kitchen and poured the cafetière into a flask. Then he left and went down to the sea.

There was no one about. Not a seagull. Not a dog. He sat immobile on the beach with his flask and the waves. Just staring out to sea at the waves. And he sat like that for a very long time. Just watching the waves rolling in. Watching their hypnotic rhythm. Curving to shore in bands of grey, then rising and holding the air and falling. In folds of foam, rushing, rushing into shore. The waves rolling ceaselessly in.

Rising, falling, rushing to shore.

His lip was trembling, but his body was utterly still.

III
lantern

The fire is low, but the room is warm. A sod of turf crumbles on the hearth. Rain is rinsing the windows in short sudden bursts. The wind is on the sea tonight and the chimney is whistling. Mozart lies stretched on the rug like a toy dog. He has a blue bandage on his left back paw. Wrapped up to the wrist. It stops the paw from bleeding. From catching a stone. His ears are alert, listening to the talk.

"That's not an Irish island," she says, looking at the painting.

He has lined a few up around the walls. It is like a private gallery. A gallery of the sea.

"No," he says, "it's an island in Maine."

When he looks at the painting, he is there again. He can feel the air, the tug of the wind, the curve and crack of every crag. The sound of the sea on the shore.

"The colors in Maine are different," he says.

He can see the sunset. The sky in flames. The sun going down, a bright red bulb in a lampshade of sky.

"And you liked America?" she says.

His eyes are smiling with the past. "Maine," he says. "I liked Maine.

Montauk," he says slowly. "Manhattan," he adds. "Manhattan. Three M's," he says and laughs. "I liked them all."

"When was all this?" she asks, intrigued.

His eyes give nothing away. But he can see the white dog with the black eye and the boy named Tom. Ten million years ago. A chance meeting from nowhere. A moment now a memory. Remembering someone he never knew. All the small fragments of moments. Echoing back through the years. Like a poem recollected long after.

"Back in the eighties," he says. "Ten million years ago."

She laughs.

"I have a sister in Maine," he says. "She was here a while back."

"And brothers?" she says. She hasn't asked him that before.

"Two," he replies. "In Australia. Peadar is dead and Mick is not well. I haven't seen him in years."

"Just you and Mozart then," she says softly.

"Mozart and memories," he says with a smile.

Mozart looks up at hearing his name. His eyes look from one to the other, then he rests his head back on the rug and sighs and settles down.

"I'm sorry I have to leave in the morning," she says.

"You have a job to do," he says. "That's good." He shrugs. "Life goes on."

Laura rises from her seat and looks around. "Will I see you in the morning?" she asks.

"The usual time," he says, and smiles. He looks in the half-light like a man half his age.

Mozart raises his head and staggers up on his paws. Something is happening. Something is up. He knows she is leaving and comes over to lick her hand.

She hunkers down and strokes his ears. His ears are soft, and his eyes look into hers. "Oh, Mozart," she says, "don't look at me like that. I'll see you in the morning." She jiggles his ears, and he rubs his snout against her thigh.

"I'll get you a flash-lamp," he says. "It's a dark, wet night."

He pulls open a drawer. The wind is battering the windows.

"Use this to get across the beach," he says. "When you get to O'Malley's, flash it twice. Then I'll know you're safe."

She nods and gives him a kiss on the cheek. Mozart has gone ahead to the porch. He is the butler, and a guest is about to depart.

"What is this?" she asks, pointing to a large painting on the floor by the door. She hasn't seen it before.

"Oh, that," he says. "I was moving things around. I'd forgotten it was there."

She moves forward and stares at the canvas. It is a large dark painting, framed in black.

Dark storm clouds and dark mountain slopes. Dark green fields and dark rolling hills.

"No sea?" she says, surprised.

"Mmmm," he says, "no sea."

"The fields are like a wet green sea though," she says. "The way you've painted them."

"Mmmm," he says again.

"I think it's rather beautiful," she says, standing back. "Dark and beautiful and different."

"There were ... quite a few ... of those," he says. "Years and years of them."

She looks at him quizzically.

He pulls a face. "Glenmalure," he says under his breath. "Ten long years in Glenmalure."

She knows not to press him any further.

"The Maine painting is gorgeous," she says.

"Ah, yes," he says slowly. "But that was before the flood."

She doesn't ask, just gives him a hug.

"Now remember," he says, "flash the lamp twice when you get across the beach."

Laura opens the door. Rain spatters down and the wind blows in. It is a messy, squalid night.

"Don't come out," she says. But he insists. She gives a wave as she leaves and looks back. Mozart is barking her away. Barking her into the night. Colin is standing by the gable end, holding a lantern.

He is like a lighthouse keeper, she thinks. *With his light in the wind.* She crosses down to the beach and feels her way across the stones. The wind blows her this way and that. She is glad of the lamp. The waves slap the stones and roll back and slap in again. The spray spangles in the air, catching her cheeks. The wind pushes and shoves her along, flattening her back, bending her neck. The walk is wet and dark and slow. But she makes it and meets the road. The bed-and-breakfast is a stone's throw away. She reaches the house and turns around. His lantern is shining across the bay. She flashes the lamp. One, two. One, two. She watches. The lantern moves and then goes out. The light in the porch disappears. He has gone back in.

She listens to the waves in her bed. The waves are so close, they could roll into the room. But she is safe in her sheets and happy and sad in her thoughts. That beautiful painting of Maine. Her eyes turn heavy with sleep. The waves crash through her brain. The foam smears the sheets. She is like a bird on a rock in the sea. She skims to sleep through the sound of the waves to the darkness of Glen-malure. Deep into the painting. The valley. The mountains and dark stormy skies.

In the morning, the sun bathes the beach in a freshly washed golden light. She waits on the bench outside the Lobster Pot. Her bags are packed. She needs to make the boat at half twelve. The island air is warm on her face. The sea is crystal clear, a mirror of turquoise blue. A light sea breeze waltzes in. A man is mending a boat on the beach. She watches him work. Bent to his task in the sun. Like one of Paul Henry's men. With the currach. She has seen it in the National Gallery. She did not expect to see it here. She checks her watch. It is easy to lose track of time on the island. She looks up. They are coming. Mozart is snuffling in the grass, lifting a leg on the wall. Then he trots ahead. Holds up his left back leg and hops. Then he sees her and quickens his pace. Trots, jumps, skips. His bad leg is holding him back. But he has her in his sights. He does a hop and a skip to reach her. He barks and barks then rubs his head against her legs. Then he wriggles in the grass and rolls over, his paws cycling the air with excitement.

"You will write?" Colin says, catching up.

"I can email," she says, "if you like."

"I'd like to get a letter," he says.

And there is something about the way he says it. And she knows it is because no one sends him letters anymore.

"I'll send you a letter," she says.

He smiles and his hair shines white in the sun.

"And I'll send you a postcard," she says to Mozart, bending down, cradling his ears.

They chat on for a while, but she has the boat to catch.

"You have a good day for it anyway," he says, looking up at the sky.

Mozart runs after her when she leaves. But he stops at the corner and barks at her all the way down the road. Until she is out of sight. Then he trots back. Colin is sitting on the bench. He waits for the dog and lifts him across the stones to the beach. Then they walk. Man and dog. Down to their spot on the shore. The same spot as yesterday. And the day before that. The man throws a stick and the dog hops and skips. He picks up the stick in his mouth and trots away down to the sea.

The pier is a few miles away, but she makes it in time and joins the small crowd. The man and the dog already seem a long way away. She climbs aboard and the boat pulls out in the harbor. Seagulls swirl in their wake as they pass the rocks and push out to sea. The mainland is visible across the waves. The houses on the island have grown very small. Her hands grasp the rails, her hair blowing about like a pirate queen. He will be having lunch now, she thinks. A bite to eat, as he calls it, listening to the one o'clock news. Mozart beside him, looking up at him. Waiting for a morsel of chicken to fall. They will doze after lunch. Then he will clean out the fire and lay turf. He might sketch for the afternoon and clean his brushes at six. Then think about dinner and switch on the news. He will sit in his chair and stare at the flames and Mozart will roll on the rug. And her seat will be empty. Because she is not there. And she stares out to sea and all she can see is Colin in his chair and the dog on the rug by the fire.

blackbird

"The calling of wild birds has always attracted me but there is nothing with such potency, to my mind, as the mournful cry of the wild geese."

—Paul Henry
"The Coming of the Wild Geese"

1

Snow was swirling across the valley camouflaging the sheep on the hills. The slopes were covered with the creeping blue shade of twilight. And the snow was beginning to freeze. Colin's kitchen lamp was the only light in the valley. His footprints in the snow to the gate clearly visible in the glow. Soon they would be covered over. But the bird was there. He held his breath.

The blackbird on the gate. Like an angel in the snow.

Every day it came. His blackbird. Today it had come in the blue winter cold. And pecked the crumbs from the ground by the table. His blackbird in white. *Is it cold,* he wondered, *in the freezing air?* The snow falling gently now, each flake a debutante at a ball. Twirling, curtsying gently down. The light fading. And then the blackbird was gone. It was dusk. Within minutes it was dark. Night had come.

Tomorrow would be Christmas Eve.

In the morning, the snow was still there, and he wondered would he be able to get the car out. He had parked it well up the track to avoid the worst of the ice. The blackbird didn't come at breakfast. He kept an eye out while he did the dishes, wondering if it was late or if he'd missed it. The cat from across the fields came in. With something in his mouth. "Jesus," said Colin. "Get out, get out." Tiger ran under the table and Colin heard the crunch of bone on the tiles. Then the cat walked away, its head in the air. Colin looked under the table. There were black feathers strewn on the floor. "Jesus," he said again, "you ate the bird." He cleared the feathers up, shaking his head.

His bags were packed, and it was time to leave. But he lingered until lunch, had a sandwich and a mug of tea. He washed up the things in the sink and looked out. The light was already starting to fade, a weak sun shining through the trees. Patterning the snow with asymmetrical light. He looked over to the gate. The blackbird was back. In the same place. A bead of black in an ocean of white. He let out a long breath of relief. It must have been a younger one the cat had caught. He had thought it looked small. The blackbird swooped down to the ground and pecked about. Then it flew up again and perched on the gate. Looking about. Looking straight at the window. The blackbird on Christmas Eve.

... *All the good times together,* she had written. He stared ahead now, all the words in the note coming back. The track was white but not steep and if he went slowly, he would make it. Join up with the road. Get to the main road. Get on his way.

... *never wanted to come, but I tried to stay ... time to think while you've been away ...can't breathe anymore ...*

The car turned out the gate. There was no traffic, no wind, and the night was pitch black, the sky pinned with stars.

... *enough food for a few days ... just let me go ...*

He drove slowly and cautiously. Anything might happen in the snow. He should have left earlier.

... *just ... let ... me ... go ...... let me go ......*

The words had haunted for him for a year. Well over a year now since coming back from America that morning the previous September. And they haunted him still. They were still in his head. Like nightmarish poetry. Unwanted but learnt off by heart. An unwanted scare in the middle of the night. And she haunted him still in his dreams. And he would wake and realize he was alone. Go downstairs and boil

the kettle in the small hours. That was when he made acquaintance
with the cat. The tabby from the house across the fields. A long, lean
country cat. A tiger on the prowl in the fields. Sometimes the cat
would come in and drink a saucer of milk. And it was company of a
sort for a while. In the soft blue hours of dawn.

... *with love and regret ... with ... love ... and ... regret* ......

He turned the car onto the main road and began to pick up speed.
That was what the note had said. He had flung it across the room.
Later he had crumpled it. Then he had kept it. One night he lit the
fire with it. But it was too late. The words were engraved in his head.
And still were. Like a sympathy card on Christmas Eve. A sympathy
card in his head tonight. Driving home to his mother from the valley.
The wilds of Glenmalure. Where he had buried himself. In the folds
of the hills. Well away from the world. From everything.

... *not your fault ... fault ... not ... your ... fault* ......

The windshield was blurring with freezing fog. His breath filled
the car and he turned the radiator up.

... *try and find ... please ... don't ... try ... and find ... and find* ......

But he had tried.

And he had found her. She had left no details. No clues. No
numbers. But he had found her. One night. Her and the cat. Her and
him. Her and the cat and him.

The glass had blurred over.

His hands gripped the wheel and he peered through the glass of
grey seeing nothing. He pulled the car to the side of the road to wait
it out. The heater was running, and the car was warm. The fog would
pass. He switched on the radio. Carols from St. Patrick's Cathedral.
Choristers' voices filled the car like a soundtrack.

... *frosty wind made moan* ...

"Monkstown," his mother had said a month after he returned
from America. Although she couldn't be sure. "Walking down the

street," she had said. So, he had gone and sat in his car on the main
street. Until the October evening had turned to night.

... earth stood hard as iron ...

The streetlamps had come on and he was yawning when he saw
them. Coming out of a restaurant and turning to the right. His arm
around her shoulders.

He had rolled down the window. Her laugh sprinkled the air
and he had bitten his lip. He had thought he might spot them. He
hadn't expected to hear her laugh. He watched them walk. They
were walking along the other side of the street. Oblivious to the car.
He sat like a statue.

... water like a stone ...

He had turned the engine on. And let the car roll gently forward.
They were turning in to a side street. And opening a gate. He heard
it clang. He watched them mount the steps to a door painted black
with a fanlight. He parked the car and sat, unable to move in the dark.

... snow had fallen ...

His eyes had seen them. Yet his mind hadn't been able to take it in.
And thoughts came again now like a blizzard in his head.

... snow on snow, snow on snow ...

He had watched the lights go on in the house. One by one by one.
And he had sat and watched as the curtains were drawn. And then
gone to open the door. But his legs wouldn't budge. So, he had sat.
Like tonight. In the car at the side of the road. Just staring at the windshield. Then the cat had come out. He watched it flick its tail and sniff
the night air. He had turned the engine on and started the car. The cat

had looked up. Poppet looked him in the eyes, and they had stared at each other. Then the cat jumped over a wall and he had driven off into the night. Every moment, every minute of it now like a silent movie in his head. Played out tonight with the soundtrack in the car.

… in the bleak midwinter, long ago …

The singing had stopped.

The news had come on. And he realized the fog had cleared. The road ahead was clearly visible now. Smooth and straight and white. Traffic was light. Glenmalure was a long way out.

Soon he was on the main road to Dublin, Santa Claus on the radio with Rudolph getting ready to take off. He was driving home for Christmas. To his mother in the dark with Santa and reindeer on the radio.

His second Christmas back home.

Traffic sped past intermittently now like stray bullets firing in the dark. Taillights disappearing like devils' eyes in the night.

*****

A few nights later he had gone back. As if lured by a sweet breeze on the air. Unable to resist or deny. And he had waited outside down the street in his car. Until he saw them come around the corner and go up the steps and go in. After ten minutes, he had followed. Gone up to the door and pressed the bell. No one came. He pressed it again and again. Still no one. He could hear voices. So, he pressed it again. There was a pause. He turned his back and stared down the steps. He knew that they knew he was here. Seen him. Guessed it. Whatever. That was the delay. The door had opened then and he had turned around.

"I don't think you should have come," Michael said.

"It wasn't you I came to see," said Colin.

"How did you find us?" said Michael, leaning against the door.

"It wasn't that hard," said Colin. "My mother saw you."

"How is your mother?" said Michael.

"She's fine," said Colin. "Why are you asking about my mother?"

"I always liked her," said Michael.

"And she liked you," said Colin. "But that was a long time ago."

"Water under the bridge," said Michael.

Colin glared at him. "Well?" he said.

"Well, what?"

"I need to see Aisling."

"She doesn't want to see you."

"You're just saying that. I need to see her. I need to talk to her."

"No," said Michael, folding his arms.

"You have no right," said Colin.

"This is my house," said Michael.

"Aisling is my wife," said Colin.

"I think you'd better go," said Michael firmly.

"I'm not going anywhere," blurted Colin.

"Fine," said Michael. "Then stay there," and he went to shut the door.

Colin stepped forward trying to wedge his way in. His foot was in the doorway. "Aisling," he called. "Aisling!" He knew she was there and he knew how pathetic he sounded. Like a child in a playground. He heard his own voice and he winced. But he knew she was listening. "Aisling," he called again. The embarrassment of it shaming him, but he had to try.

"You can't force your way in," said Michael. "If you're not careful, I'll call the guards."

"I just want to see her."

Their eyes locked together. Michael's face was flushed. He'd obviously been drinking.

"Aisling!" shouted Colin.

A shadow moved on the wall on the stairs.

"Will you please come and talk to me?" he pleaded.

"Jesus, Colin, will you just bloody well leave it?" said Michael.

But Colin was looking past his shoulder. Aisling had appeared on the stairs. Her face was pale, her eyes shadowed, her hair tumbling down her shoulders. She was standing in a green dress on the stairs like a Rossetti model. She was shaking her head.

"Not now, Colin," she said. "Not now." Her eyes looked into his.

Colin pushed against Michael, but the door held firm. He looked up. Aisling had disappeared.

"Not now," said Michael. "You'll only upset her."

"Upset her?" said Colin. "She's the one who walked out without so much as a word, just a blasted note, and you just stand there and say not now. Why the hell *not* now?"

"She's pregnant," said Michael.

Colin withdrew his foot from the door and stood back. "I don't think that's such a good idea," he said slowly.

"Why not?" said Michael.

Colin looked at him. "Oh, God," he said, "I don't even think you know the half of it."

"What do you mean?" said Michael. "What are you saying?"

Colin shook his head and looked at him. "Christ," he said, "she really hasn't told you, has she?"

"Told me what?"

Colin shrugged in disbelief. "At her age for a start," he said. Then he shook his head again. "Not a good idea." He turned and walked down the steps to the gate.

Michael stared after him. The door closed.

Colin paused and looked back. Aisling's face was framed in the window upstairs. Then she drew back. Her face disappeared. The house was shut to the night. He had walked away slowly, feeling sick, leaving the gate swinging open behind him. It had been like a dizzy carousel. London then Brighton zipping through his head. Scenes from the past but in reverse.

*****

He was closing in on Dublin now. There was no snow, only a light dusting on the grass on the side of the road. The carousel was still swinging in his head. He had to put it out of his mind. He had to leave it to one side. But it was always there now. Lurking in the cobwebs. Michael so cool and unbending, the shadow moving on the stairs, the face at the window. He pulled up outside his mother's house. It was just after seven.

"You've been a while," she said. "I was getting worried."

"The snow was heavy in Wicklow," was all he said. Nothing about the heaviness in his mind. The blackbird on the gate. The cat and the feathers under the table. The slow drive home with the turmoil in his head.

"You're in time for Midnight Mass," she said. "That's all that matters."

He could see she was pleased. The house was warm, the tree shining with lights in the hall. They had sandwiches by the fire.

*****

The church was packed. He had been there on and off through the years. The aisles were already crowded when they arrived, but they squeezed in up at the front by the Sacred Heart altar. Colin closed his eyes. A hush had fallen. Then the organ broke the silence with a groan and a hum. The sound rose through the cold air, calling people to Christmas. Latecomers drifted in from the pub. The choir began to sing. They stood up. The congregation joined in and the hymn swelled out all around them. The night had come. He stood up. He sat down. He knelt at all the right times. His mother was deep in concentration. In prayer. He went with it. The choir, the hymns, the manger and he thought of Aisling pregnant again that time. And how it hadn't worked out as he suspected it wouldn't. He wondered what they were doing tonight. *Drinking wine by the fire in that house,* he thought. He could imagine it. Poppet stretched out on the rug. The smell of Aisling's baking in the house. Candles lit, the curtains drawn, the wine flowing. Perhaps it was what she had craved after all. Michael had money. A graphic design business to his name. *Good luck to him,* Colin thought. But he didn't know whether he meant it. He certainly didn't feel it. Back in the church of his childhood. Back in his old bedroom for Christmas. A creaky car. A drafty, damp cottage down a mud track in Glenmalure. No, he didn't feel it. And he didn't really mean it either. *Goodwill to all men and all that.* He felt small and mean and hard done by. And he didn't like the feeling. Couldn't shake it off. The carousel back in his head in the church tonight. He watched his mother coming back from Communion. Her face bowed, her eyes cast down. *Older tonight,* he thought. *Tired with the years.* A smile of old age on her face and a peace that came from prayer in her eyes. And he realized how small-minded he was. Was it even likely they would be wasting their time thinking of him tonight? He tried to shake them out of his mind. The imaginary sitting room with the fire and the wine and the cat. The priest was saying a few words about times of Mass over Christmas. And the choir was beginning to sing.

In the bleak midwinter, frosty wind made moan,
Earth stood hard as iron, water like a stone;
Snow had fallen, snow on snow, snow on snow,
In the bleak midwinter, long ago.

He realized his mother had fallen asleep. It was close to one o'clock in the morning. He nudged her gently. She opened her eyes and looked at him and smiled. "Oh, Jim," she said, "I don't know what came over me." He didn't think she knew what she had said. She hadn't realized. He said nothing, just let it be. Her lips moved softly to the hymn. She had a lovely pure voice. Like a blackbird in spring. Suddenly he put his hand to his eye. A single lone tear had started to form.

In the morning, the graveyard was covered with frost. The headstones thawing in the cold weak sun. Eileen had brought a wreath and a planter of cyclamen. They stood together, mother and son by Jim's grave. Colin held her arm. Even now with the distance of years it was hard. She smiled at other visitors. She knew some of the people at the neighboring graves. She had met them down through the years. There was a bond of companionship here amongst the dead. They had been coming so long now, Colin had only vague memories of Christmas days without the visit to the grave. He couldn't imagine Christmas Day without this walk amongst the dead. His mother wanted to visit a few of the other graves. To remember them on Christmas morning. It seemed to give her a certain kind of lonely peace. Mingling if only briefly with people she once knew. People who had lived on their road or around the corner. People who weren't there now. She named them all out and touched each headstone, like she was chatting to them at their garden gates. The house was quiet when they came back. He helped her in the kitchen. He laid the fire, put music on, poured her a sherry. They ate at around three in the dining room, the lamps glowing in the windows. Later they sat by the fire and gave out presents. Then his mother fell asleep and Colin watched a film. It was a slow, quiet, happy Christmas. The carousel had stopped swinging in his head. He stayed for a few more days and they went out for walks and had turkey soup and sandwiches for lunch. His mother was sad to see him go. She waved him off and he beeped the horn. He felt a pang of sorrow watching her standing by the gate on her own.

He drove out the road. A journey he would come to know like the back of his hand. Up and down to Dublin, to his mother. Glenmalure was wild and far away and hidden from the world. His silent valley. He had looked around for somewhere once Aisling had gone. He didn't know why but he had wanted to get away from the sea. Norfolk, Brighton, Greystones, their houses by the sea. Their years together. The waves of their lives. He needed calm, somewhere still. And cheap, and he found it in Glenmalure. In summer, sun-streaked hills, the swish of grass and the cry of the skylark. In winter, spring, and autumn, the mountains in a cloak of dark blue, the fields umber brown, the earth like wet plasticine. Hillside streams and gnarled hawthorn and bright yellow gorse with ragged, torn clouds sweeping past overhead. It suited his mind. He had plans. Grow his own vegetables and fruit. But it took him years to even attempt it and then he gave up. Waterlogged clay ground. Stunted bushes. Seeds eaten by birds. Too much shade. Runner beans long and leggy and searching for sun.

*****

"You have no belief in yourself anymore," said Adeline Bell, arriving one summer on a visit.

She had come unexpectedly. His unwashed dishes in the sink from the night before. A congealed baked potato and beans on a plate. Adeline looked around as if she was visiting the poorhouse. He started to boil the kettle. "No," she said. "No, I'm taking you out for lunch. That is, if we can find anywhere," she said, "in this godforsaken, out of the way place."

"I'll get my jacket," he said, embarrassed.

"Paintings," she said. "Show me what you've been doing. Then maybe I'll understand why you're here. And then," she said, "we can have lunch."

He opened the door into his studio room.

"It's like a graveyard," she said, putting her hand to her mouth.

"Mmmm," said Colin.

"I mean, what on earth?" said Adeline, coming to a stop.

"I'm having a dark phase." He laughed.

"Dark," she said. "Dark? They're as dark as night. Paintings of the dead," she said, looking around, touching her chin. "I mean they're so gaunt." Then she stopped. "No," she said, "I lie. They're like that painting he did, what was it called?" And she paused for a moment. *"The Lake of the Tears ..."*

"*... of the Sorrowing Woman,*" he said. "Yes, Paul Henry. That was sort of the starting point."

"You've drained them of color," she said. "They're like something out of the famine."

She looked at him. He had gone quiet. She put her hand on his arm. "Now I understand, I'm sorry," she said. "So this is why you've come here, to this place. To grieve over that woman."

He nodded.

"Well," she said, "I came to cheer you up and to take you out of yourself. But now when I see these," she said, flicking her hand toward them, "I don't think I should cheer you up at all. This is some of your best work, you know. What are they doing tucked away here?"

"I've sent quite a lot up to the gallery," he said. "They've sold."

"No," she said. "There's years of work here. What you need is a proper exhibition."

They discussed it over lunch in a pub halfway to Wexford.

Adeline had rearranged a table by the window. "Well," she said, "what a find this place is. No idea where we are. There you go."

They had grilled salmon. Rhubarb crumble, then coffee. And he realized how much he had missed decent food. Apart from his visits to his mother he knew he was eating badly. Plates of fuel eaten as afterthoughts.

"You should really be having a retrospective," said Adeline.

"Retrospectives don't make money," he said.

"No, but it would remind people of who you are.. That's important, you know. People forget. It's years since the *Tower*. Which leads me to ask: Have we a name?"

Colin shrugged. "I don't know. What about *Shadows and Clouds*, or something like that?"

"*Clouds*," she said slowly. "*Shadows*." She looked out the window. "How about *The Gathering Clouds*?"

"Perfect," he said. "

The sun was setting as they drove back, the sky washed pink and bathed in gold.

"You'll have to get over all of this Glenmalure malarkey," she said. "Come up to Dublin. Mingle again. Let people know you're about. There's no point hiding down here in this valley anymore. Mind you," she added, "I'm rather glad you did, or we wouldn't have all this new work for the gallery." She dropped him off and rolled down the window. "After all," she said, "I'm getting too old for all this mucking about down here in the wilds." She blasted the horn as she trundled away. Colin raised a hand. She drove as erratically as she spoke. He watched until the car turned the bend.

The cottage was dark when he got back and he turned on the lights in the studio. The paintings looked back at him. With austere stares. Gaunt bleak slopes and hills with glowering clouds. "Drained of color," she had said. "Like something out of the famine," Tiger came in and he gave him a saucer of milk. There was a bottle of red wine on the shelf. He poured a glass. It had been a good day. Adeline blowing in like a fresh breeze from the sea. He was trying to relax and found a film to watch. But his mind began to wander. The wine was a ruby merlot and slipped down. Maybe he had deserved it. The leaving. And here he was again still thinking about it. The cottage dark and empty behind him. The film filling the room. She must have just felt there was no other way. Why else do it that way? He missed her coming home from work telling him about the kitchen. The orders, the customers, the idiot waiters. The stuck-up fart who ran the place. But half the time he hadn't really been listening. Sometimes she had managed to make him laugh. He remembered laughing. But she must have realized he was only half listening. She had wanted to be heard. He could see that now. "You're not listening," she would say. "You're not really interested. I don't think you care," she said one night, her foot on the stairs on her way to bed. He had told her not to be so dramatic. "All you care about are your paintings," she said.

"You knew I was a painter when you met me," he said.

"You had glamour then," she said. "Now you just smell of turpentine and paint. We never go out. We never have fun. You never make an effort anymore."

He poured another glass of wine. He wasn't remotely following the film.

"You never clean up," she said. "You think a bit of aftershave on Sundays is enough."

He thought about getting her out of Brighton all those years ago. Finding the cottage in Greystones. Getting the garden shed, the cat. But he obviously hadn't noticed the tide going out. There had been storms, rainy days. Days when they'd argued or barely talked. They had become islands in rooms. But he hadn't noticed the tide going out. The color draining from her cheeks. Like a boat that had lost its sail. She must have felt she was drifting. Heading straight for the rocks. That must be why she had left like that. Got out. Bailed overboard. He wondered what it would have been like if she hadn't. Burgh Island all over again. Only worse. She must have recognized the signs. She must have realized the tide was going out. He was slumped on the sofa now.

"You never talk anymore," she'd said.

He hadn't realized he didn't talk. Maybe he had become distant after all. Self-sufficient in his thoughts.

One night she had grabbed his easel. "All you do is stand at the bloody thing and stare and paint and stare and paint." He remembered the feeling. Like a mad person hijacking a plane. The easel had wobbled, and the canvas had swayed. He caught it and steadied it. The paint had smudged. "Don't ever do that again," he had shouted. He wasn't proud of it now. His face had gone beetroot. Puce. He was shaking. No one had ever attacked his work. "For God's sake, I barely touched it. I'm sure you can fix it," she said and flounced out. His breathing had come fast and shallow like a dog after a run. He had tightened the canvas back on the easel and gone out and stood in the hall. He could hear her crying in the room next door. He went to open the door to go in. But he stopped and went down to the sea instead. When he got back she was in bed, the house wrapped in a bandage of silence. Colin rubbed his eyes at the memory. The silence that masked a wound. Tiger came in now and jumped up and nestled down. Colin stroked his back and the cat stretched out like an acrobat. The film played on. He poured some more wine.

The night of his birthday he had come home from Sandycove, his head crammed with ideas, desperate to get to work. The house was packed with people he didn't really know. Faces from the restaurant, faces from next door and down the road. Her misguided, futile attempt at a party for him. The place was filled with food and people smoking and drinking in the garden. Aisling buzzing about. He was livid. He snapped at her in the kitchen behind the closed door. He was sure people must have heard. He barely spoke to anyone all night. He had been horrible. It came back to him now with the wine and the film and the dark. He could see it from her point of view. The one time she had gone out of her way. She never had again. God, he had forgotten that night. She must have been hurting inside. Drifting in her boat heading for the rocks. And this the result. All this worthless regret years later. Another night on his own with a cat who wasn't his in a cottage in a valley where no one ever came. The film was over and he turned the sound off. Let the screen fill the room with flickering light. With the flickering bandage of silence. He sat until there was no wine left.

The bedroom was cold when he went up.

He pulled the curtains to keep out the draft. The floorboards creaked. The wind sighed and the windows rattled. They always rattled. Even on a warm day in summer, they always seemed to rattle or tremble. As if they were terrified to be still. He tried to sleep. The wine helped. He dozed. Sleep came.

*****

Getting the paintings framed was a lot of work in itself. Time consuming and costly. He was extremely particular with whom he entrusted the work. Peter Fenlon in Bray had worked with him on the last exhibition and he turned to him again. The frames were hand-painted in antique gilt and bespoke to each picture. Peter Fenlon was slow and methodical in his craft but the results were worth it. Colin discussed each painting with him, and Peter adjusted the gilding to match, some of the frames darker with shades of sienna, some with red umber enriching the gilt, and some paler as if faded with age in an attic. The frames transformed the paintings. Lifted them out of themselves, out of the valley. Elevated them to new heights. Ready for the gallery walls.

Preparing for the exhibition kept him busy. He felt energized again. Up and down to Bray with the canvases. Adding some extra last-minute works. Getting the titles and the prices in place and working with the gallery on the catalogue. Adeline Bell had been right. Something of consequence had come out of his time in Glenmalure. His years in the silent valley by himself. The pictures seemed to stand apart from the rest of his work. Where the *Tower* brimmed with ghost images, these mountains were still and soulful like evensong. They were stark and bleak. But with their frames they were dramatic. And in this day and age, quite unique. Adeline Bell had never been wrong. And if she was anything to go by, the exhibition should go well. Every morning now, he took his coffee out to the garden. And listened for the blackbird. And he began to look forward to the mornings now. And the song of the blackbird. And that was a start if nothing else.

*****

He had gone back to Monkstown a few times in the first weeks after finding them that October. Driving slowly past their house. Occasionally pulling in at the curb but never stopping long. Some nights there were lights in the windows. Once or twice he saw a head move in a room. One night he saw a number of couples going in. Michael opening the door. A dinner party, he guessed. In the end, he gave up. It was pointless. He knew his behavior was becoming obsessive. He didn't want to be there. But it had become an addiction. In the end, he grew bored. Bored with the tedium and resigned to his fate. He didn't return.

Then one afternoon, that winter in January, he had come across them again in Glasthule. They were standing by a shiny black car. He was coming out of a bookshop heading straight in their direction. He thought of his shabby Cortina parked down the street. And he looked at them by the glossy black car, all shiny and new like a patent leather shoe, and he took a sharp intake of breath. Trying to steady himself for the inevitable encounter. Aisling waved a hand and turned as if about to come over. But as he watched, Michael folded her into the car. He watched him opening the door and Aisling slipping in. Michael gave a quick wave and hopped into the driver's seat. They drove right by, Aisling looking at him out the window as they passed. It had happened quickly, silently. He was left alone on the pavement with the book he had bought, the wind whirling down the street. It had happened so fast, he wondered had he imagined it.

And the thing he took away with him was the shiny black car. Not just the awkwardness of it all and Aisling staring out the window. Not just that moment when Michael had bundled her in. But the shininess of the car. The blackness. The sheer blackness of the damn thing. As if to make matters worse it had to be ultra, super, shiny black. He knew he would never have Michael's money. Michael's house. Money would come his way again. He knew that. But there would never be enough. And he was resigned to that too. He had his own success. Far and away above anything Michael could ever do. And he was well aware of that. But it didn't make it any easier.

A week later he had got the phone call.

Aisling wanted to collect her things. She said Michael would drive her. It was the first time they had spoken. There were long pauses. Aisling sounded nervous. Colin didn't know what to say and kept clearing his throat. After a brief exchange, she hung up. The line went dead. He put the phone down and stood staring at it in the hall. They came on a Saturday. The shiny black car pulled up at the gate. Aisling rang the bell but Michael stayed in the car.

"You look tired," she said. "Are you eating at all?"

"You're always asking about food," he said with a sigh. "As if that's the solution to everything." She didn't reply and went straight upstairs. She wasn't long and came down with some bags and a suitcase.

"I think that's everything," she said, looking around. She was like a visitor leaving a guesthouse. He could tell she was putting on a

show and he could see she wasn't pregnant now at all, but he wasn't
going to mention that. She looked at him then and her face told him
that she knew what he was thinking. "Don't," she said. Her eyes were
becoming red and he turned away. There was silence between them.
Now that they had the chance to speak, he didn't know what to say.
She touched his arm and he looked at her and looked at the bags and
the suitcase.

"Why?" he said. "Why?"

Her lip began to tremble. "You know why," she said. "You do. You
know we weren't happy."

"But we were," he said. "We were … happy … we were."

"You need to eat," she said, touching his arm. She placed her
hand on his shoulder and he could feel himself shaking. Then she
pulled away. "You need to eat," she said. "You won't be able to paint
if you don't eat."

"Mmmm," he said, wiping his eyes.

He helped her carry the bags out to the car. "Colin," said Michael
with a nod, getting out and opening the trunk. "Is that everything?"
he asked Aisling.

"Yes," she said, turning back to Colin. She took both his hands.
"Look after yourself," she said. Colin nodded. She looked away and
got in. Michael started the engine. In a minute, they were gone. The
street was empty. The sea glimmered like sequins at the end of the
road. He fetched his coat from inside and went on a long, long walk.

*****

The exhibition was in November.

He planned to stay the week with his mother. Glenmalure was
too far away and he wanted to be on hand every day. The bleak
winter weather was as good a time as any to showcase the work. He
was nervous driving up. The old sense of dread beginning to reappear.
Would he still be considered any good? What if people didn't come
and even if they did, didn't like it? He hadn't felt like this since

college. He had been excited and confident about the *Tower* show, but that all seemed like another world now.

His mother went to bed early. He stayed up until midnight watching the late news and weather. Sat in the drawing room flicking through the paper. The world was silent and the house was as quiet as a church. Childhood days seemed a long time ago. When the rooms rumbled with Peadar and Mick and their friends home from school and Aine in an apron making cakes in the kitchen. A long time ago. He thought of the paintings hanging all together in the gallery tonight before the unmasking tomorrow and it was a strange feeling, like thinking of the tabernacle in an empty church.

His bed was his boyhood bed.

Blankets with satin trims and the Paul Henry hanging on the wall. He closed his eyes. The sands stretched far and wide. Powdery and soft underfoot with shells like blue enamel. He was dancing up and down. Jigging about, arms whirling around like an octopus slicing the air. He stretched into sleep. The sky was blue. Azure blue and he was jigging about in the sun. But there were clouds in the sky like candy floss rolling in. Jostling about and gathering pace. He turned on his side. The sky was flooding with mauve and purple. Darkening. The sun was flickering like a candle about to be quenched. A breeze was blowing in.

"... a blasted rock ... in the Atlantic ... Atlantic ..."

His feet were dancing on shells.

"... no confidence in yourself ... in yourself ... in yourself ..." Michael was talking. He was tall and lean and tanned. They were in a pub.

His feet danced up and down. He buried his head in the pillow. The clouds were falling from the sky, swooping like raven's wings down on his head.

"... wet ... wet ......wet ... still fucking wet ..." Stanley was muttering and walking away.

"No ..." said Aisling.

"No, no, no ..." said Stanley.

A storm of sea voices. Coming through the crack in the wall.

On the wind. Voices in the deep. Underwater. Deep. Down. Deep. Strands and fronds of seaweed strangling.

"You can't go on like this," said his mother "... like this ... this ... this ..."

He was dancing and giggling, the sun bouncing around. His hair shining like silk in the sun.

"Don't stay in too long ... too long ... too long ..."

A mist and a fog and a cloud and a bird. Sea mist on water and rocks in fog.

Falling through water. Trying to climb out. Escape.

Water like stone, a glass ceiling above.

"There's no one ... no one ... no one ..."

The wind was churning the bed. He was tossing and turning. Trying to settle. Then turning again.

"No belief in yourself ... in yourself ... anymore ..."

His fingers gripping the blankets. Like mussels on rocks.

"... still fucking wet ..." said Stanley.

"... rock in the Atlantic ..." said Adeline Bell.

"No ..." said Aisling.

"No, no, no ..." said Stanley.

Beginning to fall. Through water, through glass, like a stone through a pond.

In a stream. In a gush. In a torrent.

Jigging around.

The clouds swirling in. Arms flailing around.

Coming to a stop. With a bump. With a bang.

He woke up.

"I think that's what they call a crash landing."

He swung his legs out of the bed.

"... think that's what they call a crash landing."

His father was six foot three. He was six. A boy called Lal on a beach. He was four foot two.

His hands were gripping the side of the bed. Voices blown in from his past on the wind. He stood up and went downstairs.

The moon was in the window. He watched it come and go behind clouds and sipped a glass of water. He stared at the moon, the clouds trailing past like a mantilla veil. The moon slipped in and out. Through the lace of clouds.

Somewhere out there lay the winds of his future.

He sipped the water slowly and let it trickle down his throat.

2

The poached egg was perfectly cooked, and the yolk spilled over the toast. Colin could see the beach in the mirror. The glass was glinting with sun on the waves. There was a white tablecloth with a vase of wild fuchsia in the center. His mother was clearing her plate, which was a good thing to see. Betty, the woman in the guesthouse, had white hair and a blue apron on. She was bringing more coffee and Colin refilled his cup. His mother was talking about the dog.

"I hope that dog will be alright," said his mother.

The dog had shot out of nowhere and raced with the car. Colin had slowed and began to brake. The dog was chasing the wheels. A black and white sheepdog yelping and nipping at the tires. The brakes had screeched.

"You've hit the dog. You've hit the dog," his mother had cried in alarm.

Colin had peered out the windows. He couldn't see the dog.

Then he saw it bounce out in a ball of black fur. The dog scampered away. His mother held her hand to her lips. Colin got out and stared after the dog. It was lying on the grass at the side of the road, watching him as he approached, its head resting on its paws, the eyes tracking his approach. As soon as he got near, it sprang up and started barking, its head held back. The eyes were glassy and wild. Colin put his hand out to try and coax it near, then drew back. The dog looked as if it might bite. He shook his head, satisfied, and got back in the car. They had driven on the short distance to the guesthouse. An unsettling end to their journey. His mother had been rattled and upset.

"I didn't hit the dog," he said again.

"You need to be more careful," she said, shaking her head. "Your father would have been more careful."

"That dog is always chasing cars," said Betty, coming in, clearing plates.

"You can't be too careful," said Eileen. "You just don't know the day nor the hour. None of us do."

Colin sighed very gently and looked at Betty.

"Don't be worrying," she said, smiling. "That dog is always lying in wait for new cars."

After breakfast, they went for a drive.

The road from Dooagh to Keem was steep and corkscrewed in places. The island was carved like a shard of broken glass, jagged and dangerous and patterned with changing light. The light surged in across the cliffs from the west. Clouds flew in from the sea. He drove slowly, stopping in places so he could take it all in. The views were breathtaking. His mother stayed in the car. He could tell that the drive had brightened her mood. She rolled down the window. The sea air was pure and bracing and brought a blush to her cheeks. Sheep ambled about and stared at the car. Colin took photographs of the beach at Keem. An unexpected cove of golden sand, the water transparent and blue like an aquarium tank. A beach at the base of a cliff. Tucked away in the foothills of Achill.

He had left his paintbrushes and notebooks at home for a change. Paul Henry's island was somewhere very special and he wanted to soak it in. Achill with its towering clouds and hazy blue hills. The sea crashing around its shores. He had always avoided coming. Preferring to find his own islands, his own way. Fearing he might have come and felt let down after admiring Henry's work for so long. But now they had come and he was not disappointed. Achill was a geographic world of its own. A rock of ragged bog in the ocean.

He had suggested Kerry and Cork and Clare.

But his mother had not enthused. He had tried places closer to home. Wexford, Kildare, Wicklow. All to no avail. But he had wanted to take her away, feeling it would do her good. He had fetched the picture from his wall and brought it downstairs. She had smiled when he held it up. "Well?" he said. Her eyes were bright now and she nodded. He had struck a nerve. His mother had always been enamored by the painting and he had made the right suggestion. She had seemed intrigued by the idea of visiting Achill for real. And so, they had come.

They had a bowl of soup in the village for lunch. Achill's weather was fickle and they were just in time. It poured rain while they ate. The cliffs vanished in a shower of grey. Eileen had postcards she wanted to write so they sat for a while with a pot of tea. When the skies had cleared, they posted the cards and drove on. Colin had brought a map and they headed for Slievemore. He had heard about the deserted village but when they got there, he saw it was too out of bounds for his mother. But she didn't mind waiting in the car, and he set off by himself. He could see the sea far away across the hills. The island here was sheltered and quiet, the heather purple with flower, the ground soft and mossy underfoot. The village was a like a skeleton shrine from another time. The place was lonely and he didn't linger, the stone houses like headstones nailed to the side of the hill. Broken stone walls and the remains of enclosures with lazy beds for potatoes. There was no one about, just himself and some sheep wandering around. They sprang away when they saw him. This was their village and he felt he was almost trespassing. He didn't stay long. The village, too much a reminder of the sad history of places like Achill. His mother was dozing in the sun when he got back. Unperturbed by such notions.

At dinner that night, there were candles and soft lamps and a large window with a view of the beach at Keel. Their waitress made his mother feel at home and he was delighted with that. In the candle-light, she looked like a woman half her age. But when she turned her head, he could see her neck folded with wrinkles, a thin skin of parchment across her cheeks, her eyes rheumy and faded like a star in the morning. And as he watched, she turned her head, her face half in shadow like at a masked ball. Still his mother but old, as if in disguise.

There was next to no wind when he set out the next morning for the cliffs of Minaun. He left Eileen chatting with Betty after breakfast. Talking away in the cottage like an islander. Pleased with the scenery and the holiday. He hadn't seen her so animated in a while.

"You're as well off without her," she had said at breakfast. She hadn't referred to Aisling much since the breakup years earlier in Greystones. Perhaps Achill was making her loquacious.

"They're welcome to each other," she said dismissively.

"You liked Michael once," he said.

She made a face. "People can change," she said. "You wouldn't believe it but they can."

"I don't really think people change that much," he said. "We're like leopards."

"When your father died," she said, "some people would have crossed the road rather than have to come and talk to me."

"Why would they do that?"

"A widow with young children?" she said. "People didn't want to be bothered with that."

"Mmmm," said Colin. His mother had not lost her verve.

"I'll say nothing," she said, "but believe me, Aisling would pull the wool over the Pope's eyes if she could."

"What do you mean?"

"And get away with it," she added. "As long as there was a pot of gold in it somewhere."

"And Michael's loaded, of course," said Colin.

"I know well he is," she said. "I told you Aisling wasn't exactly born yesterday, you know. She'd have made it her business to find all that out."

He hadn't thought about it like that before. "You mean she had it all planned?" he said. His head was whirring now, just thinking about it. It was so obvious.

"If she thought it worth her while," she said. "She'd have laid it on thick with a trowel."

"About what?" he said.

"About you," she said. "She'd have spun him a riddle or two."

The wind was whipping in from all sides as he struggled up the slope.

He could barely catch his breath. The bog was humming with birdsong and bees chasing nectar, the wind flapping high overhead. He could hear the sound of the sea all around.

His mother had rarely voiced such opinions. He hadn't realized she had analyzed it in such depth. Worked it all out, squared the circle. There was one thing he knew she was right about. Aisling had always hankered after the finer things in life. She had never been content with his level of existence. He had come to realize that. His paintings had always been his priority. There was a gap and a half between the cottage in Greystones and the house in Monkstown. Aisling had landed on her feet. By accident or design, that much was clear.

He made it to the top and stood looking out to sea.

The ocean billowed out like a shawl of pewter silk. He blinked and exhaled and shivered in the wind. Here at the edge of the sky.

He wondered how it had happened. Had they met by chance or had she made her advances? Had she done her homework or did it all fall into her lap? He doubted whether he would ever really know.

Grace Henry had left Paul. That occurred to him now.

Left Achill and Paul, yearning for the city, for London, for Dublin. He sat down on the grass and began to think.

Ten years they had been here. Grace, too, had been a fine painter in her own right. With a reputation of her own. Most of her paintings in Achill had been nocturnal scenes and she was often seen out in a white dress in the evening painting away at her easel. But her heart wasn't in it. Whereas Paul had been addicted from the start, to the bogs and the mountains. The workers in the fields. His decade of groundbreaking work. Grace had not been a convert. Always coming and going and returning to the lights of the city. In the end, Achill helped tear them apart. And he thought about Aisling not settling in Greystones. The village, the cottage, the paintings, none of it had been good enough for her. None of it. Not even him. He knew now that there was nothing he could have done. Her mind must have been partially made up from day one. Paul Henry had gone on to marry Mabel Young and he thought of Carragoona and that beautiful place they had lived. But he had no Mabel Young. No one to lean on.

And he wondered would he ever really find his own Achill. Form a similar attachment to a place. Somewhere he could claim as his own. A landscape he could define in new ways with his knives and his paints and his brush. Where his name might live on in some small, lasting way.

Glenmalure had its own unique beauty. He thought of it now and he understood why he had felt safe there. Safe in the enclosed silent valley, hidden from the world. But here on the cliffs of Minaun, the tang of the sea filled the air and the ocean wind filled his lungs and he felt challenged and bold and adventurous again. He would need to find a place of his own like this.

The valley had challenged him but it had been a long arduous experience. Seeing the paintings all framed and for sale in the gallery had helped restore his sense of self-worth. The reviews had pleased him and the income was welcome. But when he had packed up his things after more than a decade to come back to Dublin, he had been shocked at how little there was of him. His life packed into a car. Nothing in the cottage really belonged to him at all. The car was packed with clothes and music and books, his radio and television and painting stuff. That was it. An easel and boxes of brushes and paints. A few canvases left over, his hiking boots, tarpaulin sheets, and wet gear for painting outdoors. That was it. He was sorry to go but happy to leave. The blackbirds would sing on without him. And Tiger would just have to wait for new people to come.

His mother had become forgetful. One night she had phoned

him in a panic. The kitchen was filling with smoke and she seemed confused. He had calmed her down on the phone. She had forgotten to turn off the oven and he got her to turn it off at the wall. But he had never had a phone call like that before and it unnerved him. On his weekend visits, he began to notice she was mislaying things. Her glasses, her keys, her cup of tea. She ran out of pills. Forgot to take them. Took the wrong ones. At the wrong times. If he hadn't been alert, he wouldn't have noticed anything. Then he noticed she hadn't touched half the food in the fridge since last week. The doctor had said she was borderline anemic.

"You need to eat more iron," Colin told her.

"I know that," she said.

"You need to eat more cabbage and peas with your meals," he said.

"I do," she said. "I eat them all the time."

"No, you don't," he said. "You hardly eat anything anymore." And that's when he had decided to move home. To keep an eye out. Glenmalure was too far away.

There was nothing actually wrong with her. She was just a bit forgetful about the mundane things. The tiredness of age. She welcomed his return and it seemed to do her the world of good. He took her out more. To lunchtime concerts in the National Concert Hall. Coffee and scones in the Shelbourne or lunch in the Elk Lodge Inn. Sunday drives to Enniskerry to look at antiques or the old Powerscourt estate for a walk around the gardens or to see the waterfall tumbling down on the rocks. One night they went to the opera.

He was settling his mother in her seat when he saw them. They were some of the last to arrive. *Perhaps that was deliberate*, he thought. The doors were closing, the audience settling. Aisling was wearing something glittery blue. She looked well, he thought from a distance. The theatre was packed, his mother content, her program on her lap, her hands folded. The orchestra began to play.

Magical music filled the air, elevating the evening to a different dimension. The genius of Mozart, the quivering hum, bassoon and trombone, cello and violin sweeping in, the rise and fall like a hoverfly over a flower. The froth and frippery of *The Magic Flute* mesmerizing his mind so that he forgot to think about them sitting together not a stone's throw away.

Until the interval. Walking into each other in the bar. Michael with Aisling, Colin with his mother, guiding her gently along. He had whispered to her they were in the theatre, but she hadn't spotted them. Now they were face-to-face.

"You're looking very glamorous," Aisling ventured.

There was a confidence in her voice that made Colin wince.

"Thank you," said his mother.

"Are you keeping well, Mrs. Larkin?" said Michael.

His mother gave a nod with the trace of a smile.

And that was it. His mother had stood stock-still with a frozen look on her face. There was a brief exchange of glances. Then Michael and Aisling had drifted away. His mother had stood her ground. If anything, she had made them creep away feeling chastened and snubbed. She had not been fazed. And Colin was impressed with her calm and composure.

All the way back down the cliff, *The Magic Flute* played again in his head. His mother had surprised him that night. No one would ever have guessed how forgetful and vague she had become. That was why he had wanted to bring her to Achill. While there was still some light left in her evening.

On their last day, they took a walk after breakfast on the beach at Keel. She seemed sad to be leaving, but he felt a week had been enough. She was likely to get tired or restless or both. He was taking photographs of the cliffs when she wandered off. Down to the shore on her own. He watched her walk. Her figure bent like a tree in the wind. Her scarf blowing out like a branch. She walked through the wind. His mother on the beach by herself. He watched her walk a lifetime of steps. A little unsteady on her feet. Tracing her way down to the shore. She stood at the water's edge looking out to sea, her dark coat like a bird on the water. He followed slowly. She was a Paul

Henry figure in a painting. Alone and defiant on the shore. An old woman in the wind. Braced against the elements. Staring at the sea. He knew what she was looking for. She was looking for Jim. Even now after all these years. She was looking for Jim in the waves.

He caught up and stood beside her, taking her hand. They stood without speaking. Her face didn't move. Her eyes searched the water. As if still even now he might appear. The years fell away all around her. She wasn't here, she was there. She had always been there. On the shore by the water's edge. Keeping watch, waiting for Jim. The unbearable distance of years had not separated them. She was waiting for him still.

Colin stayed with her until she was ready. Then they turned and walked slowly back along the sand. His mother was tired now yet her face was not sad but at peace. It was as if she had found what she had come to seek.

Colin let her be and after lunch they began the drive home.

Under a trembling sky.

Pale light flooding the horizon, infusing the clouds with pink. And brushing the cliffs with sun.

*****

Summer turned to autumn. The days darkened to winter and lightened to spring. The years slipped slowly by.

He walked with her up and down the road to mass. Drove her to the church when it was raining. But she preferred the walk. "The fresh air will do me good," she would say. She always knelt in the same place, by the Sacred Heart altar. It was her special place. All the congregation seemed to kneel in the same places. *Part of the ritual*, he thought, *like desks at school.*

One morning, they stopped by Mrs. Harrigan's gate.

"It used to be such a beautiful garden," she said, placing her hand on the gatepost. "She always kept it lovely. Now look at it."

The house was empty and up for sale. The garden was overgrown, weeds on the path, brambles in the roses. "She was in a nursing home for years," she said.

"You'd think her family would smarten the place up," he said.

"Sure, they're all away in England," she said.

"She bought my first painting," he said. "I wonder where it is now?"

"Her daughter must have it," she said.

They walked on up the road together slowly, the past intruding on their present.

And the empty house kept watch every day after that as they passed. Like a clock marking time.

His mother had taken to feeding the foxes. In the winter, they came early, stealing into the garden at dusk. She liked to watch them from the dining room window.

"I think they must be at the back of the Harrigans' house," she said. "It'll be quiet for them in there. No one to disturb them."

"Until someone decides to buy it," he said.

"Shush," she said in a whisper. "The foxes have come!"

They stood quietly together, barely daring to breathe. "There's two of them tonight," she said. "That's the mother," she said softly. "She comes every night."

The fox looked up at the house and paused, then stepped forward and carried off a slice of bread in her mouth. The younger one was bolder and ate the bread on the lawn. A light went on in the house next door and the foxes vanished. The garden was black as soot and they couldn't see the foxes anymore.

*****

Colin cut the garden back for winter.

The place looked bare without his mother's summer color in the borders. But neat and framed with dark hedges. His mother wanted to help but she had begun to complain about her eyes.

"That wall is all green," she said. "And you're covered in flowers."

"It's just your peripheral vision," he said.

But it wasn't. Her eyesight was failing and causing strange hallucinations. The optician told her it was a common enough thing but his mother was finding it unnerving.

"I can't see the foxes properly at all," she began to say, and he could hear the regret in her voice. And it troubled him to hear it, because the foxes had come to mean so much.

In December, she fell ill with pneumonia and he brought her news of the foxes as she lay in bed.

"How many tonight?" she always wanted to know.

"Two," he'd say.

"Two," she'd say, her eyes closed. And he knew it was a great comfort to her now.

But later in the spring she tripped and fell in the hall and a sudden headache came like a thunderclap. He got her to the sofa and the ambulance came. But by the evening, she was gone and he sat by her bed, holding her hand. Her thin white hand with her engagement ring and wedding band. Her eyes were closed as if she was sleeping and he clung to her hand like when he was young, walking to school by her side.

And he put out the food for the foxes and waited for them to come on his own after that. Their faces in the dusk like a vigil for the dead. But he knew she could see them clearly now. Their faces peering up at the house in the dark. And he wondered did they sense she was gone.

The house became quiet. Silent and still. His footsteps seemed to echo in the hall and the kitchen. When the phone rang, it was like an electric shock.

He slept with the radio on.

Piano, violin, orchestra.

Instrumental music at night. Sometimes voices. Soprano. A choir. Benedictine monks chanting. Or nuns at evensong. Like Hildegard von Bingen. The pure sound of voices in chorus. The sound rushing in like waves flooding the sea.

Under great big towering skies.

And he slept under the skies. The clouds sweeping in across Achill. The sky flushing crimson and pink.

And the air filling up with butterfly wings. Painted ladies released from glass cabinets. The air bursting with the sound of butterflies migrating. Traveling thousands of miles through time. From beginning to end. Chrysalis to death.

And beyond.

3

Every evening, the sound of crickets crackled up from the lawns. The view from the terrace never ceased to inspire, the blue hills of Maremma just visible in the distance. As dusk settled in, fireflies flashed about.

They had spent the day in San Gimignano and the towering medieval town had not disappointed. The Santa Fina frescoes by Ghirlandaio had been the poignant highlight. But now they were tired and drinking wine in the dark on the terrace. Sitting in companionable silence.

"The sound of thousands of years," said Rosetta.

"The cricket song," said Colin.

"That is why we get on, no?" said Rosetta. "We can both just sit here without talking."

"Just listening," said Colin. "Looking and listening."

Rosetta leaned forward and poured some more wine. Behind her a vase of gladioli patterned the walls of the loggia in the glow from the tall brass lamp.

"What I do not understand," she said, "is why? Why now?"

Colin's eyes stared across the lawns. The Santa Fina frescoes had faded from his mind.

"You know why," he said. "Michael wouldn't have phoned if it wasn't important."

"But what's a few days?" said Rosetta, her face softly lit by the arc of light. "When you only have a few days left anyway?"

"I don't know," said Colin. "I don't know why. Call it duty. Concern."

"Call it love," said Rosetta.

"That too," said Colin. "That too. Or what's left of it."

"I can't stop you," she said. "You have a mind of your own."

"But you can understand," he said.

"Of course," she said, "but even so, it makes me sad to see you go."

"And Aisling?" he said.

"Yes," she said. "That makes me sad too."

"I will come back," he said. "I always do."

"Someday, you won't," she said. "We both know that."

"Mmmm," said Colin.

They fell silent again. The crickets played on. The fireflies lit up the dark. Rosetta passed him the dish of olives. He took one and drank the Brunello.

"I'll miss this," he said.

"The peace and quiet," she said.

"Yes," he said, "and the wine."

In the morning, he had his coffee in the garden. Blackbirds were singing in the bushes all around. The light was hazy and soft, the sky still half asleep behind the cypress trees. Rosetta was somewhere inside. Colin sat quietly, soaking in the rolling fields for the last time. The hills of Maremma were shawled in mist. Like an Italian Paul Henry scene. Like the fields and hills of home. And suddenly a great sadness came upon him. A shadow crept into the morning ...

where once we watched the small free birds fly

And he realized he was singing very softly ...

our love was on the wing

Words that come from nowhere …

we had dreams and songs to sing
it's so lonely round the Fields of Athenry

He hadn't realized he knew the words. It was a strange lament for such a beautiful morning.

Rosetta came and placed her hands on his neck.

"I've never heard you sing before," she said.

"Now you know why." He smiled.

"We need to go," she said quietly.

Colin roused himself and stretched. The morning had broken.

Rosetta drove quickly. The scenery flashed past like a film ending. The names on the road signs disappearing behind. Montalcino. Siena. Firenze.

"I won't come in," she said when they got to the airport. "You know I hate goodbyes."

"*Arrivederci* then," said Colin, taking his bags out of the boot.

Rosetta handed him a box. "You might need this," she said.

"Brunello," he said with a grin. "That was thoughtful."

"Go," she said, "or you'll be late."

When he got to the door, he turned to wave but the car had already gone.

He shrugged and went in. Rosetta never stayed to see him off. He came every June and September and sometimes in March or April. Three years of coming and going. Always reluctant to leave but nonetheless anxious to get on his way. To get home. Back to his seascapes and landscapes. But this was a different departure. A disruption to June as unwelcome as snow in summer. He knew that was selfish of him. But Montalcino had entered his soul now and become part of him and he always looked forward to coming, the warm memories of the place bringing a smile to his face on the cold damp days back home. Today was a different sort of departure and he didn't know what to think. And he went through the routines of the airport and flight mechanically.

*****

The summer after his mother died, he had gone to stay with Adeline Bell in her rambling villa near Siena. Tuscany was a warm escape to dappled hillside groves and long languid evenings spent alfresco. "What you need is some Latin sunshine," Adeline told him when he arrived. "You're looking thin and half-starved like a stray dog. Stay for as long as you like," she said, taking his arm and walking him out to meet the other guests on the terrace.

Adeline's villa was exactly what he needed to help take his mind off things. It took him away from the empty house and the marking of time by the ticking clock. Rosetta Garibaldi had been a frequent guest at dinner. In a white shirt and grey shawl with dark hair and red lips, she was an Armani creature, slender and striking with eyes that took everything in. A freelance editor and writer, now partially retired with a villa near Montalcino, she made him feel welcome from the first evening they met.

"Signore Larkin," she said, "Adeline tells me you are a magnificent painter, is this true?"

Colin shrugged. "Adeline likes to embellish," he said with a grin.

"No, I don't think so," she said, looking at him intently. "You have music in those eyes."

"Mmmm," said Colin, "maybe a little."

"Mmmm," said Rosetta, laughing and wagging a finger, "no maybe about it, I can tell. I am right, yes?"

They were drawn to each other from the start and soon came to an arrangement which suited them both. "This is my birthplace," she said, showing him around the Villa San Lorenzo. "This is my home, my life. I am happy to share it, but I will never leave it." He understood perfectly and he didn't think Ireland would suit her anyhow.

"Your heart is in the Emerald Isle," she said with a smile. "You are a fish out of water. Stay too long here and you wouldn't be able to breathe."

Colin had laughed. He liked her dramatic language and the way she used her hands.

"I have a wandering heart," he said.

"You paint poetry," she said. "You would not settle for long. The Italian sea is not wild enough for you. I know you Celtic types, you like your waves, your storms, your ... how do I say ... your Jamaica Inns."

And so it became.

Each visit a postcard in life. But soft lines drawn in the sand at anything more. And Rosetta proved a more than able guide. "Let me show you this," she'd say. "Let me take you here."

"Have you ever seen anything so beautiful?" she said one evening at a field of sunflowers lit by an amber sun. He had and he hadn't. It was partially why he came. To this sunlit, patchwork valley of olive groves and vines. This was a different heart-aching beauty. Of the Renaissance variety. But he had his own, more fragile beauty. His own ragged beautiful ways. And Rosetta knew that. And he knew that she understood. And he knew that she adored his oil paintings. His seascapes of changing light, the wind chasing shadows on the water. And he knew that she respected him. And that meant a thousand different things. To have love and respect and understanding. But not the tension, the grip, the feeling of losing control. And he was thankful for that.

On his first visit to the Villa San Lorenzo he had painted her portrait on the terrace and she was surprised at how full of character it was.

"It's not just the face," she said. "It's the warmth, the glow, even the Brunello in the glass, the fireflies in the dark. You have captured the atmosphere," she said. "It is a warm painting."

"It's just a postcard," he said. "My postcard to you."

"No, it is almost an Italian painting," she said, looking at him, smiling. "For an Irishman," she added. That night he stayed for dinner. A calamari salad. With breads and olives and wine. The tentative romance became an affair. With no boundaries, no ties. Just birds in flight on the whim of a warm gentle breeze.

And now this. This flight in June. Taking him back across the skies.

A few years ago, there had been a thaw. A slow melting of the ice. The day had been raining. The Saturday between Christmas and New Year. That was when they had come to the gallery. He was chatting to Richard, the owner, when they appeared in out of the rain like two wet dogs. They were laughing and apologetic at being so wet.

"We got caught," said Aisling, the drops of rain sliding down her coat onto the carpet.

"The heavens opened," said Michael.

They were the only people in the gallery at that hour.

Richard made small talk. Colin felt strange as if the place had been invaded, and said nothing. Then he realized they really had come to look at the paintings.

"Do you mind if we look around?" said Michael.

"I was sorry to hear about Eileen," said Aisling, touching his hand. "I haven't seen you since the funeral."

"Mmmm," said Colin. "I was glad to see you there."

Michael beckoned to Aisling and they moved around the room in a hush of low voices. Colin let them be. They went upstairs and downstairs and after a while came back to the desk. In the end, they bought one of his paintings. The whole episode was slightly embarrassing. He wasn't sure if it was out of sympathy or charity, guilt or admiration, or a combination of them all. He just wasn't sure how genuine it was. But he was pleased and decided it was Aisling who had wanted the painting.

Now he realized why. Why it had come out of the blue. When all those years she could have had any number of paintings if she had wanted to. But now he understood the change of heart. And that wet afternoon in the gallery seemed all the more bittersweet now.

He had told Rosetta about them on the phone that night.

"Take it as a compliment," she said.

"But I don't understand it," he said. "It just seems odd, that's all."

Rosetta shrugged at the other end of the line. "Sometimes," she said, "there is no reason. Sometimes people just do things. Out of impulse. Don't always try and see a conspiracy in everything," she said. "They wanted one of your paintings, that's good. That's all. Leave it at that."

"Mmmm," said Colin. "Well, I'm not sure if I'll go."

When they were leaving the gallery, Michael had paused and said something about a party. Colin couldn't follow what he was saying.

"Try and come," said Aisling.

Colin had stared at her. There had been a note of warmth in her voice. A warmth tinged with anxiousness. He couldn't place his finger on it at the time and he had mumbled something like he'd see if he could make it. But Rosetta had encouraged him to go.

"What harm could it possibly do?" she said.

"I don't know," he said. "It just doesn't feel right."

"Go," she said. "If you don't like it, leave."

"Why are you so keen for me to go?" he said.

"I'm not," she replied. "But sometimes, it is better to face our demons. Look on it as a fresh beginning. It's just my opinion."

*****

So he went.

To the party on New Year's Eve. With a bunch of white lilies as a gift. He knew Aisling had always liked them. Something Pre-Raphaelite about them. He could have brought a bottle of wine as well but he desisted. He still harbored a deep-rooted resentment toward Michael. He decided to just bring the flowers.

Aisling seemed delighted he had come.

"Come and look at the painting," she said, showing him into the large front room. The furnishings were expensive, chosen with taste. The place felt like a hotel. Michael asked him what he would like to drink, but Colin said he was driving. The painting was hanging in an alcove above a writing desk. It was illuminated by an overhead lamp and looked well. It was odd to see it there. Like it was in the wrong room. The wrong house.

"How are things?" said Aisling.

An awkward type of question. The words taped together. Like something one would say at a school reunion in a pub.

Colin mumbled something about Tuscany. Italy was easy to talk about and the words rushed over the silence like the crackle of crickets on the lawn.

The house was filling up around them. People arriving with flushed faces and bottles of wine and champagne as gifts. Michael was playing host. Aisling waved a hand as new people arrived. Colin had already decided to slip away early. He found himself mentioning Rosetta.

"Oh," said Aisling, pausing. "You've found someone then," and she said it in a way that made it seem unthinkable. "I'm sure she's very beautiful," she added. But the words were slipped in as a postscript.

"Mmmm," he said, wondering why he had blurted it out like that, as if he'd been trying to make a point.

Aisling stared at him. "I'm really happy for you," she said. "I really am." But again, the words seemed scrabbled together and her tone sounded thin, as if she was thinking about something else.

Michael called to her and at first, she didn't hear.

She was saying something about the new year, about good fortune, when Michael pulled her away. Colin watched as he steered her around to meet people. Laughter bounced about the room. *She looks well*, he thought, watching her mingle. Very much the hostess in a black jersey dress with bracelets jangling on her wrists. Throwing her head back and laughing. That distinctive Kinsale laugh like the sun dancing on water. Moments of Norfolk, of Aisling in the pub, on the sands, on the streets of London years ago, came now. He saw her sitting by the fire on the beach in Brighton. And it was like watching an actress in a different film. And he studied her now. His Pre-Raphaelite muse, her hair shorter and clipped in a bob. And he watched her glance and turn and greet and smile. He saw how she moved through the room. And he watched until the room grew full and she was lost in a sea of bright faces. Then he slipped away. Unnoticed. A stranger in the crowd.

The fog was creeping in from the sea. He could almost see it swirl in the light from the streetlamps. Montalcino seemed a long way away. He walked to his car.

Alone.

Rosetta far away in the Villa San Lorenzo.

Michael and Aisling together inside. Their party in full swing. Not long until midnight now. Not long until the new year.

And he drove home slowly alone.

People were gathering on the streets. The sky began to explode. He got out of the car and watched the showers of light bursting forth. And he realized a new millennium had actually begun.

*****

Dublin Airport was packed. It had a festive air like a party.

Colin waited amongst the happy throng for his bags. The luggage belt went round and round. When he got home, he made coffee and rinsed his face with cold water and looked at himself in the mirror. The late afternoon sun streamed through the window catching specks of dust in the air. His face was flushed with Tuscan sun but his eyes stared back. Solemn, reflective, and still. He felt like a priest in the sacristy before mass. An incongruous feeling on a sunny afternoon. Life juddering to a halt like a train coming into a station.

He went downstairs and dialed Michael's number. The phone rang for quite a long time before Michael picked up. His voice sounded hoarse.

"She'll be ready for you in the morning," he said. "Come by around eleven."

Michael hung up and the line went dead.

So, it has come to this, Colin thought, staring at the receiver.

After dinner, he phoned Rosetta.

"I can't believe it was only this morning," he said.

She held up the phone to the air and he could hear the crickets on the lawn down the line.

"Do you hear them?" she said. "Now go and get some sleep. You need to gather your thoughts for the morning."

They said goodbye and he went out to the kitchen and opened some wine. The Brunello he would save for another time. He turned the radio on. Cello and violin. Brahms. Then he wandered from room to room, the sound of the strings following him. The orchestra rose, the music coming and going in a series of swells. Rising and falling. Lingering then fading away. The cello took center stage. He went back to the kitchen and cut up some apples and went out to the garden. The cello caressed the night air. It was still light. He scattered the apples around the pear tree then went back in and sat in the dining room. The lawn was deserted. The blue night deepened to dusk and he poured a second glass of wine and kept vigil in the dark. The only light on was a lamp in the hall. The orchestra played on in the background. Then he froze and sat still, barely daring to breathe. The slightest movement could disturb them. A snout had appeared. Then another one under the bushes. The foxes had come. Two of them tonight. They were eating the apples. Then a third one came. They carried the last of the apples away in their mouths. They had vanished like angels into the night. The garden was curtained in darkness. The orchestra had stopped.

He listened to the news in the morning when he was shaving but didn't take anything in. His mind was elsewhere. He ate some cereal and ironed a shirt. The morning passed by in a blur. It started raining then stopped. The sun came in and out behind clouds. It was going to be a day of light and shade. Like the morning he had met her on Grafton Street.

She was coming out of Brown Thomas when he saw her. He was always able to spot her a mile away. There was no sign of Michael. Colin had spent the morning in the gallery and then gone to a bookshop. Aisling was wearing a dark coat with a fur collar. He wondered should he go and say hello. She always brought him to a standstill. And these days he usually felt tongue-tied, like a young boy in primary school. She was carrying a clutch of bags in one hand. He decided to approach her. Then he noticed her other hand. She was holding a walking stick.

"I had a little operation," she told him, and smiled. They had gone for coffee in Bewley's. His suggestion, but she had agreed without fuss. He knew it was only because she was alone. He doubted she would tell Michael.

"It's my leg," she had said. But she didn't elaborate.

And he had left it at that. She stayed for nearly half an hour. He thought she looked tired but didn't say. They talked in generalities. It was too late by now for a cross-examination and they skirted the main issues like skillful politicians. But he had felt relaxed with her for the first time since she had left him. And he thought she felt the same.

"We must do this again," he joked at the end.

She laughed. "I'd like that," she said. "It's good to be friends again."

I wouldn't go that far, he thought, but smiled instead. He watched her depart. She seemed quite lame. But she had wanted no help with her bags. Said she would get a taxi. He walked quickly away. But he wondered about the limp and the leg and the walking stick.

That's why when Michael got in touch six months later, the news came as less of a surprise. It had stayed with him as a puzzle in the back of his mind.

But going to see her in the hospital had been a shock. She had no hair. She was thinner and pale but with strange bloated cheeks. Her eyes seemed huge like a doll's. But her voice was warm and the laugh was still there. And her hand stroked his when he sat down. Michael was there for a bit then went out to get coffee.

"My leg again," she said. "My leg is crumbling away." She made light of it and smiled.

"And your beautiful hair," he said.

She smiled at him. "I was wearing a wig for a good while," she said, laughing. "It was in my breast first, you see. I couldn't find a way to tell you because of how things were. But this is different."

The jigsaw was beginning to assemble but he didn't know what to say. The sterile environment of the ward had tied his tongue.

It brought back hints of the hospital in Brighton. But he didn't bring it up. She did.

"I want to thank you," she said.

His eyes widened and stared at her.

"For looking after me in Brighton. Don't," she said, holding out her hand to stop him talking. "I want to say this. That whole … Deirdre business," she said, waving her hand. "I think I must have gone a bit off the rails at the time. And when I was pregnant …" She stopped. "You looked after me," she said. "Don't think I have forgotten that."

He was still staring at her. He didn't know what to say.

"That's all," she said. Her eyes had welled up and he handed her a tissue. "Now," she said, "tell me what you're painting. Cheer me up."

"You think my paintings will cheer you up?"

And she had laughed at that. And when Michael came back, he found them laughing.

A few weeks later he went to visit again. Just before leaving for Italy. Michael wasn't there.

"I'm going home tomorrow," she said.

"That's good, isn't it?"

Aisling looked uncertain, then smiled and shrugged. "It's funny," she said, "I'll miss the nurses in a way. You get used to their company."

He looked at her and thought she seemed sad. Not like someone who was being allowed to go home.

"You'll be glad to be home," he said. The word still felt strange to him, saying it like that. But he had developed a new perspective.

"Do you know, you're right," she said. "I can't wait to see Poppet. Poor thing, he's half blind and half deaf."

"You're mad about that cat," he said. But she seemed more alert. Less a patient all of a sudden, thinking about the old cat.

"You'll have to come over when you get back from Italy," she said.

He thought it was good to hear her making plans. Thinking ahead. And that day with the sun shining through the hospital window, the summer had beckoned and stretched invitingly ahead. And he had gone to Italy hopeful for the best, not expecting to receive a phone call.

Michael's tone had sounded off-key, disengaged almost. Or weary. Colin couldn't put a finger on it.

"What do you mean she's not well?" he said, suddenly speaking very quickly.

Michael didn't answer at first. "I told you," he said, "she's been asking for you. If you want to see her, you'll need to come." He had rung off then.

Colin had felt rattled. Michael had seemed rather distant. Abrupt. But he knew he had to go. It was like a call to prayer ... her voice coming over the waves ...

The water's wide, I cannot get over
And neither have I wings to fly

A deterioration must have come like rain on the wind. And he wondered if her sky would ever brighten again. She had chosen Michael's house as her nest and it was too late now to unwind the hands of time. He had booked the flight without delay. Rosetta had been disappointed but understanding and in the circumstances, he was impressed. It was a difficult situation all around. But he had felt Aisling's voice calling him home ...

Oh love is gentle, love is kind
The sweetest flower when first it's new

But he didn't know whether to hope or expect the worst ...

But love grows old and waxes cold
And fades away like morning dew

And now he was here.

He checked his watch. It was time to go. He splashed cologne on his neck and tucked his shirt in. He was making an effort. Aisling would like that. She would notice. He got into the car and backed out the drive, and drove down the road. With light traffic mid-morning, he should be there in twenty minutes. But the traffic lights were against him. He was behind a truck. He strummed his fingers on the steering wheel. The sun came in and out behind clouds. His fingers tightened on the wheel. A door slammed in his mind.

Aisling was storming down the stairs in Greystones, her dressing gown floating behind her.

"Where are you going?" he was shouting from the landing.

"To get a bloody glass of wine," she thundered up. "I can't sleep in that room on my own anymore."

"Why ever not?" he shouted back. "You're the one who didn't want me in there."

"You've been in the guest bedroom for five months," she said, staring at him up the stairs. "There's no sign of you coming back."

"You don't want me back," he said. "I don't know what's going on. I've just been letting you have some space."

"Letting me have some space? You just want your own space. You've no interest in me," she cried. "None. Not the slightest bit. You've no interest in anything at all except your Sandycove paintings and that bitch of a dragon called Adeline Bell."

"That's just ridiculous," he said. "You're being ridiculous."

"Am I?" she shouted. "Who else would put up with your behavior? Who? Answer me that." She started to laugh. "Jesus," she said, "no woman in her right mind would put up with you."

"Oh, go and have your drink," he said. "It's the only thing you seem to care about."

"What would you know what I care about? How would you know what I'm interested in?" she shouted back. "You know nothing about me anymore." She took off her slippers and hurled them up the stairs. One made a mark on the wall. Then she went into the kitchen and he heard the fridge open and close. He watched her cross the hall with her glass of wine. The door of the sitting room clicked and the sound of the television rose through the door.

He had gone back to bed and the slippers had lain askew on the stairs.

The lights were changing and the truck was moving.

He drove ahead. His face had turned grim. Those horrible last months in Greystones swimming before his eyes. The tension in the cottage. He had banished the images for years. They ruined the picture. A jigsaw is made of a thousand pieces, interlocking fragments that make up a whole. Like the multilayered petals of a rose.

The truck was trundling along but he couldn't change lanes. There were cars moving past him on his right.

She was crying, hugging her knees up to her chest in the hospital bed in Brighton. Her face was lined with tears like rivulets from a stream. There was a howl in her moan. Primeval, untamed like a starving, wild cat. He was holding her. She was clinging to him like a child. Like a mother who has lost her baby. For the third time. He was holding her, soothing her, calming her down but the howl escaped out. The howl was coming from the deep. And he had held her until she stopped shaking. Until the roar had subsided to a shred. Her hands had gripped his neck like someone overboard in the water, clinging on.

The traffic was edging along now. The lights changed to amber then red. A dog was in the car next door. A Labrador laughing at him through the window. The dog was panting, his tongue hanging out. Colin smiled at the dog.

Aisling was smiling. The hills of Carrigoona were bathed in sun, the sky a heavenly blue. They were wandering around outside Paul Henry's house. Her eyes were alive for the first time since Brighton. The sun caught her hair and she was holding his hand. "Such a beautiful place," she was saying, gazing out across the valley to Powerscourt. The sun beamed down on their necks and their shadows moved as one through the grass.

The truck was turning left. Colin changed gear and began to pick up speed.

The sky was bright but his mind was darkening. He was anxious now to get there. He was driving like a robot. His mind was elsewhere. In a gathering of shadows. What was the word she had used? "Meta" something or other, something like that. Michael had said it again on the phone. He had said it quickly. Something about spreading rapidly. The opposite to static. Metastatic. That was it. And Colin wondered whether Aisling had told him the whole truth. Or perhaps he just hadn't taken it in. When she had said her leg, she had mentioned her breast but hadn't gone into it. That was it. Primary to secondary. Rosetta had explained it to him. They had pieced it together. She'd obviously had it for some time. Hence the wig. Now his mind was racing to keep up. The past kept invading the present. The future was still unknown.

Aisling was singing.

Their first Christmas in Greystones. Colin was humming and Poppet was getting in the way. Trying to climb up the tree. There were carols in the background and the windows were fogged with the heat from the oven …

Joyful and triumphant

Aisling was singing, waltzing around with tinsel and baubles …

O *come ye*, O *come ye to Bethlehem*

And then she spun into his arms.

"Happy Christmas," he had said and pulled her in tight and kissed her. They had fallen into bed after dinner in the dark. Poppet had stayed on the floor. The house had grown cold, the fire burning low in the grate. They had finished the bottle of sherry and turned off the lamps. And slept a deep, long, slumberous sleep.

He was parking the car. He was here now.

He just wished it could all be simpler. Instead of strange and odd and surreal like this. He wished he was coming to just take her home. Collect her and drive her away. He hated having to come to this house in the first place and especially for this. And for a moment he wished he hadn't come.

There were plenty of parking spaces. People out at work. He opened the gate. The sun was silver white.

Aisling was walking on the shimmering, warm sand. The sands of Scolt Head, with the sea glinting to left and to right, far out away under a great big, mackerel sky. She was barefoot with sand in her toes, the wind in her hair, the sun on her cheeks and a laugh that rose like a lark in the air.

He pressed the bell.

He could see her paddling now by the water's edge, the sun all around her like a halo of light. And she was waving across the years, her arm in the air, in the sun.

There was a pause. The house was quiet. No one passed on the street. Then footsteps came down the hall. Michael pulled the door back and they stood and stared at each other.

"Come in," Michael said. "Aisling's waiting for you now."

IV
canvas

The hill behind the cottage is steep. At first there are rushes and a track rutted with stones. Her red anorak moves through the green. The ridge of the hill jabs the sky like a creel of wet turf. Clumps of grass and heather appear, and farther up as she climbs there are rocks and pools of dark water and boulders. Sheep with black faces scatter stones in their wake. There are fresh mounds of cut turf and midges swarming around. She brushes the midges away from her face. She is a speck of red paint in the bog. She can't see them yet but she knows they are here. There are slopes and hollows to navigate first.

Mozart senses her before she appears. His ears prick up and he sits on his haunches scanning the air. His ears are alert. When her anorak appears, he begins to bark. This is his hill. His bog. And he vets any strangers who come. But as she draws near, his tail starts to wag. Laura bends down and gives him her hand. He licks her fingers remembering her scent. Even though it has been a full year. Colin is sitting cross-legged in a hollow with a paint box and sketches beside him. He is drinking tea from a flask and he raises his hand in welcome.

"You're back then," he says.

Laura sits down with a smile on her face. Mozart nuzzles her hand.

"Back again," she says. "I can't believe I'm here."

"Nothing has changed," he says, gesturing with his arm across the expanse.

Laura follows his gaze. The bog is burnished with russet and umber and purple. Sunlight spatters the hills with gold. The island has lured her back. And she is here in the heather in the silence, just the wind flapping up the hill.

Colin offers her tea and she takes a cup.

"I've brought you this," she says, handing him a photograph album.

He flicks through the pages, taking the pictures in. Moments from last year.

"You have an observant eye," he says, looking at them. Colin and Mozart on the beach and in the house by the fire. Colin by the window. A portrait in shadow, his cheek edged with light.

"Mmmm," he says, handing them back. "They're good. Time standing still," he says. "That's what good photographs are."

"They're for you," she says. "And Mozart of course," she adds.

Colin smiles. "Do you hear that, boy?" he says.

And she knows he is pleased.

They spend the afternoon in the warmth of the sun in the hills. Laura wanders around taking photographs. She snaps Colin working, bending over his sketchbook. His hand moves about like a magician with paint. Mozart lies sleeping beside him. He is well used to long days of painting in the bog and on the beach. And sometimes on the cliff. Laura looks at the two of them, the painter and the dog, content with each other up here by themselves in the hills. The wind blows Connor's hair like white silk in the sun. He is oblivious to the time. Only when the sky darkens with clouds does he look up from his work.

He seems surprised to see her there. She has been watching for the past half hour. Watching him make the page come alive.

She joins them for dinner in the evening. Slices of cold roast chicken and baby potatoes with salad leaves and chives. And tomatoes that have ripened on the sill. That's all. The meal is simple but delicious. The island air sharpens the appetite. Colin has lit the small clump of turf in the fireplace. There is a drizzle wafting in from the sea. An Atlantic damp descending after the sun of the day.

She is here for two weeks. Sees them on and off most days. Spends the rest of her time taking photographs, reading on the beach, and swimming in the sea. Some nights she goes to the pub on the quay or one of the small family hotels for live music. But she prefers the nights in with Colin by the fire. With Mozart asleep on the rug. He runs in his sleep. His back legs twitching. He is running in his sleep the way he cannot run during the day. It is a sad thing to see, but he is happy in himself. Content. Sometimes he looks up to check she is there, then he rests his head down and lets out a sigh and closes his eyes. He starts to run again. His four legs twitching. He is chasing rabbits in the fields.

"He is dreaming," Colin says. "He's a dreamer that boy."

One night, she makes a bowl of pasta for dinner. There's not a lot in the kitchen to choose from, so she improvises with tomatoes and ham and mushrooms. She roasts the tomatoes in the oven with salt and pepper and thyme. Sautés the mushrooms and ham and makes a béchamel sauce. There is only dried parmesan but it will have to do. Shopping on the island is still a bit limited.

Colin opens a bottle of Brunello wine.

"You didn't get that on the island," she says.

"I have a friend in Montalcino," he says quietly and tenderly. "She brought me a box last year. I've been saving this bottle."

The wine is aromatic, intense, and tastes of berries. And strong. It is quite a strong wine.

Laura sips it slowly. The taste is delicious, addictive. Colin has a faraway look in his eyes.

"And you are in love with this friend?" she ventures.

Colin looks at the wine in his glass. "In Italian love," he says with a smile.

"Is that different?" she asks.

"Mmmm," he says, staring into the flames. The warmth, the crickets, the fireflies, flash through his mind. He is on the terrace in the blue dusk of evening, the cypress trees penciling the sky. Rosetta is moving about, in and out through the open door, lighting candles and lamps, bringing bruschetta and olives to the table. The air is scented with June. He is remembering their day in San Gimignano and begins to talk about the town.

"There is a medieval chapel with frescoes," he says, "of a young girl called Serafina."

He is back in the Santa Fina Chapel looking again at the sleeping girl on the wall, her hands clasped in prayer.

"She became paralyzed," he says, "and spent six long years on a wooden bed offering up her suffering to God."

Laura is listening, startled by his unexpected words.

"And when she died," he says, "the bed began to blossom with violets. And every spring to this day, scented violets grow all around San Gimignano."

"What a beautiful story," she says.

"I think it's a sad story," he says. "But the frescoes are very beautiful. Like life," he says, "sad but beautiful."

"Like your paintings," she says.

"Yes," he says, "the sea can have that effect, I suppose."

"The wine was meant to cheer us up," she says. He laughs and pours her another glass.

"*Salute*," he says, clinking glasses.

"Someday I'll have to go and see this chapel," she says.

Colin smiles and picks up a remote control and presses play. A CD begins to whir.

The sound of soaring voices fills the room. Colin closes his eyes.

The voices gather in strength, then soften again.

"Russian Vespers," he says.

She listens to the deep male voices and she imagines priests with long beards in Byzantine chapels and the sound sends shivers down her skin.

"A butterfly can travel thousands of miles," he says. He is mumbling a little. A smile on his face. She leans closer to listen.

"From flower to flower, they dance," he says. "Like a waltz … in a ballroom." His voice grows dim and his fingers caress the music as if he is conducting an invisible choir.

"Aisling," he says, "had butterfly wings."

"Who is Aisling?" she asks.

He smiles at her question, but his eyes are closed.

"My best friend Michael had a girlfriend called Aisling," he says. "But I fell in love with her and we ended up getting married and then one day years later she left me and went back to him."

"Your friend?"

"Well, he wasn't my friend by then."

"Why did she leave you?" she asks.

"Because I painted too much, I think," he says, and pauses. "Aisling preferred the art as a backdrop," he says, "but to me it was always center stage." He nods to himself as if he has just summed it all up correctly.

She can tell that he is still in love with this girl.

"Your Serafina?" she says.

"My Serafina," he says.

Laura knows to leave it there.

"You'll find a photograph in the bedroom," he says, and reclines his head toward the door.

She has never been in his bedroom before.

It is sparse and catches her by surprise. The room is bare. There is nothing. A bed, a table, and a chair. The only nod to comfort, the dog basket and rug on the floor. *The rug is for Mozart*, she thinks. To stop his paws sliding on the floor. There's a bottle of pills by the bed. A book and a photograph. The book is a collection of Irish poems. Well thumbed. The photograph is small in a plain black frame. A girl with curls is laughing. Her eyes light up the room. The bed is dark wood with white pillows. A grey duvet and a folded wool rug. The rug is a dark Donegal tweed with flecks of blue and green. The walls are white. A single window frames the beach. The window is the picture in the room. There is nothing on any of the walls. There is a door in the wall to another room beyond. But she does not open it. She does not like to intrude any further. She already feels like she has trespassed in here. She takes the photograph in her hand and looks around. And she imagines him. A pill before bed. A poem. The moon in the window. The dog in his basket. Then sleep. Perhaps a dream.

She brings him the photograph.

He has turned the radio on now. Irish music jigs along in the background.

"Aisling?" she says, handing him the frame.

"When she was young," he says. "When we were young."

The eyes are very much alive. A laughing smile. Head thrown back. Laura can imagine her dancing a jig.

Colin puts the photo on the mantelpiece. The flames fan the hearth in rhythm to the tune. Aisling looks down from the frame.

"Time to make a move," says Laura.

Colin walks her to the door. Mozart opens an eye, sensing movement, but is too lazy to move. He will wait until the door is open and the night air comes in.

Colin turns the porch light on and Laura glances up.

A moth is circling the bulb with frenetic abandon. The wings flitter and flip in the glare.

"Why is it doing that?" she says.

"They think it's the moon," he says. "They fly by the light of the moon."

Laura watches the moth circle and flap.

"They always fly to the light," he says, "even if it means they die."

Laura stares at the fluttering wings. "Like a martyr," she says.

He shrugs and nods.

They arrange to meet the next day and she heads off into the night. Mozart barks her away until she is out of sight.

Colin closes the door and stares at the moth. His faithful, nocturnal friend. He turns off the switch and the moth rests its wings. He does not want it to burn.

Laura meets them most mornings.

Colin's walk, she thinks, *is slowing. Mozart is stiffer too. Lifting up his back leg for longer.* She wonders if he's in pain. Sometimes, she walks with them down to the shore. To the same spot. As yesterday. And the day before that. But she does not ask why anymore.

At the start of her second week, Colin says he has something to show her.

"You'll be going soon," he says. "I want to show you something before you leave. In case I'm not here next year," he adds.

Laura is surprised by his candor.

"You just never know," he says looking at her. "No one knows."

Colin opens the door of the bedroom. The room is exactly as it was. The photograph is back in its place, the tweed rug folded on the bed. The book of poems beside the lamp.

Colin opens the door in the wall and stands back. There is another room. A completely empty room. No furniture, not a stick. The floor is dark slate and the walls are white. The room is like a side chapel, a private gallery. On the facing wall, there is one painting. The painting is unframed and takes up almost the entire wall.

Colin says nothing.

She looks at it in silence.

The painting is like a tapestry of silk. A shimmering canvas of Turner serenity. A painting of light.

There is sea. There is sky. Nothing else. And only the sense of them. There are no clouds, no waves, no birds, no rocks. There is only color. Layers upon layers of colors and shades all cut with light. And the light seems to emanate from all angles. From all around. There is no beginning and no end. The painting has a power of its own.

"What do you see?" he says.

"I don't know," she says slowly. "Light. Light drawing you in like a moth to a flame."

He nods. "Yes," he says, "that's one way of putting it."

Laura goes over and stares at the painting. Up close, the depth is mesmerizing. The quality of finish as smooth as satin. It is a breathtaking piece of work.

"I wasn't sure I could do it," he says. "Capture what was inside my head."

"And you're pleased with it?"

He smiles and nods.

The painting haunts the room like a Byzantine icon. A shining mosaic of sky and water. And somewhere far beyond.

"I spent all my life trying to do this painting," he says. "Trying to get it out of me.

"All my life," he says. "Trying to push myself to go beyond. The eye can only see what the brain tells it to see. But the mind wanders on."

"Like a moth to a flame," she says slowly, again.

"Yes," he says, "into the light. All the people in my life who have gone. Gone beyond the horizon."

Always the same spot, she thinks. *Always the same spot, looking out across the sea.*

"One day it will go to the gallery," he says. "But for now, it's here. Where it belongs, with me."

She has not heard him talk so much, so freely before. She is aware of how much he has let her in.

Laura stays for the evening and makes scrambled eggs for supper. The sky is swept clean and the light of evening is tinged with salmon pink. Like a haze upon the horizon. She leaves before dark for a walk by the shore. The night is calm, the sea like a pane of glass. Mozart's tail is wagging and he watches her until she reaches the beach. Then he turns and hops back to the cottage. Laura walks by the shore. The air is warm and smooth. The island air is like something from another planet. Her feet crunch the stones and the waves barely break on the sand. The waves are slow and lethargic tonight.

Mozart follows Colin to bed. He gets into his basket and washes his paws. Colin turns the lamp on and reads a poem. He reads it slowly.

> *Brightness was drenching through the branches*
> *When she wandered again*
> *Turning sliver out of dark grasses*
> *Where the skylark had lain*

The words are entwined with memory. More reliable than the mind. Thoughts written down on the page can focus the eye. And his eyes see through the dark grasses and he hears her in the wind ...

> *And her voice coming softly over the meadow*
> *Was the mist becoming rain*

He closes the book. The window frames the sea. He glances at Mozart. The paws are twitching. Colin smiles. Mozart is running in his sleep. Chasing rabbits down burrows. Running circles of eight in his mind. Colin yawns and slides down the sheets. Into sleep. Into rain. He is driving through rain. To a house on a hill. The windshield wipers sweep away the rain. They sweep the rain in waves on the glass. And there is someone running on the sands. He is running with Aisling on the sands. Hand in hand. And they are running through the waves. They are running through the rain. And his car is driving through the rain. There is another car in the frame. A second car driving in the rain. And he has lost Aisling's hand and she is slipping through the waves in the dark. Her smile is fading in the rain. And the cars drive on. And in the morning when he wakes, his pajamas are wet with sweat.

Laura is tired when she reaches her cottage. The painting has followed her across the beach. She can't get it out of her mind. His life's work. In an antechamber. No one knows it is there. And he has shown it to her. They barely know each other but he has shown her his most precious work. "A lifetime," he said. She hates the thought of having to leave again soon. The island is like an elixir. But the holiday is slipping away. She plans a meal. To say thank you. Before she has to say goodbye. *A roast chicken,* she thinks. He would like that. She will head to the shop in the morning. *Roast potatoes,* she thinks, *fresh vegetables and a pan-made gravy from the juices. Mozart will love that.* She smiles, climbing into bed. *I could come back at Easter,* she thinks. *March or April. Not that long away really.* She reads for a while but the painting still shines in her mind. His masterpiece. No one knows it is there. Behind the door in the wall in the cottage on the island. She feels like the keeper of the flame. She lets the book drop and sleeps an unbroken sleep.

Colin opens the door of the cottage and stretches. It is going to be another beautiful day. The sky is a pure Mediterranean blue. Only faint wisps of clouds. The waves slide in. Silent and ceaseless. There is no trace of wind. Mozart trots out and lifts his leg against the wall. Then he sniffs the air and wags his tail. Colin goes in and boils the kettle and comes out with a cup of tea. The morning is early. There isn't a soul on the beach at this hour. The island is still half asleep.

Laura is fast asleep. There are flowers bright as paint in the hedgerows. Birds flying low across the sea as the sun skims the water. Her sleep is dappled shade. She can see coral and shells and shoals of fish. The fish curve and glide through waters of turquoise green. A breeze is blowing hay in the meadows. Blowing ripples across the water. The breeze gathers strength and scatters the birds in the sky. The breeze is growing in sound. The sound is coming through the window. She opens her eyes and looks at the clock. It is just after seven. Sunlight sweeps the floor, brightening the room. The sound is coming through the window. The sound from her sleep. It is an incessant sound. She realizes it is real. The sound from the window. She is alert now and listening. She knows the sound. It is a barking sound. Laura jumps out of bed and pulls the curtains back. The barking is real. "Oh, God," she says. Mozart is barking outside her window. Barking. Barking. Barking. Her mind is racing. She grabs some clothes from the chair and begins to run.

moth

"My work as an artist had long accustomed me to early rising and although it was dark as I dressed, there was a faint flush in the east which was gradually lightening as I picked my way past the upturned curraghs at the little landing place by the harbour."

—Paul Henry
"The Coming of the Wild Geese"

1

His mother's roses by the gate were still in full bloom. Their scent caught the air like a spray of sweet charm amidst deadly thorns. Many times they had caught his fingers. A prick upon the skin drawing blood. Colin looked at them now. The multilayered petals of soft crimson velvet. *It would only take a gust of wind,* he thought, *to bring them down.* Or a sudden downpour. Tomorrow they could be squashed on the ground. Their sweet scent a memory.

It could have happened that suddenly, he thought.

And perhaps he was wrong about it after all.

Perhaps it had just happened. Like a wind in the night. "You don't know the day nor the hour," his mother had said. "None of us do." Words from beyond the grave. He put his bag in the car and closed the trunk. Perhaps he would never know. But he had to try. And he knew he had to go. Last night he had filled up the car with petrol. Checked the tires and oil and water. And bought a bag of peppermints. He would be glad of them on the journey to County Clare.

He paused. The roses flared pink against the hedge, their petals pristine, unblemished by dew. And in the morning sunshine their perfume caught him again. Like that morning when Michael had opened the door and an avalanche of scent wafted out. Michael was doused in cologne. An expensive cologne. And the scent had followed him all the way down the hall. The cologne was heady and lush and felt out of place. Incongruous. Like someone drinking gin in a hospital.

"She's in here," Michael said, opening the door into the sitting room.

Colin remembered the room from the party. Now it had a bed. Aisling was sitting up, a silk scarf around her head.

"Come in," she said smiling, her eyes pleased to see him. Her voice was warm and inviting. Michael left them to it. Aisling gestured to a chair. Colin sat down, looking around. His painting was still on the wall.

"Still there," she said, catching his glance. "Were you afraid we'd sell it?"

"No," he said. "I'd forgotten about it, that's all."

"It's good to see you," said Aisling.

But he noticed her voice was quite weak. A hoarse fraction of what it once was.

"You're looking well," he said tentatively.

"It's just a bit of paint," she said. "Underneath I'm all grey."

And Colin noticed how thin she had become. The veins in her hands were like tubes of blue and her arms were twiggy like a matchstick drawing. Her scarf added a touch of bravado and the small bit of makeup helped. But the effect, he realized, was just that little bit grotesque. And he felt awful for having thought it. Like visiting the star of a vaudeville show.

Michael brought them tea and Aisling said she was hungry.

"Hungry?" said Michael.

Aisling nodded her head. "Do you know something?" she said. "I could murder a bacon sandwich."

Michael and Colin looked at each other. "Well, if you really want one," said Michael, and he went off to make one.

"Sure, what harm could it do?" Aisling said to Colin. "I mean at this stage." She shrugged.

"How bad is it?" Colin asked.

"The end," she said quietly. "Only we don't really know when the end will come. Sometimes," she said, "it feels imminent. Other days, like today, I feel I could get out of bed and go on for years. Well, maybe not years," she said. Her eyes were beginning to glisten but she dabbed them with a tissue and smiled.

Colin held her hand.

He was holding her hand when Michael came back with a tray. "I thought I'd bring extra," said Michael. And the three of them ate quietly together. All their concentration focused on the crisp bacon. And all of them aware the triangle had come full circle.

"That was lovely," Aisling said, wiping her lips with the napkin. But she had only managed a morsel. Just a taste.

*****

The tang of bacon had stayed with Colin all summer. He hadn't eaten it since.

Last night he had made cheese on toast. Spread mustard on the bread and stood by the oven watching the cheddar melt under the grill. It seemed to take a long time. Standing there watching the cheese bubble and swell to the edge of the bread. He had opened a bottle of beer and ate sitting at the counter table. The radio in the background for company. To keep the silence at bay. To keep the image of the pillow away. The image that had started to haunt him. Disturb him. And terrify him. Asleep or awake it was hard to escape. Hard to get out of his head. It was the reason he was going down to Clare.

The routine of the gear bag and towel every morning had helped. He started swimming in his local pool and some days went out to the Forty Foot. To cold water and drizzle and old wrinkled men with white legs. And when he swam in the water, he was free. Cutting through the water like a flipper. Skimming up to the surface, ducking down, coming up for air, his hair plastered wet, the goggles pinching his nose. Swimming back and forth to erase painful thoughts from the past and the present. But as the summer wore on, he knew he was simply just drowning. Sometimes, he woke in the night. Shaking. Michael was holding him down with a pillow. The pillow was over his face. He couldn't breathe. Michael was pressing him down and he was beginning to choke. And that was when he woke up. Always the same moment. When he started to choke. And that's why he kept swimming. To erase it from his mind. But the swimming didn't work. The pillow wouldn't go away. And that's when he knew he had to talk to Michael.

After the grilled cheese, he phoned Rosetta.

"I don't think you should go down there," she said.

"I have to go."

"You are chasing demons again," she said. "You will be walking into the lion's den."

"Even so," he said, "I have to know."

*****

He had to know. And it was time to go now.

He was backing out the car when he stopped. The child from next door was standing at the gate. He had come across her once or twice before. Colin got out.

"Where are you going?" she said. Her face was freckled and she had big brown eyes that were staring at him. She was seven. Her family were new on the road.

"I'm going for a drive," he said.

"Why?" she asked.

"Because I have to see somebody," he said.

"Why?"

Colin paused and looked at the girl. "I can't move the car if you stand there," he said.

"Then stay here," she said. "Come and see my cat."

"I don't really like cats," he said.

"Well, my cat doesn't like you either," she said. "We think you're weird."

"I'm sorry your cat doesn't like me," he said. "But can you move now?"

The girl moved away, her eyes staring at him. Colin backed the car out of the drive. Slowly. Then he turned the car on the road. The girl was standing by the gate, holding the cat in her arms. Colin sighed and drove off, the girl with the cat in the mirror.

He was already feeling irritated. It wasn't a good start to the drive. Maybe Rosetta was right. He shouldn't be going. And what difference could it possibly make anyway? There was still plenty of time to turn back. But he kept driving. His face had turned grim. Before long he was on the motorway, looking for the exit to County Clare.

"Come and see me again," Aisling had said.

The bedroom appeared, clear as day.

"Of course I will," he'd said. "But you need to get some rest now."

After the sandwich, her energy had dropped. She needed to lie down. He realized she was becoming uncomfortable. Michael said the nurse was due soon and Colin made his excuses.

Her fingers traced his hand. And she gave him a wave from the bed.

"I'll come again tomorrow," he said to Michael. The tension between them appearing to have eased now after the sandwich. The breaking of bread.

"No, leave it for a bit," said Michael. "Leave it a few days. She gets tired easily."

Colin paused and then nodded and went down the steps. The door closed quickly behind him.

And that was the beginning of the thought. But he didn't know it then. The dream of the pillow and the image in his head. The repetition. In slow repetition, all summer. The door closing quickly behind him. He could hear the door closing now as the car sped along. Michael couldn't wait to close the door. Close the door on him. Shut him out.

The feeling came to him strongly now. Of Michael wanting him gone. He had been allowed in to see Aisling but the visit was over and Michael had wanted him gone. He must have had it all planned, Colin thought. All that time eating the bacon sandwich, he must have had it all planned. And all he was waiting for was for Colin to go.

"Come and see me again," she had said. And he had promised he would. "Island Man," she had said, the words escaping her lips for the first time in years. She was smiling when she said it. A faint trace of a smile on her lips as she held her hand up in a wave. "Come back to me, my Island Man," she had said, her voice growing sleepy. He had turned and looked back from the door. Her eyes were open and smiling at him. She seemed relatively restful. Content.

He knew the attraction Michael's wealth had held. He had struggled with that for years. But when she had said those words again, he knew how much she still cared. And in the end, that meant a great deal. A valedictory statement of fact.

And that was why the phone call had come as such a shock. A bare day and a half later.

"Passed away in her sleep," Michael said.

"Peaceful," he said.

The phone call was short.

Colin had to sit down. His leg was beginning to shake.

He knew she was dying. But they hadn't said goodbye. They hadn't needed to. She had been alert. Alive. It couldn't have been the end. She wasn't at death's door. She wasn't. But then he thought of the roses by the gate in full bloom. Their scent filling the air with hope. And perhaps in the night death had just come like a sudden blast of wind blowing in.

He drove steadily on. There wasn't long to go now …

Raindrops were splattering the roses by the gate. Their petals were dropping in his mind and lay smudged on the earth in the rain … the countryside was speeding past, trees, fields, cows in a blur, the sky like a scarf of blue …

Low lie, the Fields of Athenry
Where once we watched the small free birds fly
Our love was on the wing

Perhaps it had come naturally in the end after all ... or perhaps something else had taken place in the night. Death aided and abetted by a hand in the dark. That's what this journey was about ...

We had dreams and songs to sing
It's so lonely round the Fields of Athenry

It had taken him all summer to decide. And when finally he had phoned Michael, he deliberately kept it short.

Michael was in his holiday house in Doolin. "I'm here for a few weeks," he said, "sorting things out. I'm thinking of selling up. So, if you really want to see me, you'll have to come down."

Colin said he could do with a trip to get some painting done.

"Whatever," Michael said.

The road to Doolin was flanked with stone walls and small, sloping fields of green. The sky was radiant with light from the sea and the light gave the land a strange maritime feel. He could sense the ocean now as he drove. The proximity to the sea was palpable.

His guesthouse was comfortable.

A modern bathroom of white and chrome. His bedroom had a view of fields and stone walls and cows. The fields were lumpy, spiked with rushes and dotted with cow pats. The cows were red and cream and black and white. There was one grey cow moving about, swishing its tail. Like the odd one out from the crowd. Now he was here, he needed a walk. Before going up to the house on the hill.

Michael's house was visible across the fields.

A half hour's walk away. But Colin had decided he would drive there. And he went for a walk now instead. The walk took him down to the sea. He watched the tide swimming in. The sea was a bruised purple blue in the afternoon light. The light was diffused by storm clouds that had darkened the sky a rich, deep cerulean blue, and the sand glowed cream and pale under the cloak of the gathering gloom. The light was churning the sky into a turmoil of colors, the landscape seething with autumnal tones. It was a breathtaking evening and he wondered would it rain or would the clouds storm past overhead? The wild air was bracing and the freshness had lifted his mood and he felt less uptight now about why he had come. And as he walked on the beach, he realized this was the beach. With the slope of the sand and the curve of the sea. And the scenery beyond. This was the beach with Michael. And he was retracing steps from a distant moonlit night. He could see the flames in the fire and the stars sprinkling the sky like glitter in the dark. The flap of the tent and the swim in the sea. A lifetime ago. Two fresh-faced boys in their T-shirts and shorts.

Not men like now.

With their troubled minds.

He had a quick bite to eat in the village. Still with no clear idea what he was going to say. Or how he could even begin to defend or explain his thoughts. Michael would deny it. There would be words. Bad blood. And what would be the point in that? The funeral had been tense enough. Michael had barely spoken to him and afterward in the hotel, he had winced when he heard Michael laughing. Almost cheery. Drinking wine. As if he'd been glad it was the end. As if ... as if ...

The subject was closed. Michael had made that quite clear. The first phone call had been short. Later calls just as brief. He had deflected all Colin's attempts to know more. Even now, Colin could still see him at the funeral, in the hotel shaking hands and the mantra, the quick mantra ...

"... was peaceful ... peaceful ... peaceful ..."

Over and over again. The words rushed, his face flushed, shaking hands. Almost as if ... as if ...

It was nothing much to go on. Just the feeling that something was wrong. The feeling that had stayed with him all summer. That it had all been too quick. Too neat. Something no one else would understand or suspect. Even if there was there was nothing he could actually do about it. Other than let Michael know that he knew.

*****

It was coming up to seven when he began to make a move.

The rain had stayed away. But there were fresh clouds sweeping in and the light was draining from the sky. The road twisted and turned but the drive was short. Up ahead he could see the house on the hill. Michael had turned some lamps on in the windows. And the house seemed to be waiting for him. Like a skull lit up like a lantern.

Colin drove in through the gates.

The avenue was gritted with gravel with a beard of grass up the middle. Near the house there was tarmac and space to turn the car. A sea breeze was blowing in his face as he got out. The house was higher up than he thought. A good view by day, he imagined. From this isolated, windblown spot.

He knocked on the front door but it swung open into a hall with fishing rods and golf clubs and boots. An old marble washstand with a jug and basin and a mirror up above it. There were Barbour jackets hanging from the wall. He looked around, trying to get his bearings. Then a voice came.

"In here," Michael called from somewhere down the hall.

Colin found him in a room with softly glowing lamps in the corners and old sofas with cushions and throws. A comfortable holiday room.

"I suppose you want to get your painting back," said Michael. "Is that why you've come?" He was slouched in an armchair, one leg over the other, with a large glass of wine in one hand. He was holding the glass at an angle and the wine looked as if it might spill.

"No," said Colin. "That's not why I came."

"Well, what then?" said Michael. "Why are you standing there, looking at me like that?"

"Like what?" said Colin.

"Like you've got something to say."

A moth was circling the lamp, and Colin looked at it and smiled.

Michael's hand swayed and some wine tipped on the floor. "Blast it," he said, steadying the glass. "What are you smiling at now?"

"I was looking at the moth." Colin pointed.

They both looked at the moth. The wings dipped and ebbed around the lamp. The only sound in the room was the quiver of wings like faint violin strings in the air.

Michael sighed. "Have a seat," he said.

Colin sat down. Michael poured him a glass of red wine. They sat opposite each other in the lamplight. Silent and still. Both watching the other like knights on a chessboard. Colin's mind was working away. He could imagine the room with a blazing fire and Aisling coming in from outside. He could imagine her hair all blown by the wind. He could imagine her coming in now fresh faced from the sea and sitting down between them tonight. He took a slow sip of wine.

"Well?" Michael said.

Colin took a deep breath. "Look, it's difficult," he said. "I've been thinking about how Aisling died and ..."

"What about how she died?" said Michael.

"The night she died ..." Colin paused.

"Yes?" said Michael, snapping out the word.

"Did you ...?"

"Did I what?"

Colin stiffened. Michael's reaction had been too quick. Too defensive.

"Oh, my God, you did." Colin put down the wine.

"Did what?" said Michael, his eyes flashing across the room.

And Colin had the feeling that Michael had become quite unhinged.

2

It was still very early, barely even morning and the bedroom was dark, but through the slit of the curtains he could see a line of light rising across the stone walls. Somewhere out in the fields, near the red barn a calf was bellowing, and he lay now listening to the plaintive, crying, lonesome sound. And he knew what it was. It was the sound of a calf calling out for its mother. He had seen the truck yesterday parked in the yard with the tail lift down and a slow, heavy, lame black and white cow being pushed up into it. He hadn't thought about it then, but he turned his head on the pillow and thought about it now, about how the cow was being driven away for slaughter. An old mother cow, no use anymore, being taken away from the fields of the farm, from her calf, from the life and the land which she'd known from her birth. He turned his head again and looked out the window. Little birds were twirling in the air above the hedges and he watched them flitting in small arcs and curves making spirals, each spiral they made like a second on a clock.

The seconds had lengthened and crackled like static between them then. But the hours that had followed just seemed like a few seconds now. A few seconds that joined all the dots. Colin watched the birds twirling and then looked round the room. Recollection of time is a relative thing. A relativity complicated by the lack of unbroken sleep. The night had been a long shadow, the bed in the guesthouse like a board in a cell; prison or monastery, he couldn't tell. But it felt like a kind of atonement, a penance, a sentence but for what he didn't know.

Michael had stared at Colin.

Each of them knew what the other was thinking. Colin remembered how the sea kept crashing on the shore and how the roar of the water had focused his mind. The sky was racing with torn shreds of clouds and through the window he had seen the horizon, the sky sweeping down to the water.

"You did do something," he said.

And Michael had flinched at the steel in his tone. "What if I did? What of it? She was in pain."

"She was alive," said Colin.

"She was in agony."

"Not all the time."

"She was going to be," said Michael. "She was going to die." He stood up. "What the hell would you know about it anyway? You were barely even there. Well, I can tell you it was hell."

"But she was happy."

"Jesus," Michael said. "Happy to see you? That's all you care about, isn't it? How she felt about you."

"That's not true," Colin said.

"Well, why are you here?"

"Because I need to know."

"And you think I'm going to tell you?"

"Yes," said Colin. "I think you will."

Michael moved to the window and stood with his back to him, refilling his glass, looking out at the night. His shoulders had risen and fallen while he made up his mind.

The rain had started to fall then and he remembered now the soft swish of drizzle caressing the window like the first tentative notes of a symphony. By the end of the evening, it had been pouring from the sky but now here this morning, it was no more than a trickle. A faint spray of gauze on the window. *Soon it will be light,* he thought. Not quite six o'clock yet but already the red and white cows moving like shadows on the hill. Colin lay with the back of his hand across his forehead and thought about getting up. He pulled his legs out of the bed slowly, like an old man, and reached for the switch on the bedside lamp. Found the kettle in the half dark and filled and clicked it on. He poured a dribble of long-life milk from the small plastic carton into a teacup. There was a cellophane packet of shortbread and when he opened the plastic the biscuits broke, cracking in half, the crumbs tumbling through his fingers to the floor. He poured the tea and switched the television on low. And then he sat, staring at the screen, the sports news, the world news, the business news, dunking the tea with the broken biscuits. But all the time Michael was still standing by that window with his back to him, refilling his glass. Getting ready to say it. To explain it. Michael had started talking and the words had come slowly and hesitantly at first like in a confessional, and now they came through again, through the commercials, the weather, and the endless breaking news.

"After you left," Michael had said, "she slept most of the day. The next day she was worse. Very bad. The nurse came. I couldn't bear to see her like that anymore."

Colin watched him and listened. He didn't know what he wanted to hear. He had the impression that Michael found it a relief to be able to say it.

The words had come slowly.

"She was asleep," Michael said. "Fast asleep with morphine. I couldn't bear to watch her ..." He stopped.

"And what ... did ... you ... do?" Colin said in a low, quiet voice, barely over a whisper.

Michael stood looking out the window. His face in the glass looked like a frightened man, out of his depth, grabbing for words to explain what had happened.

It was a while before he began to speak. Then the words came. In a slow, dull, weary tone. As if Colin wasn't there.

"I put my hand on the back of her head," he said. "I just rolled her face into the pillow. Like she had turned in her sleep. I just helped her turn in her sleep. And I held her like that while she slept. She just passed away in her sleep. It was peaceful," he said. "Very, very peaceful. You have to believe me … it was … the best thing … to do."

He turned around and looked at Colin.

"Now do you understand?"

Colin took in a deep breath as he stared at the television. Every word, every nuance, every moment clear as day, here in the morning. Seconds of crystal-clear clarity. Recollecting every second can be an unsettling thing. An unconscious effort to sift through the evidence, rectify, alter, change it. Clarity of thought can stir up the mind like a wind rolling over the water.

"No," he remembered himself saying. "No."

Michael's eyes had looked at him, startled.

"I … eased … her … passing," he said very slowly. "That's … all." He was breathing quite heavily, struggling with the words. His voice sounded gurgled, as if he might choke.

"You had no right," said Colin.

"You have no right to say that," Michael shot back.

Colin shook his head. "I have every right," he said. "I could go to the guards."

"And do you really think anyone would believe you?" said Michael.

"Well, it's the truth, isn't it?"

"She was dying," said Michael. "That's the truth."

"No," said Colin, "that's just your excuse."

Michael brushed past him and opened the door.

"Will you please just go now?" he said.

"No," said Colin. "We're not done yet."

"Oh yes, we fucking well are," said Michael, grabbing his keys from a table in the hall.

He stormed out the door and flicked on the lights of his car. It was raining and the rain was falling now like silver needles flashing in the glare. The engine came alive and the wheels swiveled on the gravel. Colin ran out and thumped on the window. Michael was shouting in the car. But Colin couldn't hear what he was saying. The rain was falling on his face, slanting in the wind from the sea. Michael turned the wheels on the gravel and the car revved and then roared down the drive.

*****

The news was coming from India now. Colin watched the images changing on the screen. Dignitaries arriving in sleek, polished cars at a trade conference. The reporter talking directly to the camera. Behind her, behind the dignitaries, there was just the sliver of a glimpse of the bustle of Delhi. A splash of rich color penetrating the room. And he kept his eye on it, transfixed until the end of the report. He hadn't taken anything in except the mutating color, the sense of another world far away. Far away from here, from this bungalow and the cows rasping grass on the hill.

He roused himself and stretched and put the teacup back on the tray. Perhaps he shouldn't have rushed out like that after Michael. Perhaps he shouldn't have followed. But Michael had been drinking and it had been an instinctive thing to go after him. He remembered hesitating for a moment in the rain before he ran to his car. A split-second decision. There had been something unnerving about Michael leaving like that but going after him had been a crazy and dangerous thing to do. The headlights flashing on the greasy, black roads, the wipers fighting the rain on the windshield. The road twisting and turning in the dark and the *Cambria* coming into his head, the ship thrashing in the waves off Inishtrahull and the passengers crying out in the night. Michael had taken an abrupt turn to the right and Colin had followed him all the way, all the way up to the cliffs. The bleak, bare Cliffs of Moher with the wind beating in from the black churning sea. The wind had caught him full blast as he opened the door. Michael was heading up the incline and Colin had paused for a moment and then gone after him.

*****

There had been a kind of madness to it all in the windblown rain with the sound of the waves pounding and roaring on the rocks far below out of sight, and he let out a long slow breath now and took his bag out from the wardrobe and began to sort out his things. His clothes from last night were still wet and he draped the shirt and the jeans over the radiator to dry them out. He picked up his jacket from the floor and hung it on the back of a chair and placed the chair close to the heat in the hope it might help before he left, after breakfast. He realized he was hungry and the thought of bacon and eggs and black coffee suddenly seemed very good. All he wanted now was to get moving, to get showered and dressed and eat and get out of here.

*****

"Why won't you leave me alone?" Michael had shouted on the hill.

"What the hell are you doing up here?" Colin had shouted back. "Are you out of your bloody mind?" Their voices had sounded strange, strangulated by the wind tossing and playing with their words.

"Why? Don't you like it?" Michael had shot back. "Well, look all around you, Colin, because do you see all of this? This is your precious, little world—your very own fucking goddamn distant point. And do you know something? This is what drove her away from you … from you … from you." The words were coming back thick and fast now out of the night. "Take a good look around you," Michael was shouting, "because this is what's inside your head … your head … this is what she wanted to escape from … escape from … escape."

*****

Colin rubbed the back of his neck and picked up his wash bag and went into the bathroom and shut the door tightly, as if he could shut out the sound of Michael's voice in his ears. He placed his shaving cream and razor on the sink, pulled the shower door open and began to peel off his pajamas.

"You're mad," he could hear himself shouting in the wind.

"No, you're the one who's mad," Michael had shouted back. "You just couldn't leave us alone. This is what she wanted to escape from, you know. You're the one who drove her away ...... her away ...... her away ......"

He turned on the shower and the water sprayed out in a blast of hot steam. He stepped under the nozzle and just stood as the water gushed over him, through his hair, down his face, across his shoulders. His whole body felt drained. He felt cold and sick and tired. He had kept trying to tell Michael to come away, to shut up, to just leave her in peace. And he stood now and let the water hiss over him, until he began to warm up and his skin began to tingle, and a flush crept back into his cheeks.

"She's not at peace. She's dead," Michael had shouted. "There is no peace. You talk like there's some kind of heaven but there is no heaven, there's only this. This fucking wild madness." The words were raining down now on his head in the blast of the shower. "This fucking wild madness ... this place."

"Stop saying that," he had yelled. "Just stop it, okay?"

"Why not? I don't believe it. She didn't believe it. Just because you might have some mad insane belief, you think everyone else thinks the same? Well, there is no heaven, Colin. She's gone. She's just dead. There's nothing left. This is all there fucking well is."

His eyes were closed tight, his hair and his face all covered in suds. He rubbed at his scalp as if he could clean out his head and then turned the shower down from hot to full freezing cold and stood in the waterfall of ice, just letting the cells come alive and race with the shock and the rhythm. Then he moved the dial up again and felt the hot steaming water engulf him. He raised his arm slowly and switched it all off and stepped out and took a towel from the rail and began to rub himself down. Vigorously and hard until he could feel the blood running through his limbs. He looked in the mirror at his hollow dark eyes and their sockets of shadow. He stared at his eyes. He stared at the mirror, at his naked limbs. His unremarkable, slim, white body. He looked at his eyes and his eyes looked at him like two dark pools of water. He turned the tap on and and tied the white towel around him and pumped shaving cream into his palm and stood waiting for the basin to fill, watching the water making bubbles as it flowed from the tap. He turned the tap off and stood looking at the blob of foam curled like whipped cream in his hand. The bathroom was quiet now, and in the silence, he could still hear them shouting. He could see the moon shining in the sky. They had reached the summit and the moon had come out spotlighting the cliff and the grass all around and the edge. The rain had eased but not stopped. They were close to the edge and the wind was catching their breath. "There's your light," said Michael, pointing to the moon. "You can paint all of this now," he said, throwing his arm out. "There's no one's stopping you now, is there?" Colin stepped closer. The moon slipped away. "You just can't face it," Michael said. "She's dead, not fucking sleeping, Colin Larkin." And they stared at each other. "You see what's out there, behind me?" said Michael. "Your distant point, that's what. And you know something, Colin, there's nothing fucking there." And he seemed to stumble then for a moment and twisted around and let out a cry and bent over clutching his ankle.

Colin lathered his cheeks now with the cream and rubbed it all in and picked up his razor and started shaving slowly and methodically, up and down cheek and jaw, the blade cutting the foam like snow.

Michael was sitting on the grass, crouched over his leg.

"I've done something to my fucking ankle," he said.

"You need to stand up."

Michael winced and tried and squirmed and sat back. "I can't. I can't move it."

"You'll have to try and get up and lean on me, then. You can't stay here."

"I like it up here."

"No, you don't. Now get up."

"I need you to drop it first though," said Michael.

The rain was lashing all around them.

Cheek and neck, then jaw and chin. He drew the razor slowly up and down.

"All that stuff about Aisling, I need you to drop it."

Colin rinsed the razor and drew the blade down over his upper lip.

"Alright, alright," he said.

He pulled the blade up his neck now to his jaw. He was nearly done, and he ran his finger and thumb over the smooth skin to check for any stubble.

Their descent had been slow. Neither had talked. The energy had gone out of Michael and he was leaning on Colin and limping.

"You'll have to come back with me," Colin said, "you're in no state to drive."

Michael nodded. "Answer me one thing," he said. "How the hell did you know?"

"I didn't," Colin said, getting into the car, "but I needed to."

"And now?" Michael asked.

"I haven't changed my opinion," said Colin, "but can we just leave it, alright?" Michael looked at him bitterly and slammed the door shut and stared out the window. Colin started the engine and turned up the heat. The rain was showering the glass with spray. He unplugged the sink now and watched the water gurgling away. Then he rinsed the lather from the sides and cleaned the basin and wiped it and turned the tap off. The headlights had swept through the dark as they came down the hill. And then suddenly he had tightened his grip on the wheel. And he clenched his hands now, the knuckles showing white through his skin as it happened again.

"Jesus," Michael said.

Colin froze.

The road was greasy with rain and the car was skidding. The tires were skating out of control. He tried to steer the car to the right, to the side of the road to try and bring it to a stop, and the tires turned and freewheeled, and it shot at an angle into the ditch, brushing grass and then it flipped.

The car was lying on its side and Michael was tilted up over Colin. "Turn off the engine," he shouted. "Turn it off." Colin's head was pressed against the door, but his fingers found the keys. The engine shuddered to a halt. Neither spoke and they lay there like that for some time with the rain beating down.

Colin turned off the tap and dried his hands. Silence fell in the bathroom. The door of his car was dented and scraped. He would have to get it looked at. The night had snapped in two after that. The long, damp wait for help in the cold and the wet. It was the middle of the night before he had got back to the guesthouse. But the first half of the night was still as vivid as ever. "There's nothing fucking out there," he heard Michael screaming again, and he thought of the void of black over the cliff, the dizzying drop to Michael's nothingness, and the sail through the wind to the rocks. To the waves. And the tide like a battering ram at the base. He shook his head slowly and pulled on a fresh shirt in the bedroom. "Too smooth," said his mother in his ear. "Too smooth an operator for my liking. That fellow Michael," she said, "nice as pie to your face and then stab you in the back as quick as look at you." Colin shook his head again as he buckled his belt. Shook his head with regret and bewilderment. "You should eat, Island Man," Aisling was whispering. "You always forget to eat." He nodded and began to gather up his things. The sky was lightening from the east, a pale swathe of cream flooding in. "Come on," Aisling said, beckoning to him, "we're going on a picnic." And he smiled now and saw the two of them then wandering up a green hill. He watched as they climbed hand in hand across the slopes. Aisling's red dress like a splash of Monet color in a field of haze. There were baguettes of smoked salmon in a wicker basket, bunches of grapes, salt crackers and cheddar, red apples, and bars of dark chocolate. Aisling's dress rippled in the breeze. "I just hope she remembers what you did for her," his mother was saying. "It wasn't always a bed of roses, you know," he said, as he watched them ambling about on the hill. "I wasn't exactly an angel." His mother looked at him. "I know that," she said. "You were never an angel. You're difficult and stubborn and set in your ways, both of you were in your way." He nodded his head at the simple words. The words had almost brought a smile and tears to his eyes. And he could see the two of them now sitting on their rug on the hill. Aisling had earrings that dangled like shells and caught the light like a rainbow in sun. They were looking out across the downs, the green and the brown and the gold rolling hills and the sky up above a shimmering mosaic of blue. Aisling was laughing, her head tilted back on his shoulder.

And that's where he left them. On the hill with their picnic and laughter and dreams on that tranquil English evening. Her voice like a lark still singing in his heart. He gathered up his things and packed them in his bag and placed his wallet and keys together. Then he looked around the room and opened the door and went down the hall slowly to breakfast.

3

The lights from the riverbank were shining like jewels in the water. Jewels of fire in the tide. The water was flowing like a slow-moving mirror and an acrid smell of burning was beginning to rise. Colin had come early with his guide, Kishan. Crowds had been gathering in small groups since dawn and the first pyres of the morning were being lit. The air was intense and singed with flames from the piles of blackened wood and the ground was already covered with ash. This was why he had come to Varanasi. The sacred, ancient Indian city.

To see at firsthand. This ritual for the soul.

And the lights in the river came back to him now on the terrace.

A haze on the water was turning the sky blossom pink. Soon the sun would break through across the Ganges. And he had stood a long time, observing in silence the sacred vignettes. The transition from earth to beyond and the escape from reincarnation in this profound Hindu practice of moksha. The air hummed with soft prayers and chanting and the sound of bodies hissing in the flames. From a heat so intense he was already dripping with sweat. But he had found it all strangely hypnotic, the boats arriving with timber, the bodies in white cloths decorated with flowers and the never-ending flames and plumes of smoke rising as the river drifted on.

*****

Rosetta was serving dinner and he joined her at the table.

"Well, are we still thinking about India?" she said, looking up.

Colin drank from his glass and nodded with a smile.

"I didn't know what to make of it when I was there," he said, lifting his fork. "But it's stayed with me ever since."

"Did you paint?" she asked.

"No," he said, shaking his head. "I wanted to free my mind."

"And did you?"

"Yes," he said. "But I think it filled up as well."

"With what?"

"Color," he said. "Magical Indian colors. And light," he added. "The light was extraordinary. I can see a lot more clearly now, I think."

Rosetta took a sip from her wine. "Your eyes are smiling again," she said. "You'll be fine when you go back to Ireland."

"But I've only just arrived," he said.

"I know that," she said with a laugh, "but in the end, we both know you'll go. It's the way we are, you and I," and she shrugged with a smile and raised her glass in a salute.

After dinner, when Rosetta was in bed, he stayed on the terrace to finish his wine. He sat very still gazing at the cypress trees across the fields and listening to the crickets on the lawn. India was still deep inside him. It had buzzed all around him from the moment he had stepped off the plane into a blast of warm humid air. The sights and the sounds of the streets of Old Delhi were here with him now on the terrace like a carnival parade. And he knew those multicolored scenes could never leave him now. He had known he needed to get away. From that night on the cliff and the upturned car. And the memory of Aisling in bed with the scarf on her head.

The perfume of smoke from the pyres came back to him now on the breeze. And he could see Michael's shiny black car in the rain on that cold, wet, dark, black night, and the two figures on the cliff, bent in half like old twisted hawthorns in the wind. Michael talking through drink. Pent-up rage and regret. The rain coming down and the car in that downhill skid. The mobile phone call and the ambulance coming from Ennis.

The next morning after breakfast, he had called to see Michael but the visit had been brief. Michael's ankle was swollen and bandaged and his neck was all numb with whiplash. He was slumped in a chair by the window. "I just came to see you're alright," Colin said. But Michael barely moved or replied. "I'm a bloody wreck," he grunted without turning his head. "But what does it matter? You got what you came for, so why don't you just go?" And Colin left him like that, slumped in the chair by the window with the beach down below bathed in sun.

On his way back to Dublin, he knew he had to find somewhere to go. It was an instinctive thing. To want to disappear. Far away beyond the horizon. He kept seeing the scenes from the television that morning as he drove. India had just seemed like another planet and that's what he knew he needed. And so he went in the spring. To the foothills of the Himalayas in Uttarakhand and long days of treks across hills of wildflowers. The silence and remoteness of the landscape was a cleansing sensation with the sun dazzling down and the snowcapped peaks in the distance. The mountain villages were friendly and welcoming after long days of walking across the isolated hills. And from the people he met on his travels he began to understand how everything in India was sacred. Every mountain, every stone and every river. And the depth of this clear, pure philosophy began to seep in. It seemed to sum up some free, wild instinct in him which had always been there and first drawn him to painting.

And after three weeks, he made his way to New Delhi and found a guide called Kishan who agreed to take him to Varanasi. In a search for some peace he could bring back home. They traveled in an old battered car along dusty straight roads, Colin bouncing around in the back. Weaving their way through tuk-tuks and rickshaws, mopeds and white, sacred cows. To a city teeming with life from all across India with pilgrims and mourners all squeezing in through its narrow, crowded lanes and bazaars. But it was the cremation ghats down by the river that Colin had come to see. And Kishan had taken him there, past the devotees making offerings at shrines on the sides of the road, all the way down to the waterside ghats and the holy men in saffron robes, the blazing pyres and the baskets of soft, fine, warm, grey ash.

And in Varanasi he had found an awestruck peace. A contrast to the void of Michael's bleak world. And he sensed he had turned a new corner. The viscerality of the pyres had brought him up close with death. But the spectacle had filled him with a surprising serenity. His journey had not been in vain. And he prepared to go home with a new sense of calm in his mind.

And he felt calm now as he paused and finished his wine. At peace with himself and with Michael and at peace with his sense of beyond. Then he turned off the lamps and went upstairs to bed.

Rosetta was dozing when he crept in. Her arm found his hand across the sheets.

"Where are you now?" she mumbled.

"I'm here," he said. "In Montalcino with you."

Her hand gripped his fingers. "That is good to know," she said, pressing his palm. "That is good to know."

Her hand eased its grip. She was sleeping. Colin slipped in beside her and glanced around the room. The white sheets in the starlight and the shadows on the wall and the floor.

So many nights and so few like these, he thought. And he tried to stay in the moment. As if it could always be simply like this.

Then he slept.

The next day they went to the sea. A long sandy beach with the hills of Maremma close by. Sailboats glided past like wild geese on the water. The weather was warm and they walked barefoot on the sand. The seaside glistening all around like a watercolor mirage.

"So, tell me your plans," said Rosetta over lunch.

Colin toyed with the scallops in his bowl and paused, unable to bring himself to say the words.

"I'm going to sell the house," he said with a finality that startled even him.

She nodded. "I can see that makes sense. And where will you go?"

He shrugged.

"No, don't tell me," she said. "I know. You will find an island somewhere. Yes, that's where you'll go."

"And you'll come and visit me on this island?" he said, laughing.

"Will it be warm and blue and sunny like here?"

"No," he said. "It'll be cold and wet and raining and the wind will blow you away."

"Aaah," she said, "then I will come. I will definitely visit you there."

And they drank to his island against a backdrop of warm blue sea.

On their drive back to Montalcino, the dying sun set the sky on fire. And they drove in companionable silence, each lost in their own special thoughts.

*****

It took him a year to sort everything out and the day when it came was fresh with a cotton-wool sky and a wind blowing in. The boat was leaving the quay, chugging out in the waves and he was standing at the rail with a dog in his arms. The dog had come from a shelter in Galway. And he held him now close to his chest.

"And you're sure?" the woman at the counter had said.

But Colin had been certain. The dog looked like a fox. Like in his mother's garden. With the apples and bread on the lawn. He had a whiskey-colored coat and a grin like a mischievous fox.

"He has a broken hip," the woman said. "It'll trouble him when he's older."

"All the more reason," said Colin.

The boat was riding the waves, the spray catching the dog on the nose. The island was appearing now, the curve of the hills clearly visible from deck. And Colin felt free for the first time in years. The dog looked up and licked his face. The boat was heading for the harbor and the pier.

Their first night on the island, the sky was clear and studded with stars like a thousand eyes in the dark. They settled down by the fire after dinner, Colin in his chair and the dog on the rug. The Paul Henry on the wall and a jug of wildflowers on the sill.

The dog's legs were beginning to twitch.

Hop, skip, jump, and trot. Colin had watched him earlier on the beach. Hop, skip, jump, and trot. His way of getting about. And he had performed the same sequence every time. Like a perfect adagio. Never missing a beat. There was a rhythm to it, like violins in a concert hall. Now in the evening, his legs were twitching in his sleep, in time to the music on the radio. A string quartet dancing through the room. And Colin remembered Montauk and smiled. In the morning, the dog had a name. And they walked down the beach to the water's edge. Colin with his hands in his pockets, Mozart trotting along, stopping here and there, sniffing rocks and bits of wood on the sand. The tide was out, beginning to turn. The perfect spot. The epicenter of the bay, light caressing the horizon. An invisible line of sky meeting water.

Every day they came the same way. To the shore. The light different every time. A palette of interchanging blue and grey and green. And Colin's eyes scanned the horizon. And each time he saw something different. Each time the distant point changed. In rain and in wind, or in sun and in mist. And his eyes absorbed all the changes, the variations in line and tone and shade. And he thought of the Ganges and the lights flowing in the tide. Rippling away through the water. Water flowing into water. Always moving away. *Because the journey never ends*, he thought. *Because there is no beginning and there is no end.*

And her voice coming over the waves was a voice in a chorus of voices.

The sound of a peaceful lament.

Many voices in the wind on the water.

The days all began with the walk along the shore and ended by the fire in the evening. The flames of the fire throwing shadows on the wall like the pyres still burning in his mind.

And after a week, he was ready to begin.

All his life a warm wind had been calling him here.

He put a basket for Mozart in the studio. With a plaid rug and a water bowl on the floor. Then he tightened the canvas on the easel and placed his palette on the table.

The canvas was already primed with a mix of yellow ochre and titanium white. He lined up the tubes of color one by one and squeezed them out. Unscrewed the bottle of resin and linseed oil and poured turpentine into a jar. Then he stood back and looked at the canvas. Mozart watched from his basket. The sky in the window was like a cloth of light, veiling the sun. Not too bright. Just right. His father was swimming far out in the water, weaving his way through the waves. And he picked up his brush and began to paint.

V
sound

The sky is lost in a shawl of white mist. There is moisture in the air and the sea is draped with grey. Seaweed clings to the rocks and the light is low on the skyline, clouds hanging down as if they might drop. There is no one on the beach at this hour. The sand is stained mauve where the tide has slipped out. Soon it will return like a pattern of lace and cover the mauve with water. The water will reach the stones. And the beach will slip under the sea. The mist clears to a drizzle. A soft invisible rain blowing in. Then they come.

Moving slowly across the stones. A faint blur in the wind as the rain whispers in. They move together as one. Arms holding the dog like a fish in a net. They reach the sand and bend down. The dog sets off on his own. He knows the way.

His paws mark the sand. A curving line of prints etched out. She follows him all the way down. When he reaches the spot, he sits. Sniffing the breeze. Twitching his snout. His eyes stare out to sea. The gulls squawk and swoop in the air. Thin lines of waves break ranks. The water slides in and sucks back. The dog is staring out to sea. But there is nothing today. The sea is an empty basin of grey.

She takes out her phone. Scans the screen. Nothing new. She sighs and puts it away. She sits on a rock and passes a hand through her hair. She is looking at the waves but doesn't see them at all.

They have followed the same pattern every day. A cup of tea and toast first with the news and the weather and then the walk down to the shore. She has made a bed for herself in the cottage. Lit the fire every night and walked the dog in all weather. She puts new bandages on his paws every day. He doesn't mind. They protect his paws. It has nearly been a week since she had to call for help. There was a message last night. But the signal was weak and she could barely make out the words.

She checks her watch now and looks at the clouds. The morning is moving on. Clouds are gathering in. Colors darkening from the west. There is a shiver in the air. The sea is moving swiftly in. Wind rolling the waves. The beach is draining of color. She takes out her phone and tries to listen again. But the message is too faint to hear.

The dog is listening to the wind. His eyes are scanning the water. His fur is damp and he is getting cold but he does not want to move. He can hear the rain on the wind and the waves crashing in. And as he listens in the wind, he turns his head. She watches him from the rock, her cheek cupped in her hands. She watches the dog turn and get up. And the dog is away. He is running now. With a hobble, a skip and a jump and a trot. Heading back across the beach on his own. And she stands for a moment and stares. The waves are flooding in on the sand. And she hears the sound now through the waves. The sound comes into view. A car is coming down the road. A black hatchback emerging from the grey. A car is a rare sight on this part of the island. And she starts to race after the dog. The dog is heading straight for the car. She can see the wheels turning and she is sprinting in the wind. Calling to the dog across the beach. The dog is scrabbling over the stones. The tires scrunch to a halt and she can hear the dog yapping. She can see his red fur. The driver gets out. The dog is standing and barking at the driver. She is nearly there now. The driver opens the back door and helps a man out. The man stands for a moment, then steps gingerly forward. The new stents in his heart have made him slightly unsteady. The dog looks at the man. His snout quivers in the air. Then he lifts up his left back leg and hops.

acknowledgments

With thanks to Addi Black, Madeline Hopkins,
Courtney Vatis, Deirdre Curley,
Sean Thomas, Jeff Yamaguchi,
Greg Boguslawski, Megan Wahrenbrock,

Lauren Maturo, Mandy Earles,
Josie Woodbridge,

Paul and Susan Feldstein, The Irish Writers' Centre,
Caitriona Lane, Audrey Lane,

And of course, Ian and Shadow, and especially Pepe
who brought every page to life.